RAVE REVIEWS!

Jennifer Blake

"Blake's style is as steamy as a still July night on the bayou, as overwhelmingly hot as Cajun spice."

—*Chicago Tribune*

"Blake's a master at romantic fiction."

—*The Chattanooga Times*

Robin Lee Hatcher

"Robin Lee Hatcher is a natural storyteller with a gift for creating engaging characters readers will take to their hearts."

—*Jayne Ann Krentz*

"Ms. Hatcher's writing is like a fire on a cold day—warm, inviting, and you don't want it to end."

– *Affaire de Coeur*

Susan Wiggs

"Susan Wiggs is one of the best writers working in historical romance today."

– Joan Wolf,
author of *Daughter of the Red Deer*

"Susan Wiggs is a superb storyteller."

– *Romantic Times*

Harper
Monogram

A PURRFECT ROMANCE

Jennifer Blake

Robin Lee Hatcher

Susan Wiggs

HarperPaperbacks
A Division of HarperCollinsPublishers

HarperPaperbacks   *A Division of* HarperCollins*Publishers*
                    10 East 53rd Street, New York, N.Y. 10022

"Out of the Dark" Copyright © 1995 by Jennifer Blake
"A Wish and a Prayer" Copyright © 1995 by Robin Lee Hatcher
"Belling the Cat" Copyright © 1995 by Susan Wiggs
All rights reserved. No part of this book may be used or repro-
duced in any manner whatsoever without written
permission of the publisher, except in the case of brief
quotations embodied in critical articles and reviews. For information address HarperCollins*Publishers*,
10 East 53rd Street, New York, N.Y. 10022.

Cover illustration by Jeff Barson

First printing: September 1995

Printed in the United States of America

HarperPaperbacks, HarperMonogram, and colophon are trade-
marks of HarperCollins*Publishers*

❖ 10 9 8 7 6 5 4 3 2 1

CONTENTS

OUT OF THE DARK

~ *by* ~

Jennifer Blake

ONE

To have the Dark Angel appear at the ball was a stupendous honor. It was no more than a country cotillion, after all, this being the summer season when everyone retreated from pest-ridden New Orleans to the more healthful air of their upland plantations. More important, Lucien Roquelaire, the premier duelist whose deadly skill had given him his title, was known to avoid such mild entertainments.

Anne-Marie Decoulet watched the arrival of this exalted guest from her corner seat, half hidden behind a gilded and silent harp. She had never met the Dark Angel personally but knew him on sight. Invited everywhere because of his social standing and devastatingly handsome appearance, he cut a wide swath through the city during the festive winter season. Fluttering feminine hearts and shattered male egos littered his path like rose petals before a conquering hero. It would have been difficult not to know him.

There had been a time when Anne-Marie had thought Lucien Roquelaire the epitome of masculine charm. She had spun wondrous daydreams around him in which she played the part of his loyal and valiant lady, the only person who could see through the mask he assumed to conceal the torment in his soul. In her fantasies, he fought for her on the field of honor, climbed to her balcony to rescue her, swept her away with him to exotic climes and exciting experiences.

How silly she had been. The Dark Angel was no man of dreams, but rather a cold-blooded assassin. Any torment in his soul was of his own making. Anne-Marie had come to despise the code duello by which he lived and also the man who was its most notorious example.

Oh, but the hostess for the evening, Madame Picard, was so very gratified by the saturnine gentleman's appearance at her summer ball. Her smile was a beatific beam, while her breath of satisfaction threatened the overstrained seams of her coral silk ball gown. Rustling forward in haste, she was embarrassingly effusive as she made him welcome. Lucien Roquelaire bent his dark head over the lady's hand, all grace, polished manners, and condescension. It was infamous.

But as the gentleman turned to glance around the gathering with a weary air, the smiles of his hostess gave way to doubt. The lady had realized, perhaps, that it was one thing to arouse the interest of the Dark Angel, but quite another to satisfy it. How humiliating for her if he should turn on his heel and leave the house within seconds of arriving. Wild-eyed, Madame Picard searched for something or someone to offer her guest by way of entertainment.

There was not a great deal from which to choose. One of the most popular waltzes of the past winter was floating on the air, and nearly every person present, with the exception of the chaperones and elderly aunts, was on the shining parquet of the dance floor. The district boasted no true intellectual light who might engage her guest, and the few elder statesmen in attendance were sequestered in a back room, deep in games of faro and draw poker. The midnight supper hour was still several dances away, and must fail to impress in any case, being only the usual collection of meats, pastries, jellies, and ices.

It was then that Anne-Marie realized Madame Picard was staring in her direction. Her hostess grasped the arm of Lucien Roquelaire and started forward.

The blood drained from Anne-Marie's face. She glanced around for an avenue of escape, but there was none other than undignified flight. Panic invaded her chest in a choking wave.

She should have been dancing; her stepmother, the wife taken recently by her widowed father, would scold later for the way she had hidden herself away from prospective partners. Yet following the antics of her friends and neighbors from a distance had been far more preferable to venturing onto the floor in the company of awkward partners with sweaty hands and no conversation beyond horses and hunting dogs. Unfortunately it now left her available.

"My dear Anne-Marie," Madame Picard said as she came to a breathless halt before her, "here is someone who needs no introduction, since the entire neighborhood has known for days that he was visiting cousins at Bon Sejour. You will be so kind as to make him welcome, won't you?" The older woman gave the gentleman at her side a nervous smile. "And you, M'sieur Roquelaire, must prepare yourself for a treat. I assure you our Anne-Marie is something unusual in young ladies."

The Dark Angel had no choice except to invite her to dance; Anne-Marie saw that. She was under no obligation to accept, of course, and might easily have declined if she could have forced her brain to produce a reasonable excuse. Nothing came to her. In the meantime, Madame Picard was standing there looking so ridiculously hopeful that it was impossible to disappoint her.

Anne-Marie murmured something that might be taken for agreement. Lucien Roquelaire proffered his arm. As she accepted his support and rose to her feet, she felt the heat of his body and the rigid muscles covered by his coat sleeve.

A peculiar tremor ran along her nerves to lodge in the center of her being. She looked up to meet her partner's intent, assessing gaze. She stopped, standing quite still in the way she might at facing some unexpected danger.

Of above average height, Lucien Roquelaire possessed the classical features and perfect form of a Greek statue allied to the polished grace of a courtier. At the same time there was an elemental air about him, as if beneath the gloss of his appearance he was not quite civilized, something less than tame. The impression came in part from his eyes. Satirical and penetrating, they were a rich brown that caught the light with shifting gold reflections. Intelligence gleamed in their depths, along with the calm that comes from supreme self-confidence. Above them were thick dark brows that arched at their centers so that the least play of amusement across his features caused his expression to turn diabolical.

"I see you have noticed the eyebrows," he said. "Are you going to comment on the likeness to Lucifer, or be truly unusual and refrain?"

The wry inquiry released her from her odd, transfixed state. With a brief glance upward, she said, "I don't believe discussion is required."

"Just so," he said as he swung her effortlessly out onto the floor.

It was incredible to Anne-Marie that she was moving to the music in the arms of Lucien Roquelaire. Her hand was held in his strong grasp, and his gloved fingertips rested at the narrow turn of her waist. Once she would have been in transports; now she was appalled. Of course she was. The odd, unwanted sensations that chased themselves down her spine were mere animal instincts that must be ignored. She fastened her gaze at the level of his cravat while she sought composure.

It was a distinctive cravat, she saw, one made of silk in a soft and unusual shade of amber. She wished abruptly that she wore a ball gown of that color. She longed for anything, in fact, except the virginal white chosen by her step-mother, which gave her the look of a sacrificial maiden. It was embarrassing to be costumed so fittingly for her part.

She was looking far from her best, she knew that with depressing certainty. Her father's new wife had offered the services of her personal maid for the evening, an honor that could not be avoided without giving offense. Under the new Madame Decoulet's forceful instructions, the thick and curling abundance of Anne-Marie's hair had been controlled with slatherings of pomade, which dimmed the rich golden highlights to a dull brown. It had then been braided tightly and twisted into a ridiculously complicated arrangement. In addition, rice powder had been used to coat the creamy skin of her face, giving her a sickly pallor. Though she had been less than pleased by these deficiencies before, they had not seemed especially important until this moment.

Her partner, she realized abruptly, was gazing down at her with a quizzical smile on his chiseled lips. It was a moment before she could attend to what he was saying.

"I believe polite conversation is usual in this situation," he suggested. "Have you no bright conversational gambit with which to entice me? Is there nothing you have been practicing to say to your partners this evening?"

"Nothing," she replied through tight lips.

He tipped his head. "You are not precisely delighted to be dancing with me, I think."

His perspicuity was startling. "How can you say so?"

"Easily. You give no indication of being intrigued, seem in no danger of rushing like a moth to my flame."

"I should hope not." He was held in no great regard as a prospective husband, she knew. There were whispers of bad blood in his family; his father had killed his mother in a drunken rage, or so the story went. Moreover, his many affairs of honor did not bode well for a comfortable future as his wife. Though most fathers stopped short of ordering their daughters to decline his invitations, their mothers regaled them with frightening warnings. Not surprisingly, this made him wildly attractive to the more heedless belles.

"Then you are repelled," he said evenly.

A short time ago, she would have answered without hesitation. Now she was not quite so sure. "Perhaps I am indifferent."

A silent laugh shook him, for she felt it, though he was too polite to let it sound in his voice. "You make me feel like a coxcomb for expecting anything else. Is that what you intended?"

"No," she said after the barest glance at the wry smile curving his mouth.

"That's something, at least. Then if we are neither of us out to captivate or impress the other, I suppose we may enjoy our waltz in comfort."

Amazingly enough, Anne-Marie was aware of a brief longing to captivate him. It was a simple matter of pride, she was sure; she had spent too many hours in the past thinking of this man not to wish that she might arouse his interest. Still, she could not imagine what that might take. Vague visions of herself as one of the nude odalisques such as those painted by Delacroix flitted through her mind. How very intriguing that should be, here among the other dancers in their silks and satins and jewels, their cutaway coats and starched linen. She wondered how it would feel to be held naked in this man's arms as they moved together in the fine soft glow of candlelight.

"Now what," he said softly, "has caused that sudden and very becoming flush? I should like to think it was something I had said or done but cannot so flatter myself."

She drew a sharp breath as she flicked a glance upward, then away again. Her mind had a disconcerting tendency to wander off into odd fancies at inopportune moments, but few people were observant enough to notice. "Nothing," she said in compressed tones. "I was just—thinking."

"And I am unlikely to be told the subject."

"Very unlikely," she said, and controlled a shudder. Or thought she did. It was possible he felt it, however, for his hold at her waist tightened so she was brought closer to him. A moment later he spun into a turn, whirling her with the stiff embroidery of his waistcoat pressed in shocking firmness against the soft curves of her breasts.

Had he been flirting with her? The thought was nearly as distracting as his embrace. She suspected he might have been but could not be sure since she had no experience with men and precious little with balls and dancing.

The fault lay with the circumstances of her youth. At fourteen, she had been plunged into near perpetual mourning. The middle child of five offspring, she had put on black when her two younger sisters succumbed to a virulent summer complaint, then continued it two more years as the brother next to her in age died of cholera. The mourning clothes had been packed away in cedar shavings barely two weeks before they had to be brought out and refurbished for the sake of her eldest brother, just eighteen, who was killed in a duel. Then some ten months later her mother, worn out with tragedy, had passed away, extending the period of grief to the past winter.

By the time Anne-Marie had finally put aside the last purple gown of half mourning, there had been long years of crepe-hung mirrors and stopped clocks, of seclusion without merriment or the kind of quick, effortless exchange of thought and opinion that made for ease in the social milieu. Left to her own devices by a grieving father, she had become bookish. Her character, formed in virtual isolation, had turned headstrong and eccentric in a quiet fashion. She was amenable only to a point; past that, she went her own way. Her sense of justice was fierce, and she had no use for falsehoods. She especially disdained false gallantry.

As the movements of the waltz slowed again, she said, "I fail to see what interest Madame Picard's gathering can hold for someone like the Dark Angel."

"It's a distraction."

The words were clipped short. It seemed he did not care to have the name he had acquired thrown at him in public. That was understandable; upward of fifteen duels resulting in at least three deaths and any number of disabling injuries were hardly a source of pride.

She said in spurious sympathy, "Then you must have been bored beyond belief with the company at your cousin's house."

"In point of fact," he answered, his eyes cool as he gazed down at her, "I am perfectly content there. However, a summer fever has invaded the household nursery, preventing the family from attending this evening. I am here as their envoy."

"How providential you did not succumb to this sickness."

"I am never ill."

There was no vanity in the words, only a statement of fact; yet they irritated her. She felt it as an affront—his hardihood and the fact that he had survived so many duels while her brother had died. "No doubt your exemption comes from regular exercise," she said in caustic tones. "Braving the early morning damp under the dueling oaks must have tempered your constitution."

His eyes narrowed. "No doubt."

"I wonder that you felt the need to leave New Orleans since disease holds no terror for you. Think what trouble you might have saved by staying home."

"But then," he said deliberately, "I might have missed meeting you. And I'm beginning to think that would have been a pity."

Her stare was defiant. "I can't imagine why."

"It isn't often I am privileged to hear precisely what a person thinks." The quiet words carried a disturbing sound of weariness.

"And whose fault is that, pray? Fear is such a spur to discretion."

His gaze raked her face. "But you don't fear me."

"It is my good fortune that women are ineligible for contests of honor," she answered in brittle tones. She was going too far, she knew, but seemed driven to it by some half-acknowledged instinct for self-protection as well as her annoyance.

"You have not considered," he said with lethal softness. "I could always force a challenge on your father or your brothers."

"You are not known for meeting men who are your elders. As for my brothers, one died in childhood, the other on a dueling ground."

A soft sound left him, and he stared down at her with an intent frown drawing his arched brows together over his nose. When he went on, it was with an abrupt change of tone. "I am sorry for your loss. And you are quite right; I spoke from anger only. I have never issued a challenge from revenge."

She did not want his pity. "I expect the threat has always been sufficient without the deed."

"Don't spare my feelings, if you please," he said, instantly on the defensive again. "It should be interesting to see how low an opinion of me you are able to express."

"Oh, I doubt you will be inclined to stay long enough to find out."

"You are wrong." The words were smooth. "But only tell me how I must pass the time on my hands instead of remaining here, and I will go and do it."

"Whatever you like that doesn't decimate the countryside," she answered, then added in some haste, "But you will forget I mentioned leaving, if you please. You cannot go just yet."

"Can I not? What is to stop me?"

"Manners," she said stringently. "If you dance a single dance and then depart, it will appear there was nothing here to hold your attention."

"I am many things," he said with quiet precision, "but unmannerly is not one of them. Suppose I said I might be persuaded to stay for your sake. Would you walk out into the garden with me to ensure it?"

Anne-Marie stared at him. Did he mean it, or was it only a suggestion meant to confuse and embarrass her, thus putting an end to their exchange? The words not quite steady, she said, "You speak in jest, I'm sure."

"Do I?" he queried, his gaze steady upon her face. "You should know better, being no convent school mademoiselle."

Indeed she wasn't. According to her stepmother, she was perilously close at twenty to the age when an unmarried woman was advised to throw her corset on top of the armoire and accept the role of spinster.

The marriage of her father to the voluptuous, hard-eyed widow had been unexpected; they had met during Lent and were wed just after Easter. By the time they all removed to Pecan Hill, the plantation near Baton Rouge, it was plain the new wife considered Anne-Marie a thorn in her side. When her stepmother began to hint that a marriage might be arranged for her, Anne-Marie had not objected. Her father's house was no longer her home; to leave it for that of a strange man could hardly be more uncomfortable, no matter what he was like.

Or so she had thought at the time. It was possible she had been mistaken.

The words distinct, she said, "I believe it would be best if you returned me to my seat."

"Oh, I think not. There would be no satisfaction in that." He lowered his voice, drawing her nearer so he spoke at her ear. "Madame Picard was right. You are something out of the ordinary. You perplex me, and not simply because you hold me in contempt and are unafraid to say so. There is something about you that— Look at me, if you please."

She could not resist, though not because of his request. There was an intent note in his voice she needed to decipher. Slowly, carefully, she lifted her lashes.

His gaze was dark, so dark. It spoke of deep nights and banked fires, of old pain and carefully constructed defenses. It constrained her in some mysterious way, threatening to consume her. She could sustain it no more than an instant before looking away again.

"Fascinating," he said in bemused softness. "How did you come by such wanton Gypsy eyes?"

"I was born with them," she said in compressed tones. The subject was a sore one; her stepmother often made such remarks. Besides, his interest made her uneasy.

"Of course you were, and I am well served for asking," he said at once. "You must forgive the personal remark, but I was so surprised."

"In any case," she went on quickly to fill the silence, "I am not a Gypsy. My great-grandmother was Indian, of the Natchez tribe."

"That explains it, then. A wild child of nature rather than a wanton."

"Hardly!" Her stare was suspicious. Most people considered Indian blood to be cause for concern, if not scorn. She herself knew the Natchez to be a fine, proud race whose members were equal if not superior to the French with whom they had mingled their heritage. Still, she had learned to be careful of the reactions of others.

"I wonder."

His comment was musing, yet freighted with rich layers of speculation. It required no answer, however, which was just as well, since Anne-Marie had absolutely none to offer. They whirled gently for a few moments before he spoke again.

"You dance well. Actually, you are one of the most responsive women I've ever held in my arms. You follow my slightest turn without hesitation, venture any complicated step I begin. I am tempted to wonder if such perfect grace of movement would translate to—places other than a ballroom floor."

Lucien Roquelaire had substituted another phrase for the one he had intended, she thought. There had also been an undercurrent in his voice that made her suddenly aware of herself as a female, one in the arms of a male not her father or her late brother.

His hold was firm, with limitless support in its tensile strength. Their steps were perfectly matched, their bodies fitted together with exactitude. There was a sense of leashed power inside him that she responded to without conscious thought, making it easy to move with him to the music. Even through layers of petticoats and with the distancing of spring-steel hoops, she could sense the taut hardness of his muscular thighs shifting against her skirts.

She liked none of it.

Clenching her fingers on his shoulder, she gave him a slight push away from her. Voice tight, she answered, "I doubt it."

He relinquished his hold somewhat. "So do I," he said. "It seems a great pity."

They said no more as the waltz swung to a gliding halt. Her partner released her, then led her back to the chair behind the harp where he had found her. After he inclined his head yet again, he walked away.

She watched him go and sighed with relief. Or at least she tried to convince herself that was the feeling uppermost in her mind.

The evening advanced. Anne-Marie danced with her father and also with Victor Picard, the son of her hostess, a somewhat pompous young man she had known since childhood. She spent a pleasant quarter hour in discussion with the parish priest, who was of course in attendance; the two of them had a mutual interest in the novels of Dumas the Elder. Other than that, she remained alone in her nook, observing the kaleidoscope of movement and color.

Roquelaire, she noticed, became part of a small group that included the most popular belles and beaus of the

community. She had expected nothing less; it was doubtless his rightful place as long as he chose to remain in that
section of the country.

The Dark Angel did not look her way again, which
was precisely as she wanted it. She cared not at all what
he thought of her; why should she, when he was nothing
to her or she to him? He would soon go back to New
Orleans and his round of decadent amusements. And she
would shed no tears.

She wished she could go home; she felt a headache
coming on. It was caused, no doubt, by the tight braiding
of her hair. There was no excuse that would permit her to
leave, however. Her stepmother was addicted to dancing
and would not think of departing until the last waltz was
played.

The time crept past. The candles in the crystal and
ormolu chandeliers overhead began to smoke and flutter
on their sinking wicks. The number of couples on the
floor became more sparse as the dancers tired. Midnight
supper was finally announced.

Anne-Marie was not at all hungry, yet the pretense of
eating would give her something to do for a short while.
Taking the plate that was filled for her by a manservant
in lieu of an escort, she returned to her seat.

She ate a tiny buttered roll containing smoked ham,
then picked up a pastry puff filled with shrimp spread. She
opened her mouth to take a small bite.

A scream rent the air. Shrill with terror and loathing, it
was still ringing through the room as Anne-Marie jerked
around on her chair. The woman who made the noise stood
no more than ten feet away. Mouth open and eyes starting
from their sockets, she was pointing a shaking finger toward
the open French doors just in front of her.

In the darkness beyond the opening, a shadow moved.

It shifted, shimmering in the dim light, then elongated and glided forward.

Anne-Marie saw the eyes first, feral gold and faintly reflective. Then the dark shape padded into view, moving silently through the doorway and onto the gleaming dance floor.

It stopped there, poised in terrible grace on its mirror image that gleamed in the polished parquet. Black and powerful and huge within the enclosed space of the room, it bared glistening white teeth as it growled in low distress. Its baleful and hungry stare swept the room.

It was a swamp panther.

TWO

The great black cat ignored the screamer, paid no attention to the sudden oaths and cries or the scrambling, undignified retreat of those close to it. Head lifted, it quartered the gathering with a searching stare while the black pupils in its yellow-green eyes closed slowly to slits against the light.

Then its gaze stopped, centered. It raised extended nostrils while twitching a long black tail. Lifting a huge paw, it stretched into a smooth walk. Madame Picard's guests parted before it, fluttering away to safety like chickens in a barnyard.

They left a cleared expanse of floor, a shining path that marked the panther's line of sight. It led straight toward the corner where Anne-Marie sat.

She did not move; she could not. Her gaze was fastened on the advancing beast. With her lips parted in amazement and the shrimp puff forgotten in her hand, she followed his steady advance.

Oh, but he was a magnificent animal, even beautiful in a fierce and deadly fashion. The candlelight slid along his back with a glassy sheen; the muscles under his sleek skin bunched and contracted with the controlled strength of his effortless strides. Swift, silent, he glided toward her in unstoppable certainty. Mesmerized by his power and the steady light in his fixed eyes, she did not try to escape but waited, barely breathing, while he rounded the harp and bore down upon her.

As the great animal neared, he crouched a little, ears forward, nose outstretched. He put a foot on the hem of her skirt where the fragile material was spread over the floor. He stopped.

Anne-Marie could feel the heat of his body, smell the wild, outdoor freshness of him. His power surrounded her. She inhaled softly in wonder.

Pushing his neck forward toward her hand, the panther blew gently. His warm breath tickled her fingers, then he opened his mouth and reached a rough tongue to lap gently across them.

The sensation was astonishing, abrading yet warm, stimulating beyond all reason. The beast's facile tongue slipped along her knuckles, searched between them to discover areas of sensitivity she had not known she possessed. Heat began somewhere deep inside her and radiated to her skin's surface.

Anne-Marie allowed her taut muscles to relax a little so that her fingers lost their cramped curl. At that slight motion, the great black cat took the shrimp puff from her hand with delicate precision. He downed it in a single gulp.

Anne-Marie gasped, then gave a shaky laugh. "Why,

you great devil," she said. "How dare you take my supper? And where, pray, is your invitation? I fear you are a trespasser of the most pernicious sort: you do not even pretend to like the company but come merely for the food!"

Incredibly, a rough rumble, like a cross-cut saw drawn across a hollow log, came from the panther. He blinked up at Anne-Marie with his eyes glinting green-gold and its pupils expanding slightly to the shape of narrow triangles.

"Yes, it's all very well to make up to me, but I am not fooled," she scolded gently. "I daresay that morsel you just swallowed made not a dent on your appetite. I have a little pâté on my plate, if you think you could relish it."

She dipped her finger into the smooth goose-liver paste and held it out. The panther took it in a swift lick.

Somewhere in the room, a woman gave a hysterical spurt of laughter. Anne-Marie sent her a warning glance even as she spoke once more to the cat. "A fine treat, was that not? I rather expected you would think so. And what about a bit of roll to go with the next taste?"

While the cat ate the roll, she reached out, greatly daring, to touch the huge head. The hair had the silken crispness of cut velvet. Hardly aware of those around her, she went on in soothing tones. "Now this is quite foolish, coming here. What possessed you? Oh, I see that you have been in a trap; your paw looks a mess. You chewed it free, didn't you? Better half a paw than waiting for someone to come and finish you."

The big cat blinked up at her and flicked an ear. Its gaze shifted then to fasten on her plate once more.

"Still hungry, yes? Is hunting so difficult, then? I haven't touched this nice piece of chicken, if you would like it."

From somewhere in the rear of the crowd, Victor

Picard called out, "That's right, *chère*, keep feeding it. I'm going for a pistol."

"No!" Anne-Marie said, looking up with anger flashing like lightning in her dark eyes. "You can't shoot him!"

"*Mon Dieu*, but of course I can!" Victor was backing away toward the study, where his father's weapons were kept.

"There's no reason." There was an undertone of pleading in her voice.

Victor took another careful step. "He could turn on you at any moment, turn on us all."

"He won't," she said with certainty. "Can't you see he's too weak?"

"He doesn't look weak to me," the young man declared. Around him, several of his friends muttered agreement. "Anyway, what else is there? Another bite or two and you'll have nothing more to feed him."

She did not know how to answer. She was even now holding out the last tidbit on her plate, a piece of toast spread with savory cheese.

"Here is more food." Lucien Roquelaire spoke in stringent tones as he strolled from the direction of the dining room with a laden plate in his hands. "And Mademoiselle Decoulet is quite right: any sudden move is inadvisable. As for firing here in this room, I would not. The danger for your guests is too great, not to speak of the peril for the lady."

That the Dark Angel would come to her aid was so unbelievable that Anne-Marie could only stare at him. He met her gaze while his mouth curved in a slow smile. "Don't look so surprised," he said quietly as he came to a halt at her side. "Even the devil looks after his own."

"Apparently." Her gaze rested an instant on the plate piled high with shrimp puffs.

Extending the new supply of tempting morsels, he

said, "Perhaps you can give him two or three more, holding the rest in reserve. If you will rise and walk to the door where your friend entered, he may be persuaded to follow you."

It was the only possible course. A threatening grumble was rising among the men at the back of the room. At any minute, they might decide to try to kill the panther regardless of the consequences.

The very idea made Anne-Marie feel cold and sick inside. Wild as the beast might be, he was only as nature made him. He deserved to live out his allotted span of years the same as any other living creature.

After giving the panther a shrimp puff as a distraction, she took a few more in her right hand, then rose slowly to her feet. Lucien Roquelaire reached out to offer his arm, and she clasped that firm support with her free hand.

The cat flinched at her movement and shrank to a crouch with his ears laid back against his head. Men breathed curses and women cried out in horror. Anne-Marie sent a fierce frown around the room before she turned back to the panther. Speaking quietly, she reached out toward him, letting him catch the scent of the food held in her fingers.

After a moment, the great beast eased upright again. As Anne-Marie moved away a single step, then looked back, the panther glided closer, shrinking against her skirts. She took another pace. The interloper followed and even nosed her hand and the half-crushed shrimp puffs clenched in it.

Step by careful step, the three of them made their way toward the open doorway. Anne-Marie kept up a low-voiced murmur of encouragement. The cat stared up into her face now and then, twitching his ears and licking his muzzle.

As they reached the dark gallery and the animal followed them into the night, Anne-Marie gave a small sigh of relief. She turned her head to look up at the man beside her. Her eyes were suddenly bright, her soft lips tremulous with gladness.

The man at her side made a quiet sound. There was an odd expression in his eyes as he watched her, one compounded of amusement and respect and something more that sent a shiver along her nerves. The muscles of his arm under her hand hardened. She felt her heart flutter against her ribs while a flush stung her face.

And Anne-Marie was aware, suddenly, of standing between two sources of danger. Man or beast, she hardly knew which was greater. Yet in some inner depth of her mind it seemed they were the same. Beast and man, both were strong and sure in their power, both wild and untamable. To sustain the approach of either took all the courage she possessed, while against them she had no defense except soft words and her own staunch inner spirit.

The movement slow but decisive, she lowered her gaze, then stepped away from the man. Turning toward the panther, she led him the last few yards to the steps of the gallery. She extended the last shrimp puff and waited until he had swallowed it down. Then she brought her hands together in a sudden sharp clap.

"Go!" she cried as she clapped them again. "Scat!"

The panther shied, then surged around and bolted into the night. His body made a dark arc as he leaped to the brick walk. A solid thump came as his full weight struck the ground. He streaked away, a vanishing shadow. And all that was left was the night.

Lucien Roquelaire moved to her side. In quiet approbation, he said, "That was well done."

She turned to look at him. "Was it? He is wounded.

And now I may have made it easier for him to be hunted down because he will have lost some of his fear."

"While the hunters have the excuse that he is dangerous since he has dared venture close to man. Yes, I see." He went on with deliberation. "Perhaps if I called on you tomorrow, we might discuss this problem?"

"I doubt there is a solution." She glanced away into the dark. His suggestion was only a courtesy. What more could it be?

"Perhaps not," he answered in whimsical tones. "But then, don't you feel we have an obligation?"

"We?"

"Assuredly," he answered. "Having claimed the panther as my own, I cannot desert him now. Or you."

She gave him a straight look at last. "You owe me nothing."

"But I do," he said, reaching to take her hand and carry it to his lips. "You are something of an enigma, mademoiselle. Because of it, I have escaped from my dark humors for an hour or two, and seem likely to have the same pleasure again. For these favors alone you are due my humble thanks and my homage."

"I'm not sure what you mean," she said shortly.

"Don't you? Intended or not, you offer provocation that strikes me as very like a challenge. If you know anything of me, then there is one thing of which you may be sure."

As he paused, she searched the dark depths of his eyes, wondering at the fierce light that gleamed there. Her voice unaccountably tight, she said, "And that is?"

He smiled, a slow twist of sensual, well-molded lips. "I thought you might have guessed, mademoiselle. I never refuse a challenge."

THREE

Your intentions in regard to my stepdaughter cannot possibly be serious," Madame Decoulet said sharply. "Can they?"

Lucien Roquelaire thought Anne-Marie's stepmother appeared torn between amazement and disgust, hope and disbelief. He regarded the calculating glint in her china blue eyes and her upright, rigorously corseted figure while he fought the urge to return an acid answer. As much as it might satisfy him to put the woman in her place, that would not aid the purpose of his morning visit.

Shifting on the hideously uncomfortable horsehair settee that graced the parlor of Pecan Hill, he spoke in even tones. "I trust you have no objection?"

"None whatever," came the prompt reply. The woman reached out a plump hand toward a bell that sat on the side table. "May I offer you coffee and cakes?"

He declined with every civility. It was not his purpose

to be trapped into a long tête-à-tête with the woman across from him.

"Perhaps you might be tempted by something stronger? A julep, yes? . . . No? You're quite sure?"

Madame Decoulet appeared disappointed, perhaps because he had removed the excuse for her to indulge in midmorning refreshment. He shook his head as he shifted yet again while glancing around him. The parlor had recently been refurbished, or so it seemed; Gothic monstrosities of stiff mien and dark finish had been crammed in with older and more graceful Queen Anne pieces, while the plastered walls had been covered with flocked cloth figured with improbable shapes in muddy colors. He assumed the result was the handiwork of the new mistress of the house, since he could not feature the young woman he had met the evening before at the ball being comfortable in it.

Madame Decoulet favored him with a smile that was crimped at the edges. "I trust you will not regard my questions. I should be failing in my duty if I did not make some effort to discover the nature of your interest. To raise my poor stepdaughter's hopes only to disappoint them would not be a kindness."

"That is not my intention," he said with the surface politeness that often came to his rescue when his patience was most strained.

"Indeed?" The woman gave a grunt of satisfaction.

Lucien was not particularly gratified by her approval. He had few illusions about his eligibility as a future husband.

Brought up by a harsh and overbearing father, he had spent a large portion of his younger years proving to all and sundry how unaffected he was by frequent applications of the whip. Then had come the string of duels, with the bitter feelings and whispered epithets that went with them. The only thing that had ended his wild career had been the deaths of his father and elder brother in a steamboat accident. Responsibility for his father's vast holdings in land and real estate, in addition to the well-being of a younger brother and sister, had finally sobered him.

Parents among the French aristocracy of New Orleans normally looked askance at a man with such a distasteful past and uncertain future. It did not give Lucien a good opinion of Madame Decoulet to realize she was perfectly willing to welcome a libertine, gamester, and notorious duelist into the family in order to be rid of her stepdaughter.

His manner was barely polite as he spoke again. "Given your relationship to the lady, I quite understand that other matters take precedence over her welfare in your eyes. Should the situation warrant it at a later date, it will naturally be my pleasure to discuss the matter with someone more closely related."

The bosom of the woman who sat on the salon's settee across from him swelled with indignation as she took his point. She contained herself, however, most likely because giving rein to her annoyance might lose her a possible *parti* for Anne-Marie. Through stiff lips she said, "You will discover that her father is guided by me in these matters."

"Nevertheless, there may be explanations required which I prefer to make to her natural guardian. Consider it a personal preference, if you like."

"As you wish." The tone of the words did not match their content.

He inclined his head. "If you are satisfied, then, madame, I will repeat my earlier inquiry: Is Mademoiselle Decoulet at home?"

"She is about the place somewhere," the stepmother

snapped. "With such an odd girl it's difficult to say where she might be at any given moment."

"Yet you have the responsibility for watching over her," Lucien suggested with acid in his voice. "I assume she is not close by or you would have sent for her before now. If you would be so kind as to give me her general direction, I will save you the trouble of a search."

"You must do as you please," Madame Decoulet said through pinched lips. "It's possible you may run her to earth if you care to walk in the direction of the barns; there was some mention of a new litter of kittens. Don't blame me, however, if the effort is for nothing."

"Certainly not," he said, rising to his feet with a short bow. "I feel sure you are anxious for me to discover her."

Lucien did not find Anne-Marie at the barn, or at the stable, the plantation hospital, the nursery, or the dairy. She was not in the kitchen garden or any other place a daughter of the house might be expected to visit. Still, he was able to inspect all these places in the course of his rounds, as well as the cooperage and the sugar mill. The exercise was sufficient to gauge the extent of the holdings owned by her father.

Their size and prosperous condition suggested a reason the stepmother was so anxious to have Anne-Marie off her hands. The young lady would doubtless be heiress to a considerable fortune one day unless Madame Decoulet could find a way to separate Anne-Marie from her father. The circumstances meant little to Lucien, since he had no need for a wealthy bride, but it seemed that the young lady was in need of a strong husband to look after her interests.

It was his experience that plantation children were always aware of everything worth knowing about what went on around a place. Since he had collected an escort of at least a dozen grinning youngsters, he finally resorted to asking for information about their young mistress. Several knew where to find her; that much was plain to see. It was also obvious they were not inclined to part with the knowledge.

"What you want with her?"

The question came from a sturdy young black boy with a pugnacious stare. Lucien was diverted at having his intentions questioned again, this time from what appeared to be true concern. He smiled a little as he lifted a brow. "I am paying a courtesy call, or trying my poor best. It's customary after a ball, you know."

"You courting Mam'zelle?" There was no relenting in the dark, liquid gaze.

Was he? Lucien was beginning to wonder. "Now that I can't tell you for certain. It's a remote possibility."

"Maybe she don't want to see you. Maybe she don't want to see no menfolks a-tall." The boy put his fists on his hips and pushed out his bottom lip.

It appeared that Mademoiselle Decoulet had a protector. Lucien said quietly, "If she doesn't want to see me, then I will go away again. I will not hurt your mam'zelle, I promise."

The boy considered that for some seconds before he gave a short nod. "I'll show the way. But Mam'zelle must say if she wants you."

That thought had intriguing possibilities. "What are we waiting for? Lead on, my friend."

"Name's James," the boy said. Without waiting for more, he whirled and made off at a fast pace.

The way led across the wide pasture that lay behind the barn, then across a creek and down through the woods. The boy James barreled through tall grass, weeds gone to seed, briars, and vines like a puppy on a home trail. Lucien fought his way past the impediments with the help of the sword cane he wore in place of a dress cane, but he was ruefully aware of sacrificing his favorite boots to the quest.

Topping a small rise after some minutes of walking, they came to a clearing under the shading canopy of tall oaks. At the edge was a spring with mossy banks around which grew ferns so thick they blanketed the ground in rich, vibrant green. Cool and secluded, stippled by the sunlight striking through the foliage overhead, it was a perfect retreat. There they found Anne-Marie.

She was frolicking in the middle of the clearing, running and tussling with what appeared to be a large dog. An instant later, Lucien caught his breath as he saw that the animal was no dog, but the shining black panther from the night before.

The sun through the trees made a golden halo around her hair that spilled in loose waves down her back. It touched the skin of her face with the shimmering translucence of pearls. As she ran and romped in an old day gown that was minus hoops and petticoats, the light outlined the shape of her body with gentle fidelity. The pale nonentity of the night before, with the tight coiffure and tighter manners, had been replaced by a wood nymph.

Free and graceful as that classical spirit of the forests, the turns of her arms, the curves of waist and hips, had a natural comeliness that surpassed mere beauty. Her smiles were quick and unshadowed, her laugh rang out with the clear sweet sound of untrammeled joy.

At the same time there was a fey quality about her, something not quite of the mundane world with its worries about money and conventional behavior. It was not simply that she had no fear of the wild beast at her feet, but rather that she celebrated the wildness of its nature and of her own.

Lucien was lost in that moment. What's more, he had the sense to know it even if could not help himself. It was a supreme irony, he thought, that after all the wiles and traps avoided over the years he must succumb to a female who not only had no use for him, but who actually despised him.

A part of it was the challenge she represented, yes. But far greater was the invisible effect she exerted on his imagination and his emotions by her rare courage and spirit. These were things he had felt as he looked into her face the night before. They had only been reinforced as he watched her protect and defend the maligned wild creature that had come among them.

She was magnificent yet warm and human with it. He felt her attraction as a silent, irresistible beckoning. Like the great black cat, he had wanted to move in as close as possible to her, to kiss her hand, even to eat from it, and never again to stray beyond the radius of her incomparable smile.

Madness.

She wanted nothing to do with him. She might have accepted his aid the one time, but she had no use for his hand or his kiss. He wondered what it would take to make her want them. And him.

There was nothing he had ever desired in his life as much as he wanted now to come close to her wildness, to be touched by it, and to answer it with the release of his own unfettered passion.

A low rumble sounded behind him. The hair rose on the back of his neck as he recognized the sound. He had noticed moments before that the panther had left the clearing, fading into the woods. Drawing the sword from his cane in swift instinct, he spun to face the beast that had circled around to stalk him.

"No, Satan!"

It was Anne-Marie who issued that sharp command. She came toward them at a run, with a hectic wash of color across her cheekbones and laughter warring with concern in her eyes. As she met his incredulous frown, she stopped abruptly and dropped her skirts about her ankles. All expression died from her face. She lifted her chin.

Silence descended as they stood in a frozen tableau. For a single instant Lucien felt unendurably foolish as he and the boy James were held at bay by the panther while Anne-Marie stood with her hair floating around her and her gaze as coolly amused as that of a queen disturbed in her private quarters.

In dawning chagrin, he recognized the reason for her humor as his brain began abruptly to function again. He spoke with resignation. "Your pet, I presume?"

"You might call him so," she answered with some caution.

"I'm delighted to hear it since I have no wish to be his noonday meal."

She smiled, a slow blossoming. The words soft, she said, "He doesn't eat his defenders."

Lucien felt as if he had received a great and long-coveted honor. And standing there, he vowed that he would have the lady also.

He was not proud, nor was he overly scrupulous. He would win her, no matter how long it took. No, nor what means he must use to achieve it.

FOUR

"Did I do right, Mam'zelle?"

It was the cook's son, James, who asked it, an anxious frown on his face as he looked up at her for reassurance. Concern for the boy's feelings released Anne-Marie from her preoccupation. She would not for the world have had him bring this particular man to her here, but she could not let him know it.

Speaking almost at random, she said, "Yes, yes, you did fine."

"You want him, then?" the boy insisted.

She saw the flicker of brief enjoyment in Lucien Roquelaire's eyes. Unbelievably flustered, she lifted her hands to her hair, catching its fullness to wind it hastily into a knot at her nape; this she held with one hand while she searched in her pocket for her pins. Head bent so she need look at neither man nor boy, she said to James, "Never mind. You had best return to the house before you're missed from your kitchen duties."

As the boy moved off with reluctant steps, Lucien spoke. "I regret the intrusion if it upsets you, and apologize for it. Regardless, I would not have missed this revelation. Tell me how you tamed my namesake."

"He isn't—that is, he was named long before—" She stopped as she saw the amusement in his eyes and realized explanations were unnecessary. Drawing a deep breath, she said instead, "You may have escaped Satan, m'sieur, but you run a much graver risk by showing even a slight interest in my welfare. My stepmother will leap at once to— In short, if you are found here alone with me, you will be compromised."

"Is that all it would take?" he inquired with a lifted brow.

"I do not speak in jest." The words were sharp.

"I am aware," Lucien said with fleeting irony. "We have met, your stepmother and I."

"Then you can see it would be advisable for you to go at once."

He smiled. "I seldom follow advice. Besides, I believe it's too late to avoid a certain amount of speculation, and you cannot expect me to leave until you have explained."

"About Satan? It happened much as you might suppose." She moved away from him to a huge red oak nearby, then turned to lean her shoulders against it with her wrists behind her back and her hands flat on the cool bark.

"I imagine he was an orphan," he said as he restored his sword cane to its sheath. Resting the tip on the toe of his boot, he waited for an answer.

"I heard him crying from the house and found him here. Hunting the big swamp cats is considered great sport, you know. Often it's a female with kits that is killed."

"But most animals rescued in that fashion return to the wild; there is no help for it. How is it you retained your Satan's fidelity?"

"I found him here in this place nearly two years ago, and here he remained. I joined his den, you might say, bringing food, making him warm and comfortable in familiar surroundings instead of taking him back to the house. He grew away from me, of course, especially this winter while we were in New Orleans; I had hardly caught a glimpse of him this summer. He is so much larger, I was not sure it was he when I first saw him last evening. But he came, I think, because he was hurt and hungry and still looks to me for safety and comfort."

"Wise animal," Lucien said. "You have been tending his injury this morning?"

She nodded. "The paw was not as bad as I feared. I cleaned it and applied a salve, but I believe he has licked it all away." She paused. "M'sieur Roquelaire—"

"I would be honored if you would address me by my given name." The look in his brown-gold eyes was steady as he awaited her reaction.

"M'sieur Roquelaire," she repeated with some emphasis, "we are not close acquaintances, nor are we likely to be. I was just going to say that you are free to go, now that you have paid your duty visit. Please don't let me keep you."

"And what if I prefer to be—kept?"

An odd fullness pressed against her throat so that it hurt. She swallowed with difficulty. "There is no obligation to continue with your gallantry, sir. I am suitably grateful for the effort you have made, but I'm sure you have duties elsewhere. I bid you a good day."

His smile was wry. "I understand you want to be rid of me, but if I go now, will you permit me to call on you again in more formal circumstances?"

"I have warned you of the consequences."

"And the warning was duly registered. If I should dare to brave your dragon of a stepmother, is it possible you will see me?"

She opened her mouth but had no idea what she meant to say until a single blunt word emerged. "Why?"

His expression turned wary, though it was a momentary lapse. "You are an unusual young woman, and I would very much enjoy the opportunity to further our acquaintance."

"You mean I am an oddity you wish to inspect at greater leisure."

"I mean," he said deliberately, "that I am intrigued by you. The leisure to become acquainted seems the next step."

"Toward what object?" she inquired.

Exasperation crossed his face, and he ran a square, competent hand through his hair, leaving it ruffled. "What do you expect?"

"I can't imagine," she said in clipped tones, "which is the reason I am asking."

"Suppose I said matrimony."

"Impossible." She closed her lips tightly on that single word.

He eyed her with the stiffness of distrust. "Impossible to believe, or impossible to contemplate?"

"Both," she snapped, turning her head away from him to stare out through the trees.

He took a swift step that brought him within arm's length. "What if I could convince you I mean what I say?"

"Then I will tell you plainly that I have no high regard for a rake as a possible husband." She turned back to him with a defiant stare. "A man who will keep me with child while he spends his time drinking and gaming and pursuing other women is not my idea of bliss."

A shadow crossed his face, and its darkness lingered in his eyes. "You don't want children?"

"I would be delighted," she said scornfully, "if they could be brought into the world by a father who truly cares for their welfare—or else without a man at all."

He tilted his head. "What of the pleasures of the marriage bed? I would not mention such a topic to a lady ordinarily, but you did glance upon it."

"A trifling matter," she snapped with a flare of color on her cheekbones. "At least, so it appears to me compared with the outcome of it. As I have been my father's housekeeper these last few years, tending the birthings in the plantation quarters has fallen to my lot. More than that, I watched my mother give birth year after year, burying pieces of her heart with the stillborn infants, all for lack of consideration in her husband. Then her few living children died one by one, until only I was left, and I was not enough to hold her. And within weeks of removing the widower's armband from his sleeve, my father set another woman in her place."

"So I am to be denied because your father was not worthy of the woman he married?" He reached out with apparent aimlessness to brace a hand on the tree trunk beside her.

Blinking as if she had not considered that possibility, she said, "My father wasn't—that is, he is at the mercy of his male nature."

"No," Lucien said with finality. "It isn't the nature of a man to use his wife without regard for her health and comfort, or to fail in supporting her. That excuse is only a convenience for a weak man."

Her chin came up. "You know nothing of the matter!"

"I know," he said, leaning closer, "that my wife will have nothing to fear from me, that the spacing of children or their advent is something we will agree upon between us. I know that if sorrow must come, she will not face it alone. I know that there is more to marriage than pain and terror; there is also comfort and pleasure and peace, and the abiding grace of love."

The gaze she turned up to him was stark with some deep longing. It was also brief. Sweeping her lashes down like a final curtain, she said, "Fine talk, but you are still a murderer."

"A duelist, when pressed," he corrected. "And you are a woman who has never been kissed, much less suffered— or enjoyed—the marriage bed. So how can you judge the state, or a prospective mate, when you have no idea what you will be missing?"

"I don't want to know!" she began.

But it was too late. He leaned closer to circle her waist with his arm and pull her against him. Then his lips came down on hers.

Stunned disbelief held her motionless while her heart shuddered into a faster rhythm and heat radiated in waves through her body. Her senses reeled with the concentrated fervor of the contact. His lips were smooth and warm and sweet. Beneath them, her own tingled as if they were swelling. Her brain felt as if it were on fire and her blood pulsed through her veins with frantic, fantastic life. Never had she known such expanding, rampaging wonder.

She could feel the hard strength of him, sense the smoothness of the linen and broadcloth he wore, smell the soap-and-bay-rum freshness of his skin. And it was not enough. She wanted to be a part of him, to make him a part of herself. The urge was so violent that she shivered with it, while deep inside a slow, insidious throbbing became an intolerable ache.

Abruptly, she was free. Shocked beyond words, not

only at what he had done but at her own reaction, she could only stare at him while she clutched his coat sleeve for balance.

"God in heaven," he whispered, his gaze dark and equally startled as he stared down into her face.

It was an effort to force her cramped fingers to release him. Backing away, she lifted her hand to her burning lips.

"Wait," he said, moving after her.

"Don't touch me!" she said, retreating with greater haste. "I require no more demonstrations of how you will treat a wife."

"I only wanted— I don't know what came over me."

"You wanted to show me what marriage would be like, and you succeeded. I hope you are satisfied, for you won't have the chance again!"

"If that was my object, it was a mistake, since I also discovered what I stand to lose." He held out his hand. "Accept my abject apology, if you please. I promise not to trespass again."

"No, I will see to that." She whirled, picking up her skirts, and plunged away, back toward the big house.

He halted then, only lifting his voice to call after her. "Running away will do no good. I know where to find you."

"You won't, not again," she cried over her shoulder.

"I will," he said, the words low yet carrying in their fixed determination. "Always."

FIVE

Lucien was a chess player. At the board he preferred aggressive moves, a strategy that had proven useful in a number of other undertakings. He was not certain it would work with Anne-Marie but could see no alternative.

To enlist the aid of Madame Decoulet was natural since they shared the same basic goal. He did not confide in the lady, of course; that would have been unwise given Anne-Marie's feelings toward her stepmother. In any case, it was unnecessary. All he had to do was appear on the doorstep at Pecan Hill and suggest he wished to have Anne-Marie's company for an afternoon drive in his Crescent City buggy. The older woman naturally moved heaven and earth to see that his desire was granted.

"Are you comfortable?" he inquired with solicitation when he had handed a reluctant Anne-Marie onto the passenger seat, then joined her to take up the reins.

The look she gave him was less than charmed. Immediately afterward, she turned her face away so he was left with only a view of her poke bonnet brim.

"Good, we can go, then." Setting the fine gray mare in the shafts into motion, he guided the buggy out of the yard and onto the dirt track that passed for a road.

"How is Satan?" he asked pleasantly.

Silence from the woman beside him.

"And James, is the boy well?"

Nothing.

"I thought to be able to say hello to your father, but he was from home. I trust he is in good health?"

The grip of her gloved hands in her lap tightened slightly, but that was the only sign he received that she had heard.

"Sulking is a sign of immaturity, and unsatisfactory besides," he said in the tone of one pointing out an obvious fact. "If you have a bone to pick with me, it will be more useful to give me the devil while you tell me exactly what's wrong."

"You know very well," she said through set teeth.

He managed, just, to conceal his satisfaction at goading a response from her. Guiding his team around a sharp curve that gave him an excuse to press his shoulder against hers, he replied, "I could make a guess, but that isn't the same as knowing."

She wrenched away from him with her eyes glinting within the shadow cast by her bonnet. "I told you I did not care to see you again and gave you my reasons. Not only did you ignore my expressed wish, but you used my stepmother to coerce me. I may be forced to endure your company in order to avert a family squabble, but you cannot compel me to engage in idle chitchat to make the drive more agreeable for you."

"In short, you despise me more today than you did when last we met." His words, he thought, were insufferably affable. He hoped she would rise to the bait.

"Yes!"

"And there is nothing I can do to change your opinion?"

"Indeed not."

"Then it's also unlikely any action of mine can worsen it." His words were layered with silken suggestion.

Rose-red color spread across her cheeks. "What do you mean?"

"Nothing, nothing," he said smoothly, but he was satisfied. She had been reminded of his kiss and was not unaffected by the memory. The dread of having it repeated—or anticipation of it, if he wanted to be optimistic—should now remain at the forefront of her mind. If he was lucky, it would persuade her to be more amenable. If not, well, he was not too proud to use any viable excuse to repeat the exercise.

"Why are you doing this?" she demanded, shifting on the seat to face him more squarely. "I refuse to believe you have any wish to be wed, no matter what you may say. Even if you did, it's unlikely you would select a bride without a careful process of elimination. As for choosing one who holds you in disregard, that is sheer madness—and though you may be many things, I don't think you insane."

"I suppose I should thank you for that much," he said dryly. "But tell me, have you any idea how I might proceed if I fell madly in love?"

"A staggering thought." Her words were bitten off as he negotiated a bumpy curve that jostled her against him, forcing her to clutch his shoulder to prevent herself from sprawling onto his lap.

It was difficult to concentrate on the road and the conversation while the soft curve of her breast was pressed against his arm. The effort sent a twitching shudder down his back. Compressing his lips, he said, "Now, why should it be so hard to imagine? I am exactly as other men."

Drawing away the instant the road ran straight again, she evaded his gaze while she yanked her clothing back into place and realigned her bonnet. "Other men," she said with precision, "don't murder those who happen to disagree with them."

Goaded in his turn, he said, "I will grant my past is a less than sterling example of sensible conduct, but I have never provoked a meeting, never injured a man who was not trying his best to kill me."

"Oh, please," Anne-Marie said in disparagement. "All men say that, but if it were true, there would be no duels."

He did not answer immediately as his attention was deflected by distant sounds. It was, he thought, a pack of hounds baying on a trail. The dogs might have been let out of their pen to run on their own, giving chase to a deer or any other animal that might have chanced to cross their path. They could also be leading hunters through the woods. Fall might be the time generally reserved for serious sport, but the men exiled from New Orleans by hot weather were apt to accept any diversion that was offered.

In some distraction, he said, "I am sorry for the death of your brother, but as tragic as it may have been, I own no responsibility for it."

"No one suggests that you do. But you have undoubtedly caused just as much grief to others." The words were not quite as rigid as he might have expected. Anne-Marie had also noticed the chase, for she sat with her head tilted in a listening pose and a frown between her brows.

The dogs were off to the left-hand side of the road. They seemed to be following the winding course of a creek that crossed the road, then continued on to meander through the Decoulet plantation. It was possible the animal being hunted would turn and follow the open roadway when it reached it. Lucien pulled in the mare a little, holding her on a tight rein. The gray might not mind sharing the right-of-way with a rabbit or deer but would certainly object to anything larger.

Returning his attention to his companion, he said, "You appear to know the public story of my career, both on and off the dueling field. I inveigled you into driving out with me because I want—"

"So you admit it!" The words carried amazed triumph.

"It seemed the only way to persuade you to listen," he agreed. "I particularly wanted to talk to you about—"

"But that's infamous when I explained quite clearly that I—"

"Will you please allow me to speak?" he said in grim determination, even as he noted the yells and crashing sounds of a hunting party far back in the woods, riding hell-bent after a quarry. "There are circumstances known only to the parties involved which may change your view of what took place."

"I seriously doubt that anything you can say will explain away the death of a young man several years your junior."

He grimaced. "As it happens—"

At that moment a dark shadow bounded from among the trees and streaked across the road ahead of them. The mare shied with a shrill whinny and reared in the shafts. Lucien swore as he rammed his booted heel against the footboard for leverage and sawed at the reins. Anne-Marie clutched his arm, her fingers biting into his cramped muscles.

"It's Satan," she cried. "The dogs are after Satan!"

Lucien had been afraid of just that; the excuse for going after the panther had been far too good for the men of the neighborhood to pass up. He cursed himself for bringing Anne-Marie out this afternoon. If he had not, she might never have known.

"Stop! Oh, please stop," she begged. "I've got to help him."

Lucien sent her a look of incredulity. Voice rough, he said, "There's nothing you can do."

"If I call him, he'll come to me. I can protect him." Her gaze turned up to him was fretted with desperation.

"Yes, and the dogs will tear you to pieces, too."

She swung from him without answering. One hand braced on the side of the buggy, she gathered her skirts as if preparing to leap. Lucien cursed under his breath. Snatching the lines in one hand, he clamped a hand on her wrist. She wavered off-balance in his hard grasp, half in and half out of the buggy. Shouting at the gray and pulling on the lines, he slowed the vehicle.

At that moment, the hounds burst from the woods. The mare went wild. Yelping, snapping dogs leaped away from the lash of hooves. The buggy slewed across the road in a cloud of dust. Tree limbs lashed the struts and stung Lucien's face. Anne-Marie was flung against him. As she twisted out of his way, she was thrown from the seat to the floorboard, where she huddled for an instant. Bracing with gritted teeth, Lucien used both hands and every rock-hard, aching muscle he possessed to hold the mare. The buggy bumped over road ridges. Skidding, swaying, almost tipping, it skirted the ditch. It rocked violently, then shuddered to a halt.

Lucien sprung down at once and lunged for the mare's head. The bit was barely in his hand before the first horseman jumped the ditch and clattered across the road. Others boiled after the rider, shouting and cursing as they saw the obstacle in their way. They reined around it in clouds of dirt and gravel. Brief and noisy moments later, they were gone.

"Stop them!" Anne-Marie called out as she stood upright in the buggy. "You've got to stop them!"

"What do you suggest?" he demanded. "Even if I had a mount and could chase them down, they are unlikely to listen to reason. That cat of yours scared them senseless. They won't stop until he's no longer alive to remind them."

She stared at him with horror in her face. An instant later, she whirled to clamber from the wagon. Jerking up her skirts, she sprinted into the woods after the riders.

Using every vicious and profane phrase he had ever heard, Lucien dragged the mare by main strength to a sapling beside the road and lashed the reins around it with a hard jerk. He leaped to the carriage to seize his sword cane, then lunged after Anne-Marie.

He might have lost her if he had not heard her crying out to her pet. She was that fleet, had that much of a head start. Incredibly, the panther was answering her calls; he could be heard yowling far off.

It seemed the animal was circling back. His plaintive cries were definitely coming closer. And the dogs were following on his heels, baying like the hounds of hell.

By the time Lucien reached Anne-Marie, the great night-black animal was gliding through the trees. Panting, sides heaving, it streaked to her and dropped into a crouch at her feet. She bent over it, murmuring reassurance.

There was only one thing to be done. Stationing himself in front of the girl and the great cat, Lucien drew his sword cane and tossed aside the outer cover. He slashed the blade through the air to limber his arm, then set his feet. As the dogs burst from their cover, he swung to face them.

They came from three directions. With dripping muzzles and the hot, glazed eyes of the chase, they charged the cat. Lucien struck right and left with the flat of the sword, a flurry of solid blows to black-and-tan backs and flanks.

The dogs danced this way and that, trying to get past him. Finding it impossible, they backed and sidled and turned in circles before charging once more. Met by strokes that whipped the air and carried a sharp edge, they cowered with sharp yelps and whimpers, quailing before slinking back out of reach.

In the midst of the battle, the horsemen came thundering up. Their hallos and yells grew hoarse with outrage.

"What in hell's goin' on here!"

Lucien barely glanced at the riders. Voice slicing in its hard command, he shouted, "Call off your dogs!"

"Like hell! Get out of our way." The spokesman was a burly man with the rust-red hair of Ireland, the clothes of a gentleman, and the accents of a dirt farmer.

"To take the cat you'll have to take me." Lucien's face was set, and his eyes glittered with challenge. "And then explain it to Mademoiselle Decoulet."

The men looked from him to Anne-Marie where she stood above the panther with her bonnet hanging down her back by its strings, her dress ripped by briars, and her hair loose about her shoulders. They were not cruel men, nor were they unreasonable when the fire began to die out of their blood. Shifting in their saddles, wiping sweaty brows, they talked in low tones among themselves. It was plain to see their greater uneasiness was centered in the big cat that lay among them, flicking its tail and regarding them with wary alertness.

"It ain't natural," came a mutter from the rear of the semicircle of horsemen. The comment was echoed by rumbling agreement from several quarters.

It was Victor Picard who finally dismounted and stepped forward as spokesman. Dividing his appeal between Lucien and Anne-Marie, he said, "It's not that we're after the panther for no reason, you must understand that. The way we see it, the thing's a danger to everybody for miles around. Nobody can sleep for wondering when he'll come sneaking through a door or window left open for air—or what he'll do when he gets inside. We can't risk him killing somebody, or maybe carrying off a babe next time he gets hungry."

"He wouldn't do that," Anne-Marie protested, paling at the suggestion.

"Can you guarantee it?" Picard demanded in strained reason. "We can't spend night and day looking over our shoulders, listening to him screaming back in the woods. He's got to go, *chère*."

"He would never hurt anybody, really, he wouldn't." She stepped forward to put out her hand as she pleaded for the great cat.

"How do you know?" Victor shot back. "He's a mangy panther, a wild animal. You can't tell what he might do. And you won't always be around to stop him."

"He isn't wild! I raised him from a kit, and he loves me. There's no reason to be afraid."

The men exchanged quick, significant looks. It was difficult to tell whether the reaction uppermost in their minds was disbelief or wariness for a young woman who was mad enough to claim the affection of a wild beast.

Then off to one side, a man made the sign of horns, a gesture to ward off evil. Two others spoke in sibilant whispers.

"Witch—"

"She-devil—"

Lucien's chest felt hot and tight as he realized what Anne-Marie had done. A lady did not befriend a panther. A lady did not defy menfolk. A lady did not claim to be fearless in face of a danger that caused men to tremble. A lady did not, above all, mark herself as possessing strange powers over savage beasts.

Anne-Marie was already considered something of an oddity. By showing herself irretrievably as a creature beyond the ken of her neighbors, she had just made herself an outcast. If there had ever been a time when she might have contracted a respectable marriage, it was ended.

Lucien, recognizing what was happening, saw his way with sudden bright clarity. From this moment on, he knew with quiet exultation, there could be no turning back. She was in his hands.

"Enough," he said, infusing his voice with the lash of authority as he stared down the other men. "You cannot take the panther here and now without killing him in front of the lady. And I feel sure that's a bloody deed none among you wants to undertake."

There was still some muttering and a few curses, but the men noted the trenchant challenge in his face, remembered his reputation with the sword in his hand. They saw, too, that he had given them a way to save face by pretending to bow to female sensibility. It took a few more minutes of milling aimlessly, of talking under their breaths and gesticulating with low threats about how they meant to get the beast come hell or high water. In the end, however, they mounted up again and called their dogs.

From the saddle, Victor Picard said, "We'll let it go,

Roquelaire, but this isn't the end of it. You can bet on that."

"I didn't expect it would be," Lucien said, and he meant it.

Reining around, the disgruntled men kicked their mounts into movement. They vanished back into the woods.

The crashing and muffled thuds of the men's departure faded away. With the slow precision of stiff muscles, Lucien turned to face Anne-Marie.

"You saved Satan," she said quietly. Her face was pale and her gaze fastened on him in clear and steady appraisal.

He made no reply as he moved closer, stepping around the big cat. He felt odd, almost disembodied, as reaction seeped through him like a slow-moving poison. There was a prickling sensation along his spine and the jittery aftermath of overtried temper in his brain. At the same time, exhilaration fizzed like champagne in his veins.

"I must thank you," she went on, eyeing him with some trepidation. "And I would had I not the strangest feeling that, whatever you may have done in the heat of the moment, it was for reasons of your own."

He reached her then, catching her forearms in his strong hands to drag her nearer. Giving her a slight shake, he said through gritted teeth, "Lady, you need a keeper."

"Because I wouldn't sit and wring my hands while Satan was hunted down like—like vermin?" she said with unsteady defiance. "That's ridiculous."

"You could have been killed. You might have been caught between the dogs and that great damned cat and slashed to ribbons."

She flung her head back. "But I wasn't. And now Satan is safe, and that's all that matters."

"Satan may be safe, but I'll be damned if you are," he answered, his grasp tightening.

"My only danger," she began, then stopped. She glanced at his hands on her arms, then stared into his set face while her eyes widened in wonderment. In abrupt concern, she said, "You're shaking."

His gaze meshed with hers, sinking into the pools of her eyes until he felt as if he were drowning. She was right, he saw. It was a fine quivering that ran through his hands and arms and down to his toes. Clattering his teeth together, it threatened to loosen his grip on his temper.

He had felt something of the same thing after his first duel. Cool and calm while it was taking place, he had descended into rattled nerves when he had discovered it was over and he was alive and unharmed. It was a natural response to the keyed-up state necessary for facing death. Still, it had never troubled him again. Until now.

He loosened his grasp to rub his hands up and down along her arms. His voice husky, he said, "You're trembling, too."

"Am I? Oh, yes," she said as she was shaken by an especially strong rigor. "But you—" A tiny frown appeared between her brows, and she reached to touch his face with quivering fingers. "You came rushing in to protect me. You risked your life, but are used to that. It was not yourself you were afraid for, I think."

He made no reply; he could not while she brushed her cool fingertips along the plane of his cheek and traced the hard muscle in his jaw in delicate exploration. It was so very pleasant, so devastating in its offer of heart's ease.

There was the amazement of discovery in her tone as she went on. "You don't like death, do you? It gives you no pleasure. Rather, it offends you. You despise it."

"Doesn't everyone?" he answered in ragged tones.

She shook her head. "Some are terrified of it, some are fascinated, some indifferent, and others accepting. Few fight it as you did."

This was cutting too close to the bone. Releasing her abruptly, he stepped back. "The mare," he said, clutching at the first thing that came to mind for a distraction. "I had better see after her. Will Satan follow if I return you home now?"

"Yes—yes, I'm sure he will," she answered, her eyes still searching his features as if some secret were hidden beneath the flesh and bones.

"Come, then," he said, holding out his arm while he turned his face away from her.

She hesitated a moment longer, but accepted the support he offered at last and allowed him to lead her back to the buggy.

The big cat followed like a faithful dog, gliding after them through the edge of the woods, keeping pace until they reached the house once more. Satan disappeared, however, when they stopped on the front drive.

The eyes of the butler who opened the door to them widened as he saw their disheveled state. Too well trained to comment, he directed them to the salon in answer to Lucien's request for Madame Decoulet.

Anne-Marie's stepmother lacked that discretion. Rising out of her chair as they entered the room, she lifted her hands and exclaimed in tones of horror, "Dear God in heaven! What have you been doing, the two of you? You look as if you have been rolling in the grass!"

"I hope I have more concern for a lady's comfort," Lucien said in justifiable sarcasm. "In fact, we met with a misadventure."

"You overturned your buggy?" There was blank disappointment in the woman's voice.

"Rather, we had a confrontation of some moment in the woods."

The older woman's bosom lifted with her indignation. "Just as I thought! I hope no one saw your condition." She turned on Anne-Marie. "Go to your room at once, you ungrateful little wretch, while I speak to this so-called gentleman."

"Please, madame," Anne-Marie said in stringent tones, "it isn't what you think."

"I have eyes in my head, my girl!" The older woman swung back to Lucien. "Sir, whatever your habits in New Orleans, you cannot play fast and loose here with a young woman's good name and get away with it."

Anne-Marie drew a gasping breath. "It was nothing like that!"

"Quite probably it was worse; you can't fool me!"

"I regret cutting short your strictures, madame," Lucien interrupted, "but feel any explanation of this affair should be placed before M'sieur Decoulet. Is he, perhaps, at home?"

The older woman's face took on an alarming mottled color, then she met his hard gaze, saw the purpose that glittered there. Her lips parted while avid speculation rose in her small eyes.

At that moment, the door leading into the library opened. Anne-Marie's father emerged, holding a book in his hand with his forefinger marking his place. "What is this commotion?" he inquired in stern yet querulous tones.

"Nothing of great moment," Lucien said evenly as he turned toward the older man and inclined his head. "There was a little excitement along the road. I would be most happy to discuss it if you will give me leave. Then there is a matter of some importance I would put before you. In private."

Anne-Marie's father surveyed Lucien, his eyes keen and measuring. What he saw seemed to satisfy him. He nodded. "Come into the library."

Lucien moved forward. At the door, he turned with a stiff bow for Anne-Marie, who looked on with puzzlement and suspicion in her face. Grasping the door handle, he pulled the heavy panel closed behind him.

SIX

There was something going on.

Anne-Marie could feel it in the air, sense it in her father's grave stares turned upon her, deduce it from the flurry of letters sent from Pecan Hill in the care of a groom. It disturbed her in part because no one saw fit to explain it to her, but most of all because her stepmother was ecstatic over it.

She had feared at first that there might be a connection to Lucien's interview with her father following the incident involving Satan and the hunters. That idea had slowly lost sway in the past three days as the Dark Angel failed to call again and all reference to the event faded away. She had not remained in disgrace nearly as long as she had expected, however, which was another bothersome aspect.

She tried to tell herself that Lucien must have put the best possible light on what had happened on the road and in the woods, that his account had somehow mollified her parent and stepparent. His attitude at the time had not indicated that he might do that for her, but he did seem to have the instincts of a gentleman.

It was also possible, of course, that he had put the worst possible construction upon it. In that case, her father and stepmother could be planning some terrible punishment for her. That would at least account for her father's concern and her stepmother's happiness.

Her greatest fear was that she might be banished. Several possibilities as to a destination occurred, each worse than the other. There was a cousin who had married a poor farmer and given birth to seven children in nine years, so had need of another pair of hands. Or she might be sent to be a companion to her father's elderly aunt in New Orleans, an obese and raddled creature who smelled of snuff and camphor and talked interminably of her days as a belle. A last resort might be the convent in the countryside south of Paris she had heard whispers about, one where wayward females who had embarrassed their families were sometimes shut away.

To lose her freedom would be a terrible thing; the fear of it haunted her. Yet her mind wandered away to other thoughts and images with distressing frequency.

She could not stop thinking of Lucien Roquelaire. She had always felt sorry for those hapless females who sighed and wept over the men in their lives, yet her spirits were low and everything seemed dull and dreary as she accepted that he was not going to call again. It was true that the two of them had sparred and sniped at each other without letup, yet there had been an undercurrent of something very different between them. He had looked at her in a way no man ever had before; she had felt in him a fearlessness and tolerance beyond anything she had ever known. She might despise him and abhor his past, but she had also been forced to recognize his essential integrity. Almost, she had allowed herself to believe that he had an interest in her, even if it was only because she was not like every other woman he met. Because of it, she had permitted herself to wonder what it would be like to be loved.

She had ignored that possibility so long, denying it because that was less painful than yearning after it when she could not have it. Even believing it could and would come to nothing with Lucien, she found that it still hurt to have the idea of being wanted removed so quickly.

Sometimes at night she lay staring into the dark, thinking of the moment he had kissed her. She could remember the sensation as his mouth possessed hers, the taste and liquid warmth of him. She seemed to feel again the heat of hands upon her, and their sure strength, which she had recognized even through her clothing. Sometimes her imagination took flight, and she lay naked with him under the trees as her stepmother had suggested. Or else they stretched out on the pristine white sheets of her bed while he demonstrated to her all the many uses of his masculine ardor and power.

Useless daydreams. Yet they were so disturbing that she did her best to prevent them rather than retreating into them as in the past. The trouble was that they crept in upon her so insidiously that she could not always control the direction of her mind.

She had another and more insistent worry. She had not seen Satan since the day of the hunt. Though she went into the woods again and again to call him, he never came. It was likely he had retreated deep into the river's swamplands, beyond the reach of dogs and riders. Cats were notorious for avoiding water, but she had seen Satan swim creeks in flood before, and she knew he would have no trouble navigating the interconnected rivers, bayous, and wide, shallow sloughs. In any case, the water receded with the advance of summer, leaving vast areas of open grass or shady and leaf-carpeted bottomland that were reasonably dry.

She prayed that was where he had gone. If he had not— But she would not think of that. This was not the first time Satan had vanished; he would come back to her in his own good time, or else when instinct told him it was safe to be seen in this vicinity.

She was returning from another fruitless tramp through the woods when the young boy James came running to meet her. His feet were flying along the path, and he was frowning with the weight of his message. He was still several yards away when he began to yell.

"Mam'zelle! You got to come quick! They been looking for you everywhere. Madame is so mad she's 'bout to spit, and your papa is walking up and down with his pocket watch in his hand."

"What's wrong? Why do they want me?" She quickened her footsteps to a swift walk again as she met the boy and he spun around to return with her to the house. He was breathing hard, as though his search had been a long one.

"I don't know, Mam'zelle. But M'sieur Roquelaire has been talking to your papa since the middle of the morning. When they come out of the library, they say they must see you. M'sieur Roquelaire wanted to come find you himself, but your stepmama said it would not be fitting. Why wouldn't it be fitting, Mam'zelle?"

"Stupid propriety," she answered shortly. "No one mentioned why I must be there?"

"No, Mam'zelle. But your stepmama's maid has been talking with Cook in the kitchen, and I heard them say they must start at once to plan a feast."

She gave the boy a distracted smile. "I expect you liked the sound of that."

"But yes, Mam'zelle. Don't you?"

She didn't. In fact, the idea sounded quite ominous to Anne-Marie. There was no time to work out the implications, however, for they reached the back door a few seconds later and made their way into the house.

She had thought to slip upstairs to wash her face and tidy her hair, perhaps change into something less faded and worn, before going in to see Lucien. She was not given the opportunity. Her stepmother sailed down the wide central hall to greet her with hissing denunciations for her tardiness, her lack of consideration, and her determination to disgrace herself. Ordering James to the kitchen, she grasped Anne-Marie's arm and marched with her back down the hall to the salon. As she stopped at the door, her dire frown miraculously became a smile. Pushing inside, she said in tones of arch amusement, "Well, and here is the truant at last. Now we may get on with this delightful arrangement."

Anne-Marie saw her father and Lucien standing before the French window that opened onto the front veranda. They turned as one, their faces mirroring an identical preoccupation. Lucien took a step in her direction, then stopped as her father spoke.

"At last, my dear. We were beginning to think you had run away."

She tore her gaze from the visitor to attend to her father. "No, why should I?"

"Young women often take fright when they realize their future is being decided." The older man gave her a warm smile as he walked to a silver tray on a side table, where a crystal decanter of wine and four sparkling glasses sat waiting. He filled the glasses, then handed one to his guest and the other two to Anne-Marie and his wife before taking up his own.

Anne-Marie took the fragile crystal stem in numb fingers. Moistening her lips, she said, "You have been discussing me?"

Her father nodded. "Indeed. We have just finalized a contract of marriage. My dear daughter, I drink to your betrothal to this fine gentleman, Lucien Roquelaire, and to your happiness with him."

Betrothal.

Anne-Marie could feel the blood leave her face. The glass she held slipped from her hand. Wine spilled down the front of her skirt like blood. The glass struck the toe of her slipper, bounced with a musical clang, then rolled over the Turkish carpet to stop against Lucien's booted foot.

Her stepmother screamed. "*Mon Dieu*, but what good fortune it did not break! It's an omen, a sign of benediction for the marriage."

"Impossible." The word was only a croaking sound in Anne-Marie's throat. Her chest ached with the fullness inside it.

"No, no, only look here," her stepmother said as she swooped down on the glass and held it up. "I will refill it, like so, and you must drink quickly."

Anne-Marie wanted to cry out that they could not do this, that her life could not be decided without her participation or consent. But they could do it; marriages were arranged all the time. There was usually some pretense of courtship, some attempt at assuring the young woman of the benefits of the match, but the end result was the same.

Her stepmother was holding the brimming glass to her lips as if she meant to force her to drink. Pushing the woman's hand away, Anne-Marie said, "How did this take place? Why was I not consulted?"

"The initiative came from M'sieur Roquelaire when you returned from your drive some days ago," her father said. "Since then, we have been pursuing the matter of your dowry, also the amount you will be allowed for running his household and for pin money, which properties he will settle upon you, and other such financial considerations. As for consulting you, why, I thought you would surely know how matters stood."

She clasped her hands tightly in front of her. "How so, when I was given no inkling of it?"

"What difference does it make?" Madame Decoulet demanded. "All women require to wed. You should be glad for the chance."

"Glad? But surely—that is, what of his background, the—insecurity of being wed to such a duelist?" She was grasping at straws, but that was all that was left to her.

"Roquelaire has revealed his past to me, including the details of his several meetings. I have made inquires and am now satisfied. I feel sure he will explain to you also if you should ask. Have you any other objections?"

"I hardly know the man," she declared, barely glancing at Lucien's set face. "How am I to guess what else I may find objectionable?"

"My dear girl," her stepmother said in scathing tones, "you are in no position to pick and choose. People are chattering like magpies about your escapades with this beastly cat, both at the ball and in the woods. Some claim you are touched in the head, and those are the ones who are being kind. There are others who think you in league with the devil himself, that you must be a witch to be able to command such a terrible creature. They fear you and use your name to frighten children. What you need is a strong man to curb your ways. Now, drink!"

Once more, she brought the glass to Anne-Marie's

lips. As Anne-Marie pushed it away, it spilled yet again, this time splashing the older woman's cloth slippers. With a cry of outrage, Madame Decoulet drew back her free hand to strike Anne-Marie.

"That will do!"

The biting command came from Lucien. He walked forward, took the glass from the older woman, and set it on the table. Then he strode to the door and pulled it open, holding it while his gaze raked Anne-Marie's father and stepmother. "I would like to talk to my future bride. Alone, if you please."

The last words were mere politeness. It was obvious from the tempered steel in his voice that he meant to speak to her without their presence whether it pleased them or not. Or regardless of whether she herself wished for it.

As he closed the door behind her father and stepmother and turned to face her, it was all Anne-Marie could do to remain where she stood. The need to flee was so strong that her lower limbs twitched, quivering with it. But there was nowhere to go. She was trapped.

With his hand still on the doorknob, Lucien spoke in low tones. "I apologize for presenting this to you in this way. I assumed your stepmother would inform you, as is customary. Since there had been no suggestion that you were not agreeable, I thought everything was in order."

His gaze was dark with concern, yet direct. She had little choice except to believe him. She suspected that her father might also have been given the idea that she was amenable, a deliberate ploy of her stepmother's to prevent her from registering her protest until it was too late.

She said, "If you feel this is necessary because of the talk concerning our adventure the other day, then I must tell you it is not."

"My decision has nothing to do with compromising behavior, real or otherwise."

"No? Well, then what? The novelty, perhaps? Do you think having a wife who consults with animals will be sufficiently entertaining to make up for my other defects? Or do you simply feel sorry for me?"

His frown was instant as he moved away from the door, coming closer to where she stood on the Turkish carpet that centered the room. "None of those things apply. How could they? You are a beautiful and intelligent woman, one who doesn't bore me or giggle or cling. You have more courage than most men, and you don't mind showing it. You may not adore me, but you aren't afraid of me, either. If you don't like what I've done, you say so; you don't smile to my face and damn me behind my back."

"Oh, I see. You want me because I don't dote on you. You require the stimulation of a full-scale argument before breakfast every morning, and wish to feel that you are not leaving a disconsolate wife at home when you go out on your usual round of drinking and gambling with your friends."

A sardonic smile carved lines of amusement into his face. "What an opinion you have of me," he said softly. "Would you believe me if I tell you I intend to be an exemplary husband, hanging on your every word, seldom leaving your side? Can you accept that I am consumed with impatience to put my wedding day behind me so that I may keep you close at my side and the rest of the world at arm's length?"

"No," she said in steadfast disbelief.

He studied her, from the suffocating color in her face to her clenched hands at her side. "No one has ever told you that you are beautiful, have they? No one has ever said they wanted you. Are they blind?"

"Maybe it's you who are blind," she said rudely. "Or insane after all."

"I am neither. Rather, I am a man who knows his own mind and goes after what he wants when he finds it. I would have liked to proceed differently, but there is no time. If we are to save Satan, then you must marry me without delay and leave all the rest to work itself out as it will."

Her interest shifted, sharpened. "Satan? What do you mean?"

"If he stays here, he will eventually be killed. It can be no other way. If he is transferred to my house below New Orleans, he will have a vast new territory to explore. The acreage is large, a grant of several thousand arpents received from the French king more than a hundred and thirty years ago. There is no reason why your panther should ever have to see another human being. He will be safe there."

"But how could you take him? There is no way he could be captured and caged for transportation. He would not enter a cage, not even for me."

"Satan came to you when he was injured. It was as natural to him as breathing. He answers when you call, follows where you go, I think, because of the mystical connection that sometimes occurs between people and the animals they love. He would trail after you into the mouth of hell itself—or to my home, if you come as my wife."

Was it possible? She would like to think so, but who could tell?

Had he mentioned hell and his home in the same breath for a reason, or was it accidental? Did he realize she saw the choice before her in that light? He was a man of perception, with a penchant for irony. He might well take a perverse pleasure in presenting this union to her in the blackest possible light.

"Yes, I begin to see," she said, the words barely above a whisper. And she did. She saw that he wanted her. Her, personally. For herself.

He had not said so in those exact words, yet the suggestion had been in every phrase he spoke. That explanation was slightly more understandable, and acceptable, than any protestation of undying love and devotion. Desire did not require perfection, had little use for logic, cared nothing for suitability. It did not depend on morals, easily overcame antipathy. She had discovered these truths for herself since meeting Lucien Roquelaire.

She was surprised that he was willing to exchange his freedom for the prospect of attaining what he coveted. Still, was that not what men had been doing for countless ages?

His wife. If she agreed, she would drive away with him to his home many long miles away. There she would be close to him, near his side, forever. Everything would be changed; she would have a position, a new name. She would be free of her stepmother's dominion.

Free. That was a strange way of thinking about this marriage when just minutes before she had considered it a trap.

"Well?" he said, moving away toward the table where her wineglass stood. He picked it up and, returning to her side, held it out to her. His gaze steady, faintly demanding, he said, "Shall we drink to our betrothal after all?"

She met his eyes, her own dark and still and filled with cogent decision. She was breathing fast, each intake of air lifting her breasts against the bodice of her old gown as if she were in a desperate race. She studied his face as though the answers she found there could mean the difference between life and death.

Abruptly, she gave a nod. Her fingers trembled as she reached out to take the glass from his hands. So did her lips as she tried to smile. Still, her voice did not falter as she said quietly, "Yes, to us."

Touching the wine to her lips, she drank it down.

SEVEN

In a few short hours it would be her wedding day.

Anne-Marie stood on the veranda, staring into the dark and trying to make herself believe it. It seemed impossible.

Had she really agreed to be married? Could she force herself to stand composed and still beside Lucien Roquelaire while she was united with him for a lifetime?

The very idea made her feel panicky and ill with nerves. She could not think how she had come to agree; it was almost as if she had been under a spell. Perhaps he was a dark angel, after all, a being come down among them who could control people and animals and force them to his will.

That did not, of course, explain why he wanted her. She was no clearer in her mind about that point than she had been on the day two short weeks ago when they had become betrothed. She had thought it mere physical desire, yet he had made no attempt to take advantage of his privileges as her husband-to-be. It was puzzling; she had not expected him to be so punctilious.

Where had the time gone? The days had seemed to rush past like the wind, turning from morning into evening between one breath and the next. Somehow, she kept expecting that something would happen—that Lucien would change his mind or her father would suddenly discover the marriage was a mistake. Nothing did.

She had hardly seen Lucien, in all truth. There had been so much to do on such short notice: seeing the priest, writing out the invitations, planning and organizing the preparation of food and drink, ordering the wedding cake and special nougat confections to be shipped upriver by steamboat to arrive with the New Orleans guests, begging flowers from neighbors to supplement their own. Then there had been appointments with the local dressmaker for the necessary fittings for her wedding gown.

Her stepmother had offered her own wedding dress for Anne-Marie's use, a billowing, too-large creation in widow's purple satin with immense gigot sleeves. Anne-Marie had refused it outright and resisted all efforts at persuasion. She would wear her own mother's gown, which had also been worn by her grandmother. Of soft silk mousseline sewn with seed pearls and diamanté, it was a gown of simple design that had yellowed over the years to a shade of amber only a little lighter than the cravat Lucien had worn to the Picards' ball.

How marvelous it had been, achieving that point over her stepmother's opposition. It had made her think that she should have enforced her will more strongly before. She had been able to do it now, she knew, only because it no longer mattered if her stepmother was angry or her father upset by quarreling. Their displeasure could not disturb her since she would soon be leaving her childhood home for that of her husband, one that would become her own.

Yet how was it possible, after so many years of being kept close and chided for every small breach of conduct, that she would leave tomorrow to drive away with a virtual stranger? It made no sense that a few words and a piece of paper could bring about such a difference.

Behind her, a change in the light falling from the salon signaled an end to her time alone. Turning slightly where she stood at the end of the veranda, she watched as Lucien sauntered toward her.

"No sign of him?" her future husband said.

He meant Satan, of course. She wondered briefly how many of the others gathered for the wedding could have guessed she was still keeping watch for the great black cat, even after so long a time. She shook her head. Voice compressed, she said, "I think— I'm so afraid he must have been killed."

"No one has claimed credit for it." His voice held steady reassurance as he stopped a few feet away from her.

"No—but he wasn't as strong as usual. He may have run into more dogs. Or he could have crawled off somewhere to die of blood poisoning in his injured foot. Then maybe he was bitten by a snake, or tangled with a bear."

"And could be he found a mate and is enjoying a protracted . . . courtship," Lucien suggested.

She wanted so badly to be convinced that she ignored the impropriety of his allusion. "I suppose it may be possible, but he never has before."

"Some males come late to its joys. As I did, for

instance. Have I told you that you're looking particularly ravishing this evening?"

He was trying to distract her, and making a fair job of it. She glanced away from him in sudden embarrassment.

"Don't you care for compliments?" he asked, tipping his head as he tried to see her face.

"I never know what to say." The words were barely audible.

"Nothing much is required, only a polite word or two by way of acknowledgment."

"I—thank you, then."

"Very good. You should get used to that exercise because you will need it. You were attractive when we first met, but you seem to grow more so every day. And I am a man driven to salute beauty when I see it."

She gave him a brief glance. "Are you quite certain it isn't a habit you bring out when other forms of conversation fail?"

"You think I have nothing else to say to you?" He turned to place his back to the railing near where she stood, then crossed his arms over his chest. "Now that you put me in mind of it, there is a subject I've been trying to raise since we first met, only something always prevents it, or else you manage to turn it aside."

She said quickly, "So tell me then what you have heard from your letters to your family. Who among them may we expect to be present?"

"I had a long missive from my sister. She wishes us every joy, but is increasing, hoping to add a boy to the family of girls she and her husband have collected. Since it would be unwise to travel, she won't appear. My brother, ordinarily a sober citizen, fell off his horse and broke an ankle while involved in a drunken race, so sends his profound, and profane, regrets. Of course, my cousins who have been giving me house room are agog; they can't wait to fire off a description of the nuptials to all their friends. That takes care of my family. But you know full well that was not my meaning."

She did, of course. With great reluctance, she said, "I suppose you were speaking of your career as a duelist, then. You are quite right. I see no need to go into it."

"But I do. You called me a murderer some time back. To be condemned without a hearing seems hard."

"My view of the pastime is not unbiased, as you know." The words had a more placating sound than she intended.

"Certainly. But just as your brother had no alternative to appearing on the field of honor for the first time, neither did I. A loose-tongued fool raised the question of my mother's good name and why she was killed by my father. Some things cannot be left unanswered."

"I understand," she said.

He gave her a dark glance. "I doubt it. She was innocent, my mother, her death a tragic accident that turned my father into a half-deranged drunkard whose punishment was mainly self-inflicted. Being hotheaded and only eighteen, I thought only of the slur cast on my family name."

"My brother was also that age," she said quietly.

"Then you should realize that once matters reach a certain pass, there is no way, save dishonor, to draw back. The difference between my case and your brother's is that I was the one left alive when the thing was over."

"That may be," she said in neutral tones, "but it still explains just one meeting."

"You are interested in the others? My second was with the cousin of the first man I bested. He demanded revenge, you see, and was carried home on a jalousie for a stretcher. The third was over a lady's mistake. She began an affair with an actor who threatened blackmail when she tried to break it off. I intervened at her request, and her paramour objected. A puffed-up Romeo with more ego than sense, the actor would not declare himself satisfied at first blood, and so he died. The fourth man was a young fool who wagered that he could break my winning streak—he still carries his arm in a sling in damp weather. The fifth was a cardsharp who happened to be a relation of mine. He became offended when I dared speak to him about his cheating habits. The sixth— But do I bore you?"

She gave him a straight look. "I do see your point."

"I'm delighted. But having begun, I would like to finish the list for you. As it happens, it was somewhere around this time that it became the fashion to cross swords with the man people were calling the Dark Angel, and the next eight meetings fall into that category—my life was not my own until I managed to discourage that particular test of courage. My fourteenth meeting, however, was with a man I saw beating his servant boy with a riding crop; he now has trouble breathing due to a badly healed puncture wound in one lung. The fifteenth was with a sea captain whose mistake was thinking I would be less able with an old-fashioned cutlass than with my usual sword. Then there was the last man."

"Number sixteen? I had not realized the count went so high."

"Actually, it is a recent affair, one that I pushed without mercy. My opponent was an arrogant rake who seduced the daughter of an old friend, then watched her leap to her death from a steamboat deck after he denied responsibility for the child he gave her. I meant to correct his manners, and perhaps interrupt his career of seduction by a mark or two on the face, but he was as much a coward on the dueling field as in his private affairs. As the challenged party, he chose pistols. We were stepping off the normal ten paces when he turned at the count of eight and fired. He missed, and was killed by his own second for that breach of the rules—a second who happened to be his brother."

"Dear heaven," she said with a shudder. "What a terrible thing dueling is."

"It is. And you can be sure I remember every meeting, every man, every drop of blood spilled and last breath of life taken by those I fought. Yet the practice ensures that men remember their manners and deal fairly with their fellow men or suffer the consequences. It's the inescapable code we live by. If I have killed, it is because the only other choice was dying. And I am not ready to die."

"No," she said in constricted tones, "but neither was my brother." She could see him still in her mind's eye, laughing, teasing, full of life. Yet he had been bloodlessly pale and cool when they brought him back from his meeting in the dawn.

"For that loss, I am desperately sorry," Lucien said. "I would take it from you if I could. But I am not to blame. Death is a natural thing, whether for a man or a panther; it always comes in its time. Whether it arrives early or late is in the lap of the gods. It is only left for us to feel gladness for being alive instead of guilt, to celebrate the joy rather than fear the pain."

"Sixteen," she whispered. "You fought sixteen times and survived every meeting."

"And came to be named an angel of death for it."

"Or an avenging angel," she said in quiet contemplation.

"Perhaps on occasion. But I am just a man, not an immortal, and I don't want to fight anymore."

"It could be—" She stopped, uncertain of the wisdom of speaking the thought that had come to her. It was important enough, however, that it must be ventured. "You believe, then, that having a wife will give you an excuse to turn away from any further challenge that might be pressed on you?"

"I pray that it will—but that isn't the reason I am marrying you," he said with emphasis. "It is you, the woman you are, who moves me. I wish you would stop looking for excuses and believe that simple fact. Or perhaps you do believe it, and are so disturbed that you are out here making up your mind to call off the wedding if your pet doesn't reappear."

"I gave you my word," she said. Which was not the same thing as denying that he was right.

"So you did," he said grimly, "but not without coercion or second thoughts."

She barely glanced at him. What he said was true in a sense. She was marrying the Dark Angel for the sake of a cat. She must be the one who was mad. But if Satan did not come back, then it would have been for nothing.

Oh, but would it? Did her reasons really have anything to do with Satan, or was it something else entirely? Was she fated always to love what was dark and uncontrollable and dangerous?

Love.

In some haste, she said, "Would you take it as proof that I am resigned if I told you I would like to leave for your home immediately after the reception?"

"Resigned." He repeated the word as if it had a bitter taste.

"Anxious, then, if you prefer."

"I do, infinitely, or would if I could believe it." He paused, then spoke again in more normal tones. "But what of the two weeks of seclusion required of a new bride to show her modesty? Madame Decoulet will be scandalized if you are seen abroad before they are over. Tongues will clack up and down the river about the depravity you have fallen into for my sake."

"Yes," she said on a defeated sigh.

"Of course," he said in considering tones, "you would not be around to hear it."

"You—you wouldn't mind if I became the subject of scandal?"

"My dear Anne-Marie," he said, a corner of his mouth turned up in irony, "how can I fault you when I've seldom been anything else?"

"Very true." Her gaze brightened as she straightened her shoulders. "Anyway, it would be a shame to rob everyone of their entertainment, don't you think? They will be looking so hard to see if either of us does anything strange."

"They may conclude, of course, that you were influenced by my wicked ways."

"Would that trouble you so much?" Her gaze turned serious.

"Oh, desperately," he said. "Though I'm sure that you can see to it that I am—resigned—if you make a diligent effort at it."

He was teasing her in his grim fashion. She gave him a darkling stare while color rose to her hairline. "If you are expecting to be persuaded by a display of affection, then you will be disappointed. Such things are best left until after we are wed."

He arched a brow. "Then I should expect a sudden change from coolness to fevered passion, is that it?"

"I never said—"

His smile turned feral. "But I think you did. And I await tomorrow evening with bated breath."

She met the dark amusement in his gaze for long, paralyzing moments before she turned her head. Her voice tight, she said, "You're trying to distract me again. And just now you spoke of the death of—of man or a panther. You really think Satan is gone for good, don't you."

He reached for her, gently drawing her close and encircling her in the comfort of his arms. She tensed for an instant before she relaxed, accepting his hold.

"I don't know where Satan is and refuse to guess when there is no proof one way or another," he said, speaking against the softness of her hair. "All I know is that wild things risk pain and loss of life every day; it's the price they pay for being free. But whatever happens, you have given the panther two years of love and caring. Because of you, he attained his full, splendid growth and gained the chance to prowl the woods, to mate and pass on his legacy of power to the next generation. That's all any of us are given."

"It isn't enough!" It was a cry from the heart.

"No," he answered as he stared over her head, smoothing his hand gently up and down her spine while his smile faded. "No, it isn't nearly enough."

EIGHT

It came, her wedding day, dawning bright and clear and hot. Perfect.

Anne-Marie thought of getting up quietly and leaving the house, of tracking through the grass that was wet with dew, making her way into the woods to Satan's clearing. And going on then until she could go no farther.

She thought of staying where she was without moving. When her stepmother came, she might turn her face to the wall while the woman ranted and raged at her to get up.

She thought of Lucien and what he would do when informed that she refused to leave her bed to be married to him. No doubt he would come storming up the stairs, fling into her room, and then . . .

She tumbled out of bed.

After that, it was not so bad. Since it was her day, she

was cosseted with a breakfast tray in her room. When she had finished her coffee, the preparations began in a desultory fashion. There was no need to hurry since it would naturally be an evening wedding; it was considered too embarrassing to have newlyweds hanging around the house for long after the ceremony. She and Lucien would stay only to have their health and happiness toasted, to cut the wedding cake, taste the food, dance a few waltzes. Then they would leave in his carriage for Baton Rouge. A steamboat would be docked there overnight on its regular run between Natchez and New Orleans. Lucien, last evening after they talked, had sent to reserve a private cabin. There they would spend their wedding night. With the morning, they would be on their way downriver to his home.

Anne-Marie would have preferred to have someone close to her to assist with her toilette. There being no one who qualified, she accepted the services of Madame Decoulet's maid. Everything would be done as she wished it, however; she made that clear from the start.

Her hair was washed in soft rainwater, then brushed dry in the sun. It was then polished by being rubbed with a length of silk and arranged in a crown of curls without a trace of pomade. Her nails were carefully shaped and buffed until they were pink and smooth and shining, then afterward her hands and arms, shoulders, knees, and feet were smoothed with scented lotion. When the maid had finished, she and Anne-Marie packed the last remaining items into her trunks, then saw them strapped and carried downstairs. By then it was noon, and a tray with a light meal was brought up to the bride's chamber. Afterward, she was left alone for a period of rest and repose.

This was the time when most brides knelt at the prie-dieu that adorned every bedchamber and prayed for hap-

piness, fruitfulness, and mercy. Anne-Marie tried dili-
gently, kneeling on the small velvet-covered bench with
her rosary between her knitted fingers and her gaze on the
crucifix hanging on the wall above it.

But the image of Lucien's face kept coming between
her and her devotions. She found herself thinking,
instead, of what it would mean if she were to make herself
over into a proper wife.

No more rambling in the woods. No more running
with wild creatures. No more hanging back in company
and pretending to be shy. No more watching the world
and its odd antics instead of joining them.

No more ignoring the future. No more thinking only
of herself. No more privacy. No more sleeping alone.

She rose from the prie-dieu and paced the room that
had been hers all the long years of her childhood but
would never be hers again. At the window, she rested her
forehead against the cool glass, staring out toward the
woods that lay beyond the barn.

Her father found her there as the sun canted toward
the west. A troubled look on his face, he came to her and
put his arm around her, saying in gruff tones, "Are you
well, *ma chère?*"

"Yes, of course." What other reply was there, now?

"This marriage, it's to your liking?"

Lucien was right, she saw that clearly. Her father was not a
strong man, had never been one. He liked his comfort and his
pleasures. He did not deal well with emotions. If he had doubts
about what he and the woman now his wife had arranged for
her, he had chosen a poor time to express them, now when it
was almost too late. Yet he was just a human being trying to
muddle through the business of living as best he could. He had
endured his sorrows and gone on to rebuild on the ruins of the
past. He was her father, and he was concerned for her.

"It's what I want," she said in quiet reassurance.

"Good." He drew a long breath. "That's good, then." He gave her arm a squeeze, then ran his hand up and down it as if still distracted. "I'm going to miss you, you know. You'll write?"

"Certainly, as often as there is news."

"Or even if there is none, just to let us know that you are alive and safe?"

"Yes." She swallowed on a rush of tears.

"And if Roquelaire doesn't treat you as he should—not that I expect it, mind, for he's a gentleman—but if things should not turn out as you like, then you know you have only to send word. I will come at once to bring you home again."

"Oh, Papa." She could not say more.

He heard the distress in her voice and was nervous of it. Giving her another quick hug, he said gruffly, "That's all right, then, as long as you remember. I just want what's best for you." Then he turned and went out, closing the door behind him.

Everything seemed to move at a hectic pace after he had gone. She had her bath. The maid returned and she was encased in corset, hoop, and petticoats. Her gown was lifted over her head in a quick flinging movement, then fastened up the back and settled around her. Her mother's veil of fine Valenciennes was pinned in place and a bouquet of late summer roses placed in her hand.

All too soon, she was descending the staircase and moving toward where Lucien stood with the priest. She reached for his arm as if grasping a lifeline. As his hand closed warm and firm around her chill fingers, she shivered once, then was still.

The rest passed as in a dream: the vows, the blessing, then the food and wine, the music and dancing. Too soon, she was handing over her bouquet to her father to be placed on her mother's grave. The last good-byes were said. She and Lucien moved down the steps and out to the carriage that was decorated with knots of ribbon. The final good wishes were called after them as they bowled away down the drive.

Before she knew it, the white wedding-cake pile of the steamboat loomed ahead of them at the dock. They pulled alongside, and she was helped down by her new husband. The narrow gangplank shifted under them with the easy motion of the river's current as they boarded.

Cordial greetings were extended by the captain himself. They were turned over to a steward then, one who led the way through the great main cabin with its Wilton carpeting in rich, jewel colors, its massive brass chandeliers and archways hung with ornate stalactites of woodwork. The door of their stateroom was reached, and a coin changed hands. They stepped inside, and the heavy door beneath its painted transom closed behind them.

She and Lucien were alone. Together.

The accommodation was doubtless the best the boat had to offer, being a corner stateroom with cross ventilation from two sets of windows and a double view of the river. However, it was barely large enough to contain its marble-topped rosewood washstand, small table with matching side chairs, and mahogany four-poster bed draped with mosquito netting. The tole-shaded lamp that burned on the table shed its light easily to the four corners.

Anne-Marie, suddenly beset by nerves, busied herself removing her gloves, then unpinning her veil and folding it carefully. Her trunks had been delivered earlier; they sat in a corner along with a strange one of leather-bound brass that must belong to Lucien. She lifted the lid of her smallest trunk and placed the veil inside, then took out her nightgown and hairbrush that she had left ready to hand.

From the corners of her eyes, she saw Lucien remove his hat and gloves and lay them aside with his cane. He stripped off the tailcoat of his evening suit and he draped it across a chair then walked to the casement window that stood open. As he pushed aside the jalousies a soft night wind off the water drifted into the room, bringing welcome coolness and the shimmer of moonlight on the water.

Resting one shoulder against the window frame, he spoke without turning. "You need not be wary of me; I'm not going to spring at you."

"I never expected it," she said, her voice not quite steady.

"No? I feared you might after our last conversation. But never mind. It will be best if we take a little more time to come to know each other before embarking on the intimacies of marriage."

She put her hairbrush on the washstand, then began to pull the pins from her hair so that it fell in soft, luxuriant waves to her waist. In the washstand's beveled mirror she could see the stiff set of her husband's wide shoulders. She had never seen a man without a coat other than her father on occasion or field workers; it was fascinating to follow the taut ridges of Lucien's back muscles under the soft linen of his shirt. She had never had occasion to notice the way his hair clung in soft, shining black waves to the back of his head, either. Her fingers tingled with the abrupt urge to trace a path from the crown of his head to the hollow of his back just above his close-fitting pants.

She compressed her lips with some force before she opened them to speak. "Is that what you would prefer, to wait?"

"What I prefer doesn't come into it," he said after a long moment. "I want you to be comfortable with me, and with what takes place between us."

"Comfortable," she echoed in hollow tones. She did not find the word particularly enticing.

He turned slightly to put his back to the frame. In stringent emphasis, he said, "I don't want you to be afraid of me."

"I thought we had established that I am fearless."

"You seem so, but the marriage bed is another matter."

"It—holds no particular terrors that I can see." She stared down at the pins she held as if she had never seen them before.

His gaze flicked toward her and away again. "Is that the truth, or only bravado? You must be very certain, because some things cannot be mended."

He was speaking of her maidenhead, which was considerate but also patronizing. Her voice taut, she said, "I am well aware of it."

Some of the strain eased from his stance. "I suppose you must be, if you have attended birthings. But between man and wife are other things just as important. Trust, faith, affection, bone-deep ease, rank high among them. I would rather allow time for these than have immediate gratification."

She took a shallow breath, all that the constriction in her throat would allow. Her voice a husk of sound, she said, "You don't want—that is, you don't desire me tonight?"

"God," he whispered, his gaze hot on her back, "there is nothing I want more." His voice hardened. "But I have no use for a martyred bride, will not trade my desire for your hatred."

She swung then in a smooth swirl of skirts. "My

hatred? You must have some odd ideas about this marriage if you think I could come to that. I am not here, Lucien, because I was forced to be. I don't hold you in contempt, or even dislike."

"You think I have blood on my hands."

"I thought so once," she corrected him. "You explained how it came about, and I was glad to listen, but by the time you spoke to me on the subject it was no longer important."

"No?" His gaze was startled.

Her hair gleamed around her face in the lamplight as she shook her head. "I've come to know you in the past weeks. I don't believe you would do a mean thing, nor would you allow temper to sway your judgment or prevent you from acting with due regard for the principles of fairness and right. I know that you did not kill indiscriminately or without mercy, for you could not." Her voice faltered, and tears rose to rim her eyes. "I have wished—I wish that it could have been you my brother faced that day on the dueling field. I know if it had been, he would still be alive."

In the quiet that lay between them could be heard the endless wash of the river along the steamboat's hull. A concertina played somewhere on the bank, the music drifting out over the water. When Lucien spoke, his voice was rich and low. "That is a rare compliment. Never have I had one I value more."

"I wanted you to know that I respect you," she said, looking past his shoulder at the dark night beyond the window. "I would not have married you otherwise."

"I am astounded."

So was she, in all truth. She had not planned to say those things; they had come unbidden from some unplumbed recess inside her. Still, she recognized their source. She had given him absolution for his transgressions and her assurance of his worth because she felt his need. She felt his need because she cared.

"I think," she began, then stopped and looked down at the pins she held so tightly they were nearly bent in half. Her gaze not quite focused, she tried again. "I think I may shock as well as astound you. Would it be too outrageous if I said that I would prefer not to delay the—the intimacy between us?"

He did not move so much as an eyelash. His voice like a violin string wound too tight, he said, "The dread is so much to bear, then, that you think it will be better to have it behind you?"

With a small sound of distress, she said, "Rather because I want—I need so much to be close to something or someone, and. . . and you—"

"And I forced my way into your life. Since you have no choice, you will accept the role of dutiful wife and trust there may be some small compensation in allowing me near you."

She met his gaze, her own shadowed yet valiant. "Not at all. I should not say so, perhaps, but I have often thought that you remind me of Satan. When you are with me, I—I feel for you some of the same wonder, know the same joy that you might need my care or my—my affection. Are you offended?"

"God, no," he said in low fervor as he moved to her with steady strides and caught her hands. He took the pins she held and tossed them to the washstand, then drew her carefully into his arms. "I am honored beyond reckoning to be placed in his company in your mind."

She rested her forehead against his collarbone while tears rose in her eyes. "I did love him," she said in soft, unsteady tones. "And he cared about me, really he did. I taught him to trust me, to accept my touch. With me, he always sheathed his claws and was as gentle as a kitten. He was my friend and my playmate. I talked to him and laughed with him, told him all my secrets. And I will miss him so much. I think—I think he is gone, really gone. And I don't know what I am going to do."

"Take me instead," Lucien said, his voice a rough murmur in his throat. "If you need something uncivilized to tame, tame me. If you need a devil to turn into an angel, I am here. If you need something or someone not quite whole to make well again, use me. If you need someone to care for and share your secrets, to keep you from the dangers of the dark and the future, then please—please let it be me."

Somewhere deep inside her, a knot of lonely anguish began slowly to dissolve. It pushed the tears over her lashes so they seeped into his shirtfront to wet it. Over the aching tightness in her throat, she said, "You won't mind?"

"I will be honored," he said as he smoothed the cloud of her hair that tumbled down her back in loose ringlets and curls. "But I should perhaps warn you that I may not always be content as your pet."

"No," she said, brushing her fingers over the firm muscle above his heart in a small, convulsive gesture. "Still, if you will allow me to love you, at least a little, then perhaps—"

"If you will give me even a minuscule portion of the love you gave to your panther," he said unsteadily, "then you will have all my devotion for all my life long. And one day, when I am old and gray and near to leaving this life, I hope you will miss me even a little for all the reasons you miss your Satan, and weep for me as you soothe me on my way to death. For you are my wilding mate and my only love, and I am lost without you."

It was what she needed, all that was required. She drew back to meet his gaze for one long, heart-stopping

moment. Then her attention drifted down to the generous and resolute contours of his mouth. Her lips parted on
a soft breath.

He needed no other invitation. Bending his head, he
took possession of her mouth, invading in full, liquid
sweep. She slid her arms around his neck and rose on tiptoe to receive him. The sudden surge of blood in her
veins made her giddy. At the same time her heart was so
full, she swallowed salt tears of both old grief and new joy.
Then the sweet, perilous rise of desire wiped away all
thought, all doubt, leaving only the piercing certainty of
bodies attuned and vibrant with recognition.

They were two parts of a whole, wandering mated
souls matched at last. If he was wild, then so was she, for
they melded together in a fury of need that pressed them
closer and closer against each other.

Still they could not be close enough, could not touch
as completely as necessary. Stepping to the bed, they
brushed aside the mosquito netting and sank onto the
mattress. He turned her so her back was to him, sweeping
her hair forward over her shoulder as he worked at the
row of tiny buttons on her gown with swift competence
and only a few muttered imprecations. Pushing his hands
inside her open bodice, he brushed his lips across the top
of one shoulder while he cupped her breasts gently.

She drew a soft, hissing breath and arched back against
him as he took her nipples in his fingers to knead them as
carefully as tender, juicy berries. As she tangled the fingers of one hand in the waves of his head, he leaned over
her, turning her to take her lips once more.

Clothes, there were endless layers of clothes. Slippers
and boots, close-fitting pants that had to be peeled away.
Gowns that slid and sagged in heavy folds. Stockings and
hose, petticoats and stiff hoops, cravats and underdrawers:

each item required the learning of new skills, at least for Anne-Marie; each called forth a salute of kisses upon the skin newly bared. Like drifts of refuse on a beach, the discarded garments collected around the bed.

Lucien sprang up then and closed the jalousies, extinguished the lamp. Returning, naked and gilded by moonlight, he lowered the mosquito netting around the mattress, then joined her inside it. With their eyes like dark pools of promise and yearning, they hovered in silent questioning. Seeing their rich, mutual welcome, they came together again, heart to heart, mouth to mouth, mind to mind.

Still, they did not hurry but moved at their own sweet pace to learn the texture of skin and the flavor of it, explore scents and sounds and sensitivities. Playful and cavorting, or grasping in hard, internal convulsions of feeling, they sought for true intimacy with hands and tongues, lips and souls. And discovered it in soft, sweet whispers and pleas, in quick, flicking licks and slow, absorbing assaults that plumbed resistance and endurance, readiness and mercy.

When they came together, the small physical barrier to penetration gave way with warm, liquid ease, aided by his careful penetration, her infinite trust. Locked in tight conjunction, they tried each other, learned each other. Then, moving together, rising, falling, seeking and finding a mutual rhythm, they sought the final glory.

And discovered it. Discovered, too, the release from their aloneness, from their grief, their worry and pain. For in loving was the benediction and the reward for choosing life. Even if it was not everlasting, it was still, finally, enough.

They were caught close in each other's arms as the steamboat slipped its moorings with the dawn. Rocked by the movement, soothed by the steady heartlike beat of the steam engine, they slept on while everything they had known slipped away behind them.

It was a slow passage, but they came at last to Lucien's house set among ancient oaks on the vast and spreading lands below New Orleans. They settled in, taking their time, growing used to each other by wondrous degrees. Summer passed into autumn, and the nights grew cooler. Still, it was a night of pleasant warmth when Anne-Marie woke to see her husband standing in nude splendor at the French doors that opened onto the upper gallery from their bedroom. He appeared transfixed as he stared out over the lawn.

"What is it?" she asked, smothering a yawn.

He turned his head but did not answer. Touching his finger to his lips for silence, he made a quick motion for her to join him.

She slid from between the sheets at once, as naked as he as she glided to his side and curled an arm about his waist. She rubbed his shoulder with her cheek an instant before turning to follow the direction of his gaze. For a moment, she saw nothing unusual. Then she caught her breath.

There under the trees of the lawn, in the strong, copper light of a harvest moon, dark, dangerous shapes glided in and out of the hard-edged shadows. There were two— no, three. Sleek, sinuous, with coats shining like cut-pile velvet, they were a family of panthers, male, female, and a single kit.

"Oh," she said softly, while gladness rose in her heart, filling it to send warm tears tracking down her face.

It was Satan. It had to be. Didn't it?

Below her, the largest of the great cats stalked into the open area and stopped in the full, flooding path of the moon. Powerful, beautiful in his grace, he stood twitching his tail while he lifted his head and stared straight up at the window where they stood.

"He found you," Lucien said quietly as he turned his head to look down at her.

"You said he would," she answered, and met his gaze a long moment before turning once more, drawn to where the panther who had once been her pet stood like a sleek ebony statue.

He was safe. He was whole. Now he could live in peace on these wide lands without being hunted. He could come and go as he willed, if he willed. He and his family.

Now his mate had seen them there at the window. She was nervous. Gathering her kit, she faded into the shadows and was lost almost immediately in the deep black of the woodland beyond. At its edge she called, a plaintive demand.

Satan turned his head to look, then swung back toward the window once more. If she herself called, Anne-Marie thought, he might come, might stay, might come close to be petted and loved, even as wild as he had become.

She did not move. Satan had his mate and his territory; she was near if she was needed. But he was no longer dependent on her as he had once been, and in truth she no longer looked to him as a symbol of her wilding urges or for loving affection.

One moment the panther was still there, the next he was gone. The lawn lay empty again under the brazen and benevolent light of the moon.

Anne-Marie put her head on Lucien's chest and closed her arms around him, holding tight. He brushed a kiss across her hair.

"Sleepy?" he said.

"No." The answer was definite.

"Shall I ring for warm milk with brandy? It might do the trick."

"I don't think so."

He glanced down at her with a faint, tantalizing smile. "What, then?"

"Come back to bed," she said, nuzzling the hollow below his collarbone.

He turned more fully against her so she could feel his arousal against the smooth skin of her belly. "That sounds like a she-panther's call to me."

"Exactly," she said, and nipped his skin, then soothed it with her tongue. "Are you going to answer?"

His laugh rumbled, vibrating in his chest. Leaning, he slid an arm under her knees to lift and carry her back to the bed, back into the wild yet gentle darkness.

New York Times best-selling author **Jennifer Blake** lives in the rolling hills of north Louisiana. Eight acres of hardwood and pine trees, dogwoods, wild azaleas, camellias, and antique roses surround the house designed by her and her husband, Jerry, as a replica of an old Southern planter's cottage. According to Jennifer, "Jerry and I have the perfect relationship: I dream, he draws. As fast as he finishes a home project, I conjure up another one. Whenever he makes an open space by cutting trees, I come along and plant something in it." Gardening is fine mental and physical therapy for someone who spends six to seven hours per day sitting in front of a computer. Still, Jennifer's favorite form of exercise is the quarter-mile walk from the house to the mailbox at the end of the drive.

A WISH AND
A PRAYER

~ *by* ~

Robin Lee Hatcher

PROLOGUE

Having four legs and claws had its benefits, Angel Emeline thought as she scratched a hard-to-reach spot with her hind leg, but she would never admit it to Archie. If she did, the archangel in charge of prayer assistance would always be giving her this sort of assignment, and next time he just might send her into a less desirable creature than the noble cat.

When the itch was gone at last, she straightened and looked about her, wanting to get acquainted with her surroundings. The small house was simple, attractive, and scrupulously tidy. She'd have expected nothing less from Miss Felicity Blessing of Appleton, Idaho.

Felicity was a dressmaker, a woman of thirty, never married. She had lived in this house since the day she was born and had cared for her father—a drinker of strong spirits—ever since her mother had died eighteen years before. The task had become particularly difficult after

Samuel Blessing, drunk as usual, fell from a moving wagon, crippling his right leg and leaving him bitter, a bitterness he'd taken out on his daughter until the day he died.

That was the sum of what Angel Emeline had learned about Miss Blessing before arriving here in answer to Felicity's prayers.

At just that moment the door opened, allowing golden sunlight to spill across the rag rug as the subject of Angel Emeline's thoughts entered the house. The woman's dark mahogany hair was pulled back from her face in a severe twist and was topped with a straw hat that had nary a speck of decoration. Her tan-and-brown linen shirtwaist was equally plain and dull. Not even a bit of lace to lessen its severity.

My, my, Miss Blessing, she thought as Felicity closed the door. *However am I to help you if you don't help yourself?*

For a moment, she wondered if this were a job too big for an angel, third grade, to handle. But handle it Angel Emeline must if she wanted her promotion.

With a mental nod, she rose and arched her back, then meowed for attention.

ONE

Felicity pulled the long hatpin from her bonnet as she glanced at the white cat standing on an overstuffed sofa near the wood stove. "Hello, Angel. Are you hungry?"

She dropped her straw hat onto the table near the door, then crossed the room and lifted the feline into her arms, rubbing her cheek against Angel's long, soft coat.

"Mrs. Babcock gave me two more orders today. The work will pay enough to see us through the month." A sigh escaped her. "But I don't suppose you worry about such things, do you? It must be nice to not have a worry in the world."

She stroked the cat, remembering how empty her house had seemed before Angel had come calling at her back door, a tiny, miserable-looking kitten with a matted coat and a voracious appetite. Felicity hadn't been as lonely since that stormy night over a year ago.

Not *as* lonely . . . but still lonely.

With another sigh, she set the cat on the floor and walked into the kitchen, where she put the kettle on for tea. Standing by the stove, she closed her eyes.

Long ago, when she'd still believed wishes could come true, she'd wished for someone to talk to, someone who could talk back just once in a while, someone to dispel the silence.

Her throat tightened.

Once, when she'd still believed in answered prayers, she'd prayed for someone to love her, someone she could love in return.

Angel brushed up against her skirts. Felicity smiled sadly as she glanced down. "You've always loved me, haven't you, pet?" Then she frowned.

Self-pity was most unbecoming, and it wasn't like her to give in to it. She'd chosen to be the mistress of her own life. She hadn't wanted to be some man's wife. After her father died, she hadn't wanted to give up her new-found freedom. She liked making her own decisions. Angel was all the family she needed.

And it wasn't as if Felicity had never had an opportunity to marry. She'd received her share of proposals over the years. Women were still at a premium in these parts, and even a plain-faced one like Felicity was desirable to a widower with a cold bed and half a dozen children who needed tending.

Don't marry for any reason but love, Felicity. It was eighteen years since her mother had spoken those familiar words to her, but it seemed like only yesterday. *Better to be an old maid than to marry for less than love.*

The kettle began to whistle, bringing her abruptly out of her dark thoughts.

"I *won't* feel sorry for myself," she muttered as she

reached for the delicate china cup she always used when she was blue. "I *won't*."

"Reow."

Once again, she glanced down. Angel sat and cocked her head to one side, as if questioning her mistress. A bitter laugh rose in Felicity's throat.

So this was what she'd come to. Talking to herself and her cat while puttering around the kitchen. There was no doubt about it.

She *was* an old maid.

Prescott Jones rode his buckskin gelding along the wide, dusty main street of Appleton. It was an ordinary western town—two churches, a mercantile, red-brick bank, one saloon, dress shop, a doctor, small schoolhouse. Just about everything the citizens of a town might need. Even its own newspaper.

But one thing was missing, especially for a place surrounded by acre upon acre of fruit orchards. A cannery.

Prescott was there to rectify that omission.

He pulled back on the reins when he saw the small shingle announcing his destination: Walter L. Johnson, Attorney-at-Law. He swung down from the saddle, wrapped the reins around the hitching post, then stepped onto the boardwalk. Once more he glanced down the length of the town, thinking he liked what he saw. There was potential for growth here, potential for a good life if a person was willing to work for it. It was a place where a man could put down roots, take a wife, start a family.

To Prescott, nothing could have sounded better. He'd been alone too long. He wanted to belong—to some place and to someone.

Without further hesitation, he opened the door to the office and stepped inside.

His boyhood friend was staring down at his desk, squinting through thick glasses at a sheet of white paper filled with small print. The past twenty-five years hadn't changed Walt much. He was still slight and wiry, just as he'd been as a boy at the orphanage. Even the familiar smattering of freckles over the bridge of his nose was the same. The only sign of his real age of thirty-five was the touch of gray at his temples.

"I'll be with you in a moment," Walt said, still studying the papers before him.

"No hurry. I'm here to stay."

Walt glanced up, and at the moment of recognition, his mouth curved into a welcoming smile. "Prescott! I wasn't expecting you for another week." He rose from his chair and stepped around the desk.

They clasped each other by the upper arms as they stared at one another, finding the boys they remembered behind the faces of the men they had become. The years melted away, and memories of Prescott's childhood flickered through his head.

"It's good to see you, Pres. Been a long time."

"Too long."

"I'm glad you decided to come."

"So am I." He released his grip on Walt's arms, then removed his dusty Stetson and tossed it onto a nearby chair. Raking his fingers through his hair, he asked, "Have you bought the property?"

Walt looked uncomfortable. "Most of it."

Prescott raised an eyebrow in question.

His friend motioned to another chair. "Sit down. I'll tell you all about it." Walt moved around his desk, and when they were both seated, he continued, "I've heard from the railroad. They're close to making a decision. I think they'll bring the spur this way regardless, but a cannery will clinch the deal. They won't have to worry about all that fruit spoiling if anything slows down delivery to markets."

Walt wasn't saying anything Prescott didn't already know. "And the property?" he prompted.

"I found the perfect location on the far end of town, just like I told you in my last letter." Walt motioned with his hand toward the west. "I've been able to buy all the lots we'll need . . . except one. There's a house on it, and the woman who lives there refuses to sell." He frowned. "Problem is, it's smack in the middle of the other lots. I'm afraid I made a mistake in buying the other property before Miss Blessing had agreed to sell, but I was afraid word would get out about the railroad and prices would go up beyond what we could afford. If that had happened, we'd be in worse shape than we are now."

Prescott closed his eyes for a moment. Had he come all this way just to fail? He set his jaw. No. He wasn't going to fail.

He met Walt's gaze. "What's the woman's reason for not selling?"

"I don't know. I made her a good offer. The best offer of all, because there's a house and a deep well on the land. The house would just be torn down, but having that well would save us plenty before we're through. But she won't even talk about selling." He shook his head. "I'm sorry, Prescott. I'd hoped to have this matter cleared up before you got here."

"Maybe she plans to hold out, thinking we'll pay her more than the land's worth."

"I don't think so. She doesn't seem the type. Keeps to herself most of the time. Except for Sundays when she goes to church or when she delivers her sewing to the dress shop, I've hardly seen her leave that house of hers. I guess she was born there, and she must intend to die there, too."

Prescott rose to his feet, then turned and reached for his hat. "I think I'd better have a talk with this Miss . . ." He looked over his shoulder at Walt. "What did you say her name is?"

"Blessing. Felicity Blessing."

"Miss Felicity Blessing." He envisioned a tiny, white-haired woman. Surely she was someone who could be reasoned with. He set his hat on his head. "Maybe I can convince her to sell." He turned and walked toward the door.

"Good luck," Walt called after him, but the tone of his voice said he didn't hold out much hope for Prescott's success.

Angel Emeline sat on the window ledge and stared out at the town. She was berating herself for not getting more information from Archie. She should have asked him more questions. It would have helped if she knew who it was she should help Felicity find. She was certain Archie had someone particular in mind. If she hadn't been in such a blasted hurry to get here . . .

No doubt Archie had noted her failure to do proper advance preparation, too. Nothing ever got by him. Nothing.

She glanced toward Felicity, who was seated on her straight-backed chair near the other window, sewing on a pretty blue dress. The color would have been splendid on Felicity, much better than the tan blouse and dull brown skirt she was currently wearing. But, of course, the blue dress was for some other woman.

Angel Emeline wondered how she was to answer Felicity's prayers when the woman was so adept at telling herself she was content with her life just as it was. It didn't take an angel to see that she was lonely.

And that was why she was here. To help answer a secret prayer, a prayer uttered in a vulnerable moment but heartfelt and true. That was the prayer that had brought Angel Emeline into the body of Felicity's cat, a cat so appropriately named Angel.

She returned her gaze to the window, wondering again how she was supposed to help. Felicity did her best to appear unattractive. She stayed inside and spent her days cleaning her little house and sewing pretty dresses for other women. How on earth was Angel Emeline to help Felicity find someone to love when she closed herself off from the world? Surely she needed to go out in order to meet someone. Surely he wasn't going to walk right up to her door and knock.

Or, then again, maybe she was wrong about that, Angel Emeline thought as she saw the answer to Felicity's prayers stride into view.

TWO

The knock on her door caused Felicity to look up in surprise. She so rarely had visitors, especially in the middle of the day. She set aside the dress she was making for Mrs. Babcock's shop and rose from her chair. As she approached the door, Angel jumped from the windowsill to stand beside her.

"Who is it, pet?" Felicity asked softly.

She opened the door, expecting to see a familiar face. She didn't.

"Miss Blessing?" the stranger asked.

He was tall—a good six inches taller than Felicity—with hair the color of ink, intense blue eyes, and chiseled features so handsome they made her heart thump involuntarily. He held a dusty Stetson in one hand, and his clothes bore evidence of travel, yet he didn't look unkempt.

"Miss *Felicity* Blessing?" he asked again.

"Yes," she replied.

Here's a man you could love.

Her pulse quickened at the thought, and she felt her skin grow flushed.

"My name's Prescott Jones. I'm Walt Johnson's business partner. I'd like to speak with you a moment if I may."

Felicity felt a sting of disappointment. "If it's about selling my home, Mr. Jones, you're wasting your time."

Angel darted out the door and wound her way around the visitor's legs, meowing for attention.

Prescott grinned as he reached down and picked up the cat with one hand. "Seems your cat's willing to listen." He met Felicity's gaze, still smiling. "Won't you at least give me a chance?"

Listen to what he has to say, Felicity. What can it hurt?

She felt that odd thump in her chest again. It seemed impossible to refuse his request. She held the door open wider. "I suppose it wouldn't hurt to listen, Mr. Jones. Please come in."

He entered, and as he walked past her, she was amazed at how small she felt beside him. She had always been self-conscious about her height. It was hard not to be when she towered over all the women in town—and most of the men as well.

"Please have a seat," she said. Her voice cracked slightly, making her feel even more flustered.

Still holding the cat with one arm, Prescott sat on the sofa and placed his hat on the cushion beside him. Angel purred loudly as she rubbed her head against his chest. The action surprised Felicity, since Angel normally was standoffish with anyone other than her mistress.

Lucky cat, she thought.

She blushed, horrified by the image of her own head pressed against that chest. What in heaven's name was the matter with her?

"Please don't feel you have to spoil Angel by holding her," she said in a prim voice as she sat on her own chair. She held herself stiffly—her back ramrod straight and her shoulders squared—unnerved by her erratic thoughts and unsettled by the way the visitor watched her.

"I like cats. Seems Angel likes me, too."

You wouldn't be lonely with a man like him around. He's got shoulders a woman could lean on.

Again his devastating smile, and again the rapid thumping of her heart.

Felicity's tone was sharper than she meant it to be. "You wished to speak to me about Mr. Johnson's offer?"

Prescott's smile faded. "Yes. Miss Blessing, I'm sure Walt told you how we intend to use the property. A cannery would mean employment for many people here in Appleton. It would mean increased profits for the farmers hereabouts." He leaned forward, his forearms resting on his thighs, his eyes filled with enthusiasm for his topic. "It could even mean the railroad would bring a spur up this way. That would benefit everyone who finds it necessary to travel as well as those shipping to market."

"But there must be other land—"

"Not as perfect as this site. Close to town. Close to the orchards. Right on the main road. Not far from the river."

She glanced down at her hands. "This is my home, Mr. Jones."

"You could have a better one."

This house . . . it's the one thing I can leave to you when I die, Felicity. Her mother's voice echoed in her mind. *Don't sell it. Don't ever leave it unless you leave it for love.*

Don't ever let your pa take you away from here. This is your home. You remember that.

She did remember. She tried always to remember what her mother had told her.

Prescott saw a look of pain flit across Felicity's face. It was not a beautiful face. It was too long and narrow for that, and her brown eyes were too widely spaced, her mouth too full and generous. A plain face, perhaps, but not unpleasant. Her thick, mahogany hair was worn in a severe bun, and he couldn't help wondering what she might look like with it loose and soft about her shoulders.

He also wondered why she seemed determined to remain in this cramped house when accepting his offer could provide her with something better. The house was sparsely furnished. It had no more than three rooms—the sitting room, a kitchen, and a bedroom. She could own something better, if only she'd listen to reason.

She looked up then, the odd sadness still present in her large brown eyes. "I can't sell, Mr. Jones. Not for any price."

Irritation flared unexpectedly. "Do you realize we've purchased the land surrounding yours?"

She shook her head.

"We're going to build a factory here, Miss Blessing. If you don't sell to us, you'll find yourself living in the middle of it."

Her eyes widened.

He set the cat on the floor and rose from the sofa, hat in hand. "We've no other choice."

"But, Mr. Jones, surely you can't mean—"

"I'm afraid I do."

Her face was as white as chalk. "I suppose you must do as your conscience guides."

"Damn right I will," he replied in a low, harsh tone.

She said nothing more. She simply continued to sit with her back stiff and straight, her gaze meeting his, the quiver in the corners of her mouth barely discernible.

Prescott smothered another curse as he turned abruptly and left the house, closing the door behind him.

Blasted female! Did she think the threat of a few tears would change his mind? If she did, she was about to learn how wrong she was.

Long, determined strides carried him back toward town.

Why couldn't she see how truly important this factory was to the people of Appleton? Didn't she care about the rest of the community? Was she so self-centered that she gave no thought to others?

His pace slowed as he pictured Felicity as she'd looked just before he'd left her house.

Self-centered? No, he rather thought frightened and uncertain described her better.

He felt a twinge of guilt but shoved it aside. He'd come to Appleton to build his cannery and settle down. From the moment he'd read Walt's letter, the one telling him of the town's need for a cannery, Prescott had known his days of wandering were over. He was going to find everything he'd ever wanted here—a business, a home, a wife and family. He knew it with an unshakable certainty.

And Miss Felicity Blessing was not going to keep him from it.

Felicity stared at the door long after it had swung shut behind her unexpected visitor. Her heart still pounded in her chest, and try as she might to tell herself it was because of his threat to build his factory around her, she wasn't fooled. The truth was, it was the man himself who'd caused her pulse to race.

This time it was her father's voice that taunted her. *Don't waste your time wantin' what you can't have, daughter. The men hereabouts won't take you to wife except out of desperation. Just like I took your ma. You listen to me now, Felicity. I'm tellin' you this for your own good.*

What her father had said was true. No man had ever looked at her unless he was certain there was no one else available. No one had ever wanted to love her. She'd seen it happen with her own eyes, felt it happen with her own heart.

She straightened her shoulders, then reached for her sewing.

She wasn't going to feel sorry for herself. She *wasn't!*

But before she could pick up the fabric, Angel jumped into her lap, purring loudly.

"Traitor," she muttered, remembering the way the cat had warmed to their visitor.

Angel rubbed the top of her head against Felicity's chin, and suddenly Felicity couldn't bear the hollow ache any longer.

Gathering the cat close to her, she pressed her face against the soft, white fur and wept.

THREE

Walt opened the door to his two-story house and ushered Prescott inside. "Rebecca?" he called, and a moment later a petite blond woman appeared at the top of the stairs. "Rebecca, this is my good friend, Prescott Jones."

Prescott watched as Walt's wife gracefully descended the stairs, her hand extended in warm welcome. "Mr. Jones, you cannot imagine how pleased I am to meet you at last. For years, I've been listening to stories of your boyhood escapades with my husband." Her eyes twinkled mischievously. "I'll be most interested in hearing your versions." She paused, smiling, then added, "You are most welcome in our home."

"Thank you," he answered as he took hold of her hand.

Walt hadn't exaggerated. Rebecca Millard Johnson

was an extraordinary beauty. If her sister was even half as
lovely, Prescott would consider himself lucky.

It had been Walt's last letter that had finally made up
Prescott's mind about moving to Idaho immediately.

> *Rebecca's sister will be visiting us for the entire sum-*
> *mer. Charlotte is as beautiful as my darling wife. If she's*
> *like Rebecca in other ways, any man would be lucky to*
> *gain her affections. Certainly my wife has been a blessing*
> *and helpmeet to me. She makes my home a place of joy*
> *and comfort and is a good companion at all times. Could*
> *her sister, raised by the same parents, be any different?*
>
> *Come to Appleton, Prescott, and meet her. Perhaps,*
> *if you do, we shall really be family one day. If you were*
> *to marry Charlotte, I could call you brother.*

So here he was, hoping Charlotte would, indeed, be
like her sister.

"We weren't expecting you for another week or so."
Rebecca cast her husband a reproving glance. "I'll need
some time to prepare your room. Why don't you and
Walt sit down in the parlor while I get things ready?"

"Don't go to any trouble for me. I—"

"Nonsense," Rebecca interrupted. "It's no trouble at
all." With a smile toward Prescott and another gently
scolding frown at Walt, she went back up the stairs and
disappeared into a room near the top of the landing.

Walt clapped a hand on Prescott's shoulder. "Come
on. We'd better do as she says." Wearing an amused grin,
he turned and led the way down the hall. "I've learned it's
wise never to argue with Rebecca. She finds the most
interesting ways to have retribution if I do." A chuckle
belied the ominous sound of his words.

Prescott followed Walt into a spacious parlor. The

room had large windows that let in the late May sunlight. The sofa and chairs were upholstered in bright florals that matched the window draperies. The fireplace mantel and tables were covered with china figurines and lamps with tasseled shades. It was a room that bespoke its master's success and its mistress's penchant for knickknacks.

For some inexplicable reason, he thought of Felicity Blessing's sitting room—plain, simple, tiny—and found it more to his liking than this more elaborate one.

"Sit down, Prescott," Walt urged. "How about something to drink? I've got an excellent brandy."

He shook his head. "No thanks." He wandered across the room and glanced out the window.

The yard behind the house was cluttered with signs of children—a ball and bat, a swing tied to the branches of a tall tree, a couple of dolls. Not far beyond were fruit orchards, and past them, a stark, gray-brown bluff signaled the course of a winding river. In the distance, wrapped in the haze of afternoon, a purple mountain range rippled across the horizon, the peaks still dusted with snow.

"You still haven't told me what reason Miss Blessing gave you for refusing our offer," Walt said, his words accompanied by the splash of brandy being poured into a glass.

Prescott envisioned Felicity, sitting so stiffly on her straight-backed chair. "She didn't give me one. Just said she couldn't sell."

"Are you really going to build the cannery around her house?"

He turned from the window. "I don't have any other choice. Too much money is tied up in that land. Unless you've got unlimited funds . . ." He watched the other man shake his head, then said, "Neither do I. So I guess that means we proceed as planned."

Walt lifted his glass in a salute. "To the J and J Canning Company."

"To our success," Prescott added, determined it would come true.

Felicity sat at her small table and stared at the food she'd prepared for her supper. The simple fare looked unappetizing, not because it wasn't good, but because she wasn't hungry. She couldn't get thoughts of Prescott Jones out of her head.

She set her fork on the table and folded her hands in her lap, clenching them tightly.

It was only because of his threat. That was the reason for her distress. It was only because he could very well build his factory around her, and she was helpless to stop him.

Yet it wasn't his warning she remembered. She kept seeing him standing in her doorway, towering above her, his shoulders broad, his body lean and strong. She envisioned the ink-black color of his hair, shaggy around the collar of his shirt, the slight cleft in his chin, the straight line of his dark eyebrows above startling blue eyes.

She shook her head, trying to dislodge his image from her mind.

Suddenly, Angel jumped up on the chair opposite her.

"Get down," Felicity ordered, surprised by the cat's actions. "You know better than that. What's the matter with you?"

Angel simply stared at her.

When was the last time a man was in your home, Felicity?

Her breath caught in her chest.

It was nice to have him here, wasn't it?

She forgot the cat sitting at the table, wanting only to

rid herself of the unwelcome questions she could hear so clearly in her head, so clearly Felicity could have sworn someone was in the room asking them of her.

You liked his smile, didn't you?

A tiny groan escaped her throat as she rose from the chair and walked back into the sitting room.

Maybe he'll come back.

Her pulse quickened.

"Maybe he'll come back," she whispered, realizing she hoped he would and dismayed because of it.

Rebecca's sister joined them for supper, and Prescott discovered she was as beautiful as he'd been told. Charlotte Millard, all of twenty years old, had the same silver-blond hair, the same delicate features, and the same slender figure as her older sister. She even had the same warm smile.

As the four adults sat around the table, enjoying the best meal Prescott had eaten in the better part of a year, Charlotte listened to every word that came out of his mouth as if they'd been dipped in gold. She laughed often and told Prescott he was tremendously amusing. She asked him questions about himself, about his work, about his travels.

"Of course, I've only been in Appleton a short while myself, but I think you're going to like it here," she said in her wispy voice. "I almost wish I didn't have to return to Seattle at the end of summer."

Prescott thought Charlotte was just the sort of girl any man would dream of marrying. The bachelors of Appleton would be buzzing around her door all summer long. If she wanted a husband, she'd surely have one easily enough.

"Perhaps you'll decide *not* to leave, Miss Millard."

Charlotte smiled softly before looking down, long lashes brushing her cheeks. "Does that mean you hope I'll stay, Mr. Jones?"

"Charlotte," Rebecca admonished softly.

He would have answered affirmatively if he'd had the opportunity.

"Reow."

Everyone turned toward the open dining room window to find a white cat perched on the sill.

"For heaven's sake," Rebecca said. "Where on earth did he come from?"

"She," Prescott interjected, then explained, "That's Miss Blessing's cat. Angel." He rose and walked toward the window. "What are you doing so far from home, girl?"

Angel seemed to leap into his arms as he reached to pick her up.

He turned toward the others. "Friendly, isn't she?" He stroked Angel's head.

Charlotte held a handkerchief up to her nose and sneezed. Once, then again and again. When she could catch her breath, she waved her handkerchief in Prescott's direction. "It's the cat. They make me sneeze." She gulped several quick breaths of air, her nose wrinkled. "Oh, do put that dreadful beast outside where . . . where . . . where it be . . . belongs." She finished with a string of sneezes.

You'd better take her back to Miss Blessing. A wagon could hit her in the dark. You wouldn't want that to happen.

"I'd better just take her back to Miss Blessing," he said, echoing the small voice he'd heard in his head. "I won't be long."

He left the house to the sounds of Charlotte's sneezing.

Outside, the air was sweet with the smell of blossoming spring flowers. Night had settled over the earth, bringing with it the singing of crickets and chirping of frogs. Yellow lamplight spilled from windows to form an uneven checkerboard pattern along the main street of town.

She's not really your sort, that Charlotte Millard.

Prescott's pace slowed, and a frown furrowed his brow.

Why would he think such a thing? A man would be lucky to have a wife like Charlotte. True, she was seventeen years younger than he was, but that didn't seem to trouble her, so he didn't see why it should be a problem.

She doesn't like cats. She thinks they're dreadful beasts.

True, but how could he fault her for that? She couldn't help it if they made her sneeze. Charlotte seemed sweet-natured and was obviously eager to please, and there was no denying she was pretty to look at. What more could a man want in a wife?

Intelligence, for one. A kind heart, for another. What about Miss Blessing?

He nearly laughed out loud. Miss Blessing? Now *there* was a woman who wasn't his sort. She was a stubborn, stiff-lipped old maid. And pretty darned plain to boot. She couldn't hold a candle to Charlotte.

With more determined steps, he left the light of town behind, his way now guided by the full moon rising at his back.

He had intended to do no more than leave the cat on the stoop, but just as he drew close to the house, the front door opened and Felicity stepped outside. Moonlight caused her white wrapper to glow, accentuating the feminine curves beneath the flowing fabric. Dark hair spilled over her shoulders and down her back.

"Angel?" she called softly.

"She's here."

He heard her gasp, saw her hand flutter to her chest as her eyes found him.

"Sorry. I didn't mean to startle you." He drew closer. "Your cat wandered into town. I brought her back."

Felicity held out her arms to take Angel from him. "I don't know what's gotten into her. She's never run off before."

Prescott gave her the cat, saw the gentle way she cradled the animal against her bosom.

"Thank you, Mr. Jones," she whispered.

The moonlight had softened her features, making her seem less stiff and formidable. He'd been right about her hair, too. It was beautiful cascading over her shoulders instead of pulled back from her face so harshly.

"It was kind of you to bring her back."

"Glad to do it."

"I . . . I wouldn't want to lose her."

You ought to kiss her.

He cleared his throat, surprised by the wayward thought, and took a step backward. "Well, I'd better get back to the Johnsons'. Good night, Miss Blessing."

"Good night, Mr. Jones. And thanks again."

Her voice lingered in his head long after he'd left her little house behind.

FOUR

Prescott was out at his property just after dawn the next morning. With precise steps, he began walking off the perimeter of the main factory building, marking it with stakes. Of course, the U-shape was a bit odd, but he didn't think it was going to be too great an inconvenience for the workers.

And if Miss Felicity Blessing wanted to live smack-dab in the middle of a canning factory, that was her decision, not his.

He paused and glanced toward the house, wondering again about the woman inside—and wondering *why* he continued to think about her. Last night he'd been unable to shake the memory of her standing in the moonlight. Even being with Charlotte hadn't driven Felicity's image from his mind.

As if in answer to his thoughts, the back door of the tiny house opened and Felicity stepped outside, carrying a pail as she walked toward the pump at a rear corner of the house.

The place wasn't even plumbed into the kitchen, he realized, but the thought was fleeting, replaced by another. Her hair was still down, and it was even more lovely by daylight. It flowed like a dark waterfall over her shoulders and down her back, a stark contrast to her simple white wrapper. The luxurious mahogany strands glowed in the sun, reflecting shades of red and gold amid the umber.

Suddenly, Angel ran out the open door and headed straight toward him. Felicity's gaze followed the cat, and when she discovered Prescott watching her, her cheeks turned scarlet and her hand stilled on the pump handle.

He touched the brim of his hat. "Good morning," he called.

She nodded and pushed her loose hair over her shoulder with one hand.

"I thought I'd better get an early start." He motioned toward the stakes.

The blush paled.

He rubbed his chin as he considered what he should do, then strode toward her with purposeful steps. "Miss Blessing . . . "

She clutched the front of her wrapper with one hand and pressed her body back against the side of the house, looking for all the world as if she expected him to assault her on the spot.

He stopped, irritation flaring. "Miss Blessing," he said, carefully controlling his tone of voice, "isn't it time we tried to find a solution to this problem? If we could just talk—"

"Talk would not change my mind, Mr. Jones. I can't sell my home." She gripped the handle of the pail with both hands and hurried toward the house, her head tipped forward and her eyes downcast.

Blasted, stubborn woman. Why on earth wouldn't she listen to reason? Why was she being so . . .

She's afraid.

But what had she to be afraid of?

She stopped in the doorway and looked back in his direction. He thought for a moment she'd changed her mind, that she would say they could talk about it after all. But it wasn't Prescott she spoke to.

"Angel. Come inside, pet."

She needs a friend.

He glanced down at the animal near his feet. As crazy as it sounded, Angel's green eyes seemed to offer an apology for Felicity's behavior. Then she dashed after her mistress.

Prescott shook his head, wondering at his peculiar train of thought, then returned his gaze to Felicity just as she closed the door behind her.

What had she to be afraid of? he wondered again. He wasn't trying to turn her out into the street. She needn't leave Appleton and her neighbors. She could live right in town, but in a nicer place. She could have a bigger house with water plumbed into the kitchen. Her refusal made no sense. No sense at all.

Prescott shook his head again. If Felicity Blessing needed a friend, she was sure going about it the wrong way where he was concerned.

With that, he turned and continued walking off the perimeters of the factory, hammering stakes into the ground as he went.

Felicity sat on a kitchen chair, her hands shaking, her breathing rapid. She kept remembering the way she'd felt as he'd stepped toward her, the way her knees had threatened to buckle, the way her mouth had gone dry, the way her body had tingled with sensations both wonderful and terrifying.

If she closed her eyes, she could still see him as clearly as if he were standing in front of her. And he would be outside her door every day, building his factory and then running it.

Why didn't she just sell her house as he wanted? His offer was fair. More than fair, even. Why didn't she sell?

Don't ever sell it. No matter what happens, don't ever sell this house unless it's 'cause you've found real love.

"Oh, Mama."

She pictured Naomi Blessing as she'd last seen her. Her mother, worn down by time and her father's ever-present disapproval and harsh words. Her mother, lying in her bed, the promise of death written in her feverish eyes as she held her young daughter's hand.

I was so lonely, I didn't care that he didn't love me. But I was wrong, Felicity. I should have cared. I was better off alone.

Felicity remembered so clearly the feel of her mother's fingertips as they'd brushed her cheek.

If he'd ever loved me, he could have had so much.

"I love you, Mama," she whispered now, just as she had then.

All the riches Sam's ever wanted were here, if only . . . It's here, Felicity. It's right here. Don't you do what I did. Don't you ever settle for less than love.

With a sigh, Felicity rose from the chair, one hand pushing her hair over her shoulder, just as she pushed away the old memories. She had no time to dwell upon the past. It was time she washed and dressed and got on with her day. She needed to deliver the blue dress to Mrs. Babcock before noon, and there was her weekly laundry to wash and her mending to do.

But before Felicity left the kitchen, she was drawn irre-
sistibly to the window, where she peered around the edges
of the curtains, just enough to find Prescott as he marked
off the boundaries of the canning factory. He walked with
a long, easy stride, the stride of a man with confidence in
who he was and what he was doing. A man unafraid to go
after what he wanted.

*Always wanting what you weren't meant to have, aren't
you, girl?* Her father's voice, full of scorn. *Your ma filled
your head with nonsense.*

She turned her back to the window.

Her father had been right. Long ago, Felicity had often
wanted things she couldn't have. But over the years she'd
stopped wanting, stopped hoping for the impossible.
She'd been content with her life the way it was.

Angel brushed up against the hem of her skirt, her purr
echoing noisily in the small kitchen. Felicity glanced
down at the cat. Angel was watching her, looking as if
she knew exactly what Felicity was thinking.

Who says you can't have what you want?

"I have what I want, Angel. I like things just as they
are."

Squaring her shoulders, Felicity left the kitchen and
performed her morning ablutions with deliberate care,
finishing them by smoothing her hair back from her face
and winding it into a tight bun at her nape. Afterward,
she prepared her breakfast without ever once returning to
the window to see if Prescott was still outside.

When her meal was finished and the dishes properly
washed, dried, and put away, she put on her bonnet,
picked up the blue gown she'd finished late last night,
and left the house, her head held high, certain she had
banished any more thoughts about a certain newcomer to
Appleton.

• • •

Prescott stepped out of Walt's office just in time to see Felicity walking along the boardwalk, coming straight toward him. Everything about her was stiff, from the straightness of her back to the firm line of her mouth. He saw nothing of the woman in a flowing white wrapper whom he'd glimpsed last night and again this morning.

She looked up and saw him, and her pace faltered slightly. Then he saw the proud tilt of her chin as she proceeded forward. His own stubborn streak asserted itself, keeping him right where he was, in the middle of her path.

"Good morning again, Miss Blessing." He bent his hat brim and gave her a smile.

She was forced to stop. "Mr. Jones."

She was tall for a woman, making it easier for him to look her directly in the eyes. Hers were a delicious chocolate brown, and behind them, he saw something . . .

"Prescott!"

He stepped back from Felicity and turned in the direction of Charlotte's voice, curiously annoyed by her use of his Christian name. He watched the pretty blonde crossing the street, her sunshine-bright smile all for him.

"Oh, I'm so glad I found you here," she said as she stepped onto the boardwalk. "Rebecca has decided we should all have a picnic down by the river. Do tell me you'll join us. I should be devastated if you weren't there."

"Well, I . . . "

She turned toward Felicity. "Good morning, ma'am. I'm sorry if I interrupted, but I was so excited to have found Prescott, I completely forgot my manners. Please do forgive me."

"Of course," Felicity replied softly.

Charlotte slipped her hand into the crook of his arm. "Isn't it exciting about Prescott's plans? He told me all about the cannery last night at supper. I know he's going to have wonderful success." She glanced up at him. "The whole town will be indebted to him and my brother-in-law."

Felicity's gaze moved from Charlotte to Prescott. "I'm sure that's true."

Charlotte's words should have made him feel proud. They didn't. Not when he was looking into Felicity's eyes.

Felicity stepped forward then. "Please excuse me. I really must deliver this dress to Mrs. Babcock."

Prescott had no choice but to step out of her way. He wasn't even sure why he'd tried to keep her there in the first place.

Charlotte's fingers on his arm drew his attention back to her. "Do say you'll come with us on our picnic."

She was pretty and warm and full of promise. She was exactly the sort of woman he'd always had in mind when he'd thought of a wife. Thanks to Walt's words of praise for his sister-in-law, Charlotte was one of the reasons Prescott had come to Appleton. Nothing had happened to change that.

"I'll come," he replied, resisting the urge to turn and catch one last glimpse of Felicity as she hurried along the boardwalk toward the dress shop.

Solving a human's problems was not as simple as Angel Emeline had expected, but things did seem to be going rather nicely. Prescott Jones was obviously the answer to Felicity Blessing's prayers. Equally obvious to Angel Emeline was the woman's attraction to him. Time, she supposed, was all that was needed now. Time and her continued suggestions to Felicity and Prescott.

If she was able to handle this assignment without asking Archie for assistance, her promotion to angel, second grade, would be in the bag. Since these two people were just right for each other, how could anything go wrong now?

Angel Emeline rose from her place on the floor and stretched before pattering across the sitting room and jumping onto the window ledge. She sat down and allowed her long tail to wrap around her paws, secretly enjoying the silky feel of it.

She turned her gaze out the window, and as if on cue, a buggy appeared on the road, carrying two couples toward the river. Prescott was included in the merry little party. So was that Charlotte Millard. Felicity wasn't.

Hmmm. *This* was what could go wrong.

It seemed Angel Emeline was going to have to do a little more than make mental suggestions to Felicity and Prescott if they were ever going to find out just how right they were for each other. And judging by the attractive young woman seated beside Prescott, she was going to have to do something soon.

But what, exactly? What was it she could do to bring them together?

As the buggy passed by the little house, an idea sprang to mind. Now, if she could just get the timing right . . .

FIVE

Prescott drew the team of horses to a halt at the far end of the factory property. He pulled the heavy leather reins over his head and looped them around the plow, then turned to view his handiwork.

He'd spent the past two days clearing and leveling the land. He'd done this work himself, but when they started to build the cannery, he would need to hire others. And it wouldn't be long before construction began. In fact, he was expecting a load of lumber today.

He couldn't resist a satisfied grin. The J and J Canning Company would be a reality by midsummer. From all appearances, the fruit crop would be a healthy one, which would mean a solid business for the cannery come harvest. It seemed the years of scraping by, making do, scrimping and saving and investing, were about to pay off.

And if Walt and Rebecca Johnson had anything to say

about it, Prescott would be engaged by September. Their pleasure in seeing Prescott and Charlotte together was unmistakable, and it certainly seemed Charlotte was willing to comply. She already watched him with an adoring expression. Sometimes a bit too adoring, he thought, then told himself he was wrong. After all, how could a woman be too adoring?

For his part, he realized, it was too soon to feel anything akin to love or to bring up the subject of matrimony, but he expected both would happen, given time. What wasn't to love about her? He only had to look at Walt and Rebecca and their children to see what his future with Charlotte would be like. Wouldn't it?

His gaze strayed to the little house in the midst of his property.

He hadn't seen Felicity in the past two days, not since their encounter on the boardwalk outside Walt's office. He wondered if she'd given any more thought to selling her house. She had to be aware of the work he'd been doing out here. When the lumber came and the actual building began, surely she wouldn't want to remain.

Maybe he should talk to her again.

He debated the idea for several more seconds, then wiped his forehead with his shirtsleeve and raked his fingers through his hair in an effort to look more presentable before walking toward the house. He was nearly there when he saw the lumber wagon coming down the road from town. He raised his arm and hailed the driver. The driver slapped the reins against the backsides of the team of horses, quickening their pace.

Prescott wasn't aware the door of Felicity's house had opened until he saw a blur of white fur dart out into the road, right into the path of the team of horses. He heard a woman scream. The horses squealed as they reared back in their traces. Felicity hurried toward the road, skirts and petticoats flying. The wagon stopped.

Prescott reached Angel first. The white cat lay limp and still, one leg lying at an odd angle. He thought she might be dead.

"Angel?" Felicity whispered as she knelt on the dirt road beside Prescott. She reached out and touched the cat lightly, then drew her hand back and clutched it to her chest.

The animal didn't stir.

Felicity glanced up.

He found the look in her eyes unbearable, so he returned his attention to the cat. He held his finger against Angel's throat and found a weak pulse. He also saw the blood that was quickly turning the white coat red. "She's still alive. Does Appleton have a vet?"

"No."

"What about the doctor? Will he treat animals?"

"He's gone to the capital city to visit his son."

"Well, let's see what we can do for her." He slid his hands beneath Angel and gently lifted her off the ground.

Felicity led the way into the house. She directed Prescott into the bedroom and motioned for him to lay the cat on the bed.

"We'll need some water, scissors, and a needle and thread," he said as he examined the wound. "And some bandages."

"I'll get them."

When she returned with the requested items, he trimmed away the hair from the wound and cleansed the gash, then sewed it closed. He bound the cat's torso with strips of white cloth, then wrapped her front left leg with care, hoping, if she survived, that she wouldn't be crippled. Angel didn't move or protest throughout the process, but Prescott thought her pulse seemed stronger when he checked it.

"Where did you learn to do that?" Felicity asked softly as he washed his hands in the basin near the bed.

He met her gaze. "Practice."

She waited, her silence encouraging him to continue.

"I had a cat of my own when I was a boy." That was stretching the truth, of course. The orphanage hadn't allowed pets. "I called him Scrapper 'cause he was always getting into fights." He shrugged. "I sewed him up a time or two."

She stroked the cat's head. "You saved Angel's life."

He started to deny it.

"If you hadn't been here, I couldn't have helped her. She might have died. How can I ever thank you?"

The notion popped into his head to suggest she could thank him by selling her house, but the look in her eyes stopped him. It was almost as if he were looking into his own heart. He understood her, understood why she couldn't bear to lose Angel. Because the cat was all she had.

Felicity looked away, as if guessing what he'd seen.

"Well." He stepped toward the bedroom doorway. "I guess I'd better see to my lumber. The driver's probably anxious to be on his way, and I've got a lot of work to get done." He paused, then added, "I'll check back this afternoon . . . if you'd like me to."

"Thank you," she replied softly. "I'd like that."

Felicity knelt beside the bed and continued stroking Angel's head. "You'll be all right. Prescott took good care of you."

He'd take good care of you, too, if you'd give him a chance.

She remembered his strong but gentle hands as they'd tended the injured animal.

He understands about being lonely.

Now, why would she think that? She didn't know anything about him.

Why don't you do something different with your hair? Prescott would like it down.

She rose and walked to the mirror hanging on the wall. She stared at her reflection, wondering if a man like Prescott Jones would notice anything she did to her appearance.

Why should he? she wondered, remembering the lovely Miss Millard. Felicity was thirty years old. Compared to Charlotte Millard's youth, she must seem ancient. The difference in their looks didn't even bear thinking about.

She turned away from the mirror.

Don't give up without trying, Felicity!

She had gone beyond being an eccentric old maid, she thought as she turned once again and began removing the hairpins. She'd gone completely mad. It was one thing to talk to her cat. It was entirely another to hear voices in her head . . . and then do what they told her to do!

She picked up her brush and began stroking it down the length of her hair. The slow motion of her hand and the gentle tugging at her scalp was somehow soothing.

Closing her eyes, she allowed her thoughts to drift back to a happier time, when life had seemed so simple. She saw them as they'd been so long ago, her mother on the chair near the wood stove, Felicity settled on the floor at her feet. As Naomi had brushed Felicity's hair, she'd shared stories about Felicity's grandparents, about how they'd come west, about how Grandpa Greer had built their first shelter—just a hut, really—from the cottonwoods that grew near the river, about how he'd planted the saplings he'd brought with him from the family fruit orchards back in New York. She'd told Felicity how they were alone for so long when Naomi was a child, about how Grandma Greer had schooled Naomi, just as Naomi had schooled Felicity, teaching her to read and write and do her sums. She remembered the way her mother had stroked her head and told her she was going to grow up to be pretty and smart, how she was going to marry a man who would treasure her.

The remembrance changed slowly, so slowly that Felicity scarcely noticed. Then she realized the picture in her mind was vastly different from her favorite childhood memory. She imagined Prescott standing behind her, brushing her hair, one large hand on her shoulder. He was standing so close she could feel the heat of his body upon her skin. She could see something in his intense gaze . . . something akin to desire.

Her eyes flew open, and she looked at her reflection in the mirror. Her face was flushed, her eyes bright, almost feverish. Her hair fell in waves around her shoulders, the ends curling softly just above her breasts.

She imagined Prescott's hands brushing across her breasts as she'd once seen Mr. Tyler do to his wife when they hadn't known anyone else was in the mercantile. She felt a strange tingling sensation.

"Ohhh." The word came out on a whisper of air as she twisted her hair quickly into a bun and jabbed the pins into place, then turned away from the mirror before any other unwelcome images could spring to mind.

It was a good thing cats purportedly had nine lives, Angel Emeline thought as she lay on the bed, aching all over. She obviously had used up one for this poor animal.

Her timing was abysmal. She hadn't meant to actually

run beneath that dreadful horse's hooves. She'd meant merely to make it *look* as if she'd been hurt. At least she'd been partially successful. Prescott had said he would come back in the afternoon.

She opened her eyes slowly, glad to see the bedroom was empty. Then she closed them again. She needed to rest, she decided, so she'd be ready for Prescott's return.

SIX

As he worked, the afternoon sun beat relentlessly down upon Prescott's back, and the earth threw the heat up into his face. Not a single cloud marred the vast expanse of blue sky to serve as a temporary respite from the glare.

Sweat had left darkened patches on Prescott's shirt, and he could feel the grit on his face. But he only had one more row to drag and then he'd be finished for the day. Tomorrow he would start hiring his construction crew.

Clucking to the horses, he guided the team in a tight turn. He was just about to smack the reins against their rumps when he saw Felicity approaching him, bucket in hand.

She stopped near the horses. "I thought you might be thirsty. It's so unusually hot for this time of year." She held the bucket slightly away from her. "Would you like a drink of water, Mr. Jones?"

He lifted the reins over his head. "This is kind of you, Miss Blessing."

"It's the least I can do after what you did for Angel."

He lifted a dipperful of water from the bucket and drained it in several quick gulps, then repeated the action two more times. The fourth time he raised the dipper above him and let it pour out over his head. When he opened his eyes, water dripping off his hair, he found her smiling as she watched him.

She had an unbelievable smile. It touched not only the corners of her mouth, but her eyes as well. He couldn't help grinning in return as he passed her the dipper, their fingers touching briefly in the exchange.

She took a small step backward, her smile already fading. "You're welcome to help yourself to the water whenever you like." She turned to leave.

"Listen," he said quickly, stopping her, "why don't I come have a look at Angel now? Give the team a rest." He pointed to the bucket. "Then I'll fill that up and give the horses a drink, if you don't mind."

"Of course I don't mind."

"Good." He wished she'd smile again. "Here." He reached out and took the bucket from her hands. "Let me carry that."

As they fell into step beside each other, Felicity said, "Angel's slept most of the day, but she drank a little cream a while ago."

"That's a good sign."

"Is it?"

"Yes." He opened the door, then waited for her to lead the way into the house.

A quick glance took in the kitchen as they passed through. The room was as small as he'd expected it to be. There was barely enough space for the black cooking stove, the dry sink, an icebox, a small cupboard, and a table with two chairs. But it was neat and uncluttered, just like the other two rooms of the house.

In the bedroom, only a few steps away from the sitting room and kitchen, he found Angel where he'd left her that morning. When he stroked the top of her head, she opened her eyes and meowed weakly at him.

"Maybe you learned a lesson today," he told the cat as he sat on the edge of the bed.

"Reow."

He checked the bandages. The one around her chest was still clean and white, which meant his stitching had held and the bleeding had stopped. He wasn't as certain about what he'd done for her leg, although there didn't seem to be much swelling.

Felicity sat on the opposite side of the bed. "My father hated cats. If they weren't mousers, then the only use for them was drowning."

He glanced up, wanting to say her father was an idiot.

"I never had a pet until Angel. She showed up at my door one night. It was pouring down rain and she was cold and half-starved. I couldn't leave her outside. And once she was in, she just never left."

"That's the way cats are. They make their homes wherever they want. It's not up to us."

Her smile returned. "What about Scrapper? How did he come to live with you?"

"Scrapper didn't really live with me. He made the streets his home. But when he wanted company, he'd climb the tree outside my window and I'd let him in." He didn't say how glad he'd always been to see that mangy-looking animal, how he'd hidden Scrapper beneath the covers on his cot and held him close, feeding him whatever scraps of food he'd managed to sneak up to his room.

"Did your parents know?"

"My parents were dead."

Her voice softened. "I'm sorry. I didn't know."

"No reason you should've known. Besides, it was a long time ago."

"My mother died when I was twelve. My father passed on last year."

He hadn't talked about his family in years, but there was something about her tone of voice, about the way she watched him with her dark brown eyes, that made him want to confide in her. "I was six. The youngest son. I had three older brothers and two younger sisters. It was a fire that took them and my parents. I still don't know why I got out alive and the others didn't. I just remember wandering around outside in the middle of the night with the blazing house lighting up the sky."

"How tragic," she whispered.

The worst part for Prescott was that he could no longer remember what any of them had looked like. He hadn't been able to keep their images in his mind, no matter how hard he'd tried. Sometimes he thought he heard a woman's voice that sounded like his mother's or heard a laugh that reminded him of his father, or he saw children playing in a schoolyard and it seemed that he had done the same thing with his brothers. But when he tried to recall their faces, he couldn't, and that saddened him.

But he still remembered the warmth that had filled their big old farmhouse in Illinois. He remembered how happy he'd been, how often everyone had laughed. And he remembered the love. When he married, he wanted a home like that. He wanted a home filled with laughter and warmth. He'd wanted it for a long time. He'd been saving and working toward it for years.

"Where did you live after they died?" Felicity asked gently.

This memory was clear in every detail. "There wasn't

any other family, so I was sent to an orphanage in Chicago." He remembered the massive brick building and the coldhearted matron who ran the place. He remembered being lonely. He remembered being scared. "That's where I met Walt. Puny little kid with big glasses. We were thick as thieves for the year he was there. Then he was adopted and moved away from Chicago. We kept in touch over the years. I could always count on letters from Walt, no matter where he was, no matter where I was."

"You never left the orphanage?"

"Not till I was sixteen." He shrugged. "It wasn't so bad once Scrapper came around."

"When was that?"

"Not long after Walt moved away. He showed up one night in the tree outside my window, meowing and making a fuss until I let him in. Scrapper always seemed to be there when I needed a friend."

Felicity envisioned the small boy with his alley cat friend and felt her heart squeeze. She understood what he'd left unsaid, better than he would ever know.

Or maybe he did know. There was something about the way Prescott looked at her sometimes that made her think he could see right inside her soul, made her think he understood her, too.

"Well." He rose from the bed. "I'd better get back to the horses. There's still work to be done, and I'm expected for dinner at the Johnsons'."

She remembered Rebecca Johnson's pretty young sister and suddenly felt foolish for sitting on the bed with Prescott, exchanging memories of their childhoods, thinking there was some sort of connection between them because of their cats.

Smoothing her skirt with both hands, Felicity stood and led the way to the back door. She opened it and stepped outside. "Thank you again for looking after Angel."

"I'll stop by in the morning, see how she did through the night."

Again, she remembered Charlotte. "I don't want to put you out. I'm sure she's out of danger."

"It's no trouble. I'll be working out here anyway."

Her throat felt tight, too tight to speak, so she simply nodded, then watched as he walked away.

Charlotte saw Prescott leaving Miss Blessing's house. So did Laura Tyler.

"Isn't that Mr. Jones?" Laura asked. "I thought he was courting you, Charlotte. I wonder what he was doing in Miss Blessing's house?"

Charlotte's cheeks grew warm with humiliation and anger. How dare he embarrass her this way? Was he calling on that frumpy old maid when everyone knew he was expected to propose marriage to her before summer was over?

Well, she wasn't going to sit still and let him get away. Prescott Jones was going to be a rich man. Soon, according to her brother-in-law. And Charlotte was determined to marry a rich man.

She didn't care what she had to do. She was going to marry Prescott.

SEVEN

Lying in her bed, Felicity watched as the first streaks of daylight moved across her ceiling. She had spent a restless night, her thoughts returning again and again to Prescott. She kept seeing him as he'd poured that dipper of water over his head, kept remembering the play of his muscles beneath his shirt, the look of his sun-browned forearms as his fingers raked the wet hair back from his face. She kept hearing him talk about the orphanage and Scrapper. He'd said so little and yet so much.

And some time this morning, he would come knocking at her door again. He would come to check on Angel's progress. He would come into her house, into her bedroom. His piercing blue eyes would look at her, and he would smile, making her heart thump as he always did.

She closed her eyes and rolled onto her side, trying not to imagine more, for her thoughts were far from what was proper for a single woman. She didn't want to imagine what it would be like to have Prescott Jones kiss her, to have him hold her and touch her in ways she'd never been held or touched.

But she did imagine it.

She told herself he was a stranger, an outsider. He'd been in Appleton no more than four days. She, on the other hand, had been born here. She could count on her fingers the number of times they'd spoken to one another. She knew little about him. There was no reason for her to be thinking such things, feeling such things. And there was no hope that such things would ever happen.

But she went on imagining them. She went on wanting what she couldn't have.

With an exasperated groan, she tossed aside the bedcovers and sat up, lowering her feet to the floor. Dawn had managed to overtake the bedroom by this time, and Felicity's gaze immediately found Angel, lying on the bed of blankets Felicity had made for her the night before.

Angel raised her head and meowed.

Felicity smiled, recognizing the familiar demand for food. "You *are* feeling better, aren't you, pet?" She stood and stepped across the room, then knelt to stroke the cat. "Thank God I didn't lose you."

Angel purred her concurrence.

Felicity's heart lightened considerably at the sound. "I'll get you some cream."

She rose and hurried into the kitchen. As she opened the icebox and removed a small pitcher of cream, she noted the need to purchase more ice. She mentally counted the money she had hidden in the crock on top of the cupboard. She decided she could afford a block of ice today. She would have the pink frock finished by Monday, and Mrs. Babcock was always prompt in paying her when she delivered her gowns.

She poured a generous amount of cream into a saucer, then carried it back to the bedroom. She set the saucer close to Angel and watched as the cat licked it clean.

Shouldn't you get ready? Prescott will be here soon.

She pressed the heels of her hands over her ears, as if she could shut out her thoughts, but it was too late. Her pulse had already quickened. Her mind was already envisioning him again.

Put on something pretty. It can't hurt.

Couldn't hurt? It *was* crazy! She was an old maid, too tall, too thin, too plain. She hadn't anything to wear that could disguise the truth.

She reached for a brown calico.

Not that one.

Her hand stopped in midair.

Wear the new green one.

Mad. She was undeniably, indisputably, stark, raving mad.

She selected the green dress.

She washed and dressed and even dabbed on some cologne. Then she brushed her hair and began to twist it into the bun she always wore.

No! He likes it down.

But she couldn't possibly know how Prescott Jones liked her hair. He'd probably never even *noticed* her hair. Still, instead of the hairpins, she selected the bronze combs that had been her mother's favorites and used them to pull her hair back from her face at the sides, leaving it falling down her back.

"I look ridiculous," she muttered as she stared at her reflection. "I look like I'm trying to be a girl again."

She might have talked herself into pinning up her hair and changing her dress if the knock hadn't sounded at her door at just that moment.

Heart pounding erratically, she went to answer it.

"Good morning, Felicity," Doc Gordon said as the door opened. "I understand your cat had an accident yesterday."

She stared at him dumbly, disappointment stealing her ability to speak.

"May I come in?"

"Of . . . of course," she stammered, stepping backward. "I . . . I was just surprised to see you. I thought you were in Boise City."

"I got back last night. Happened to run into Mr. Jones, and he asked if I might have a look at your cat this morning." He walked past her into the sitting room. "Mr. Jones was afraid he might not have set the animal's leg properly."

This was what she deserved for thinking Prescott might care what she wore or how she combed her hair. It only went to prove how useless something like vanity was for a woman like her. False vanity, for she had nothing to be vain about.

Shoulders squared, she led the doctor into her bedroom.

Prescott slipped the worm onto the hook, then handed the fishing pole to Stanley Johnson. With a great flourish, Stan cast the line out into the river.

"My dad showed me how to do that," the boy said proudly.

From behind them, he heard a gentle warning. "Suzanne, you stay back from that water."

Prescott reached out and took hold of the little girl's hand. "Your aunt Charlotte's right. Let's go back to the blanket. We can watch your brother from there."

Suzanne grinned at him. "Up," she demanded. "Up."

He laughed as he lifted her into his arms, then pivoted and strolled back to the blanket where Charlotte sat, her yellow-and-white skirt spread around her like a sunflower in full bloom.

Charlotte smiled prettily as they approached. "Dear heaven, I don't know how Rebecca manages when all four children are at home. I can scarcely keep up with Suzanne."

He set the three-year-old on her feet. "She's a lively one all right."

"Now, Suzanne, you sit down and stay put for a while. Here. Aunt Charlotte brought you a doll to play with." She pulled a porcelain doll from the wicker basket. "You take care of her, or Aunt Charlotte will be very displeased with you."

Prescott settled onto the blanket, keeping one eye on Stanley.

"Are you hungry?" Charlotte asked. "Would you like to eat now?"

What he would like to do was get back to Appleton, but he merely answered in the affirmative.

When Rebecca had asked him to take her sister and two youngest children fishing this morning, he'd known he was being maneuvered into spending more time with Charlotte, but he hadn't protested. Of course, he hadn't expected time to pass so slowly, either. Charlotte had little to talk about except for her well-to-do friends in Seattle and the wonderful dances and parties they gave. He'd attempted to introduce a few new topics, but she never seemed to know what he was talking about. She would simply ask him his own thoughts, deftly turning the conversation back to him.

He wondered why that trait no longer seemed as flattering as it had the first night they'd met.

The truth was, he found Charlotte more than a little boring. To put it simply, she was a spoiled young woman with few interests beyond herself. Oh, she was well trained in the art of flattering any male who might be near her at the time, but it was superficial at best.

As he reclined, bracing himself on his elbows and forearms, he wondered what Felicity Blessing would have to say about such topics as Idaho giving women the right to vote the previous year or about what differences the railroad might mean to the people of Appleton. For some reason, he was certain she would have plenty of things to say should he ask for her opinion.

What was she doing this morning while he was held captive here by the river? he wondered. What might they have talked about if she'd come with him and the children? Was she still worried about Angel? He wondered how the cat was faring.

"What are you thinking about, Prescott? You haven't heard a word I've been saying."

He blinked, then looked at Charlotte. "Oh, I was just wondering about Angel."

"Angel?"

"Miss Blessing's cat. I hope the doctor was able to take a look at her."

"Oh, that dreadful animal." She shook her head, her golden hair whispering over her shoulders. "I cannot imagine anyone making such a fuss over a cat."

"Miss Blessing's cat is rather special."

"Well, I'm sure that must be true if you've taken such a liking to it. Still, I couldn't bear one of those creatures in my home. I nearly start sneezing just thinking about it." She giggled, a lyrical sound that drifted away on the breeze. Her smile was fetching as she leaned toward him.

Prescott looked at her for several heartbeats, wondering why he didn't feel any desire to kiss her, especially when she was so obviously inviting him to do so. Any man who wouldn't grab such an opportunity must be an idiot.

Maybe he *was* an idiot, because he didn't intend to kiss her.

Rising to his feet, he said, "I'd better help Stan with that pole if he's ever to catch a fish before we start back. I've still got a work crew to hire this afternoon." Then he walked away from Charlotte without a backward glance.

Kneeling on the kitchen floor in her oldest dress, Felicity scrubbed with a vengeance. She had discovered some years ago that a deep-down cleaning of the house helped her to think more clearly.

Dark strands of hair had worked free from her bun and clung to the moisture on her neck. Water splashed onto her bodice and skirt and left dark spots on the faded gray gown, but Felicity didn't care. She would look a whole sight worse before she was finished scrubbing the house from one end to the other.

She supposed she was most angered by her own foolishness. Allowing her imagination to take flight. Thinking she might please Prescott with the way she wore her hair or by putting on a new gown. Why should he notice Felicity when he had a pretty girl like Charlotte fawning over him?

And why should she want him to? She was perfectly content with her life just as it was.

Are you?

Yes, she was. Perfectly content.

She pressed harder on the scrub brush and tried not to think about the tall man with ink-black hair and eyes the color of the Idaho sky, the orphan with a cat named Scrapper who, for a moment in time, had seemed to understand her as no one ever had.

EIGHT

Although Felicity's house fairly sparkled with its top-to-bottom cleaning, the work had done little to improve her state of mind. Felicity scarcely heard a word the minister said during the church service the next morning, especially since she knew Prescott and the entire Johnson family—including Miss Millard—were seated just two pews behind her.

When the service was over, she slipped as quickly as possible away from the other worshipers, careful to avoid making eye contact with anyone. She had intended to go directly home, but for some reason her feet carried her toward the apple orchards just down the slope from her place. She walked slowly through the mature trees, enjoying the cool shade the leafy branches provided. She kept walking until she reached the last row of fruit trees. Then she sat down and stared at the winding river.

Don't waste your time wantin' what you can't have, daughter.

She closed her eyes. Her father had been right. Wanting what she couldn't have only led to heartache. She was better off this way. Look how unhappy her mother had been.

"Miss Blessing?"

She gasped in surprise as she twisted to look behind her.

Prescott drew closer. "I hope I'm not intruding."

Felicity shook her head.

"It's quite a bit cooler here, isn't it?" He sat beneath the neighboring tree. "How's Angel doing?"

"Very well, thank you." Her wretched heart was pounding so loudly she could hardly hear him.

"Sorry I wasn't able to look in on her yesterday."

Don't want what you can't have, she warned herself silently. "There's no reason you should feel obligated to do so, Mr. Jones. I'm sure you have many other things to do to occupy your time." Realizing how petulant she sounded, she added, "The doctor says she'll mend just fine."

"I'm glad." He removed his suit coat and rolled up the sleeves of his white shirt to his elbows, then leaned back on his forearms, his eyes turning toward the river. "This is prettier country than I'd expected. I like the open spaces, too. Never could abide the big cities."

Curiosity got the better of her. "I've never been to a town bigger than Boise City, and that was many years ago, when I was just a girl. What was Chicago like?"

"Noisy. Lots of buildings. People everywhere. Crowded streets." He shrugged. "It's just not for me." He turned his gaze upon her. "I don't think you'd care for it, either, Felicity."

She felt the color rush to her cheeks at the sound of her name on his lips.

The blush on her high cheekbones was attractive, Prescott thought as he watched her. Placing more weight on his left arm, he leaned toward her. "Tell me about your life here. What was Appleton like when you were a girl?"

She was silent for some time before replying, "There wasn't a town when I was born. Just a few farmers, like my grandfather was before he died. My grandparents were the first to arrive along this stretch of river, and they were alone for many years, just them and my mother. Grandpa Greer planted these apple trees and dug the first irrigation canals himself. My mother sold the orchards when I was quite small, but Mr. Simpson, the farmer who bought them, allowed me to come here whenever I wanted."

A tender smile played across her mouth, and Prescott realized it wasn't too full, as he'd thought the first time he'd seen her. Instead, it was lush and just a bit provocative when curved upward as it was now.

"My mother used to tell me about the Indians who came to trade with Grandpa Greer, his apples for their animal hides. I always hoped I'd get to see one of them, but I never did. I suppose, by that time, there were too many people living here. Or maybe the Indians were all on the reservations already. I don't know."

"Do you have any brothers or sisters?" he asked.

"No, it was just me. There weren't even other children nearby until I was nearly grown."

"What about school?"

"My mother taught me to read and write." Her voice softened. "Mama taught me everything she could before she died."

He waited a few moments before asking his next question. "Have you ever wanted to leave Appleton?"

She shook her head, then turned her gaze toward the

river and western horizon. After a moment of silence, she shrugged her shoulders. "Where would I go? This is my home. I don't suppose I'll ever leave."

There was so much she wasn't telling him, and for some reason he wanted to know. He wanted to know why she'd never married. He wanted to know what had put the sadness in her dark, chocolate-colored eyes and what could be done to take it away.

He wanted to kiss her.

He sat up, his eyes still watching her, testing the idea that had popped so unexpectedly into his head.

He wanted to *kiss* her?

Amazingly enough, the thought wasn't all that surprising. In fact, it seemed quite reasonable.

Prescott rose and stepped over to her. She glanced up at him, her eyes wide with uncertainty.

He held out his hand. "Come on. Show me some more of your grandfather's orchards."

She hesitated a moment, then slipped her cool fingers into his waiting hand and allowed him to pull her to her feet.

He transferred her hand to the crook of his arm, then started walking, following the westernmost edge of the orchards. He noticed how easily she kept pace with him, her long legs matching his stride. He also noticed how comfortable it felt to be with her. He was in no hurry to get back to his work, as he had been yesterday with Charlotte. He didn't bother to wonder why. He just knew it was true.

He liked being with Felicity Blessing.

Felicity felt strangely at ease. Oh, her heart was still beating more quickly than normal, but it was a pleasant sort of feeling.

"Tell me, Felicity. What do you think about Idaho giving women the right to vote?"

She looked at him, not quite certain she'd heard him correctly. It seemed such an odd question. Of all the things he could have asked her, he wanted to know about women voting?

She couldn't help herself. She laughed.

Prescott drew them both to a stop and met her gaze. "You find the right to vote amusing?"

"No." She shook her head as her laughter faded, but her smile remained. "It just seemed so . . . so out of the blue. I thought you wanted to know more about the fruit orchards."

"I do, but first answer my other question."

"I think women should have the right to vote in all elections, not just those for the state. There are so many others like me, men and women, who must earn wages and support themselves. Too many have no say in the matters which affect us. Are we women less important than other wage earners because of our gender? What the government does affects us as much as it does men. We should have a say in those decisions." She paused, realizing how fervently she'd responded. More softly she continued, "I'm grateful this state government has seen fit to give women the vote, and I don't intend to ever waste the opportunity."

There was a twinkle in Prescott's eyes. "Admirable sentiments, Miss Blessing. And what do you suppose having the railroad come to Appleton would mean for its citizens?"

She cast a mock frown in his direction. "Mr. Jones, has anyone ever told you your mind works in a peculiar manner?" Then, unable to keep from it, she smiled again.

"Miss Blessing"—he placed his hands on her upper arms and drew her toward him—"has anyone ever told you that you have an irresistible mouth?"

Her breath caught in her throat when she realized what was about to happen. Her knees threatened to buckle, but Prescott's grip on her arms steadied her as he drew her closer to him.

His mouth upon hers was warm and tender. As the kiss lengthened, deepened, his lips parted slightly, and the tip of his tongue traced the sensitive flesh of her mouth, sending sparks shooting through her veins.

A part of her knew she should be appalled by his audacity, by his boldness. He had no right to be kissing her. She had not given him leave to do so. But neither could she make him stop. Never had she imagined a man's kisses could make her feel quite like this.

When at last he lifted his mouth from hers, she opened her eyes to find him watching her with an intense gaze. Then, with the fingers of one hand, he removed her hatpin and Sunday bonnet, dropping them both to the grass at their feet.

This couldn't be happening, of course. Not to her. Not to Felicity Blessing.

Her hairpins followed the hat, and soon her hair fell free about her shoulders. Prescott threaded his fingers through it, then leaned closer until his face was pressed close to her head.

A white heat flared in her, a yearning that cried out to be satisfied. The sensation both frightened and tempted her.

"You should always wear your hair down, Felicity," he whispered near her ear, causing gooseflesh to rise on her arm. "It's beautiful." He pulled back and looked her full in the face. "*You're* beautiful."

Prescott only realized how true the words were as he spoke them. He wondered why no one else had ever seen the beauty there. He wondered why *he* hadn't seen it before now.

He watched as tears pooled in her eyes, then slipped

onto her cheeks. Tenderly, he kissed the tears away before claiming her mouth once more with his.

He felt a fierce desire to cherish this woman, to be with her always, and wondered how he could feel so strongly about someone he'd known for such a short time. But wondering how it had happened didn't change what he felt.

It was Felicity who broke the kiss, who withdrew. Confusion played across her face as she stared at him. She touched her mouth with her fingertips, her eyes wide with wonder.

"Felicity." He reached for her.

She put out a hand to stop him. "I . . . I think it's time for me to go home." She bent down to retrieve her bonnet and pins.

"I'll go with you."

She shook her head.

"I should look at Angel."

"Not today, Prescott," she whispered, then turned and hurried back through the trees.

For a long while after she'd gone, Prescott remained standing at the orchard's edge, remembering how she'd felt in his arms, remembering the sweet taste of her mouth, remembering the luxurious feel of her hair. Most of all, remembering the way he felt.

Prescott Jones had fallen in love.

•　　•　　•

Charlotte slipped deeper into the orchard, scarcely daring to breathe for fear Prescott would hear her. She clenched her hands together, trying to subdue the indignation that consumed her.

So it was true. Prescott and Miss Blessing, kissing in the orchards. How could he do that to Charlotte? How could he humiliate her this way? She'd nearly thrown herself at him yesterday, wanting him to kiss her, but he'd acted the perfect gentleman. And now here he was with Miss Blessing!

Well, they weren't going to get away with it. Charlotte had never in her entire life had a man choose someone else over her, and she wasn't about to allow it to happen this time.

He was supposed to propose to her, and Charlotte wasn't going to let him slight her this way. Somehow she was going to get even.

NINE

Angel Emeline felt quite proud of what she'd accomplished in so short a time. Not, of course, that she'd had anything to do with the kiss by the river. That had been entirely Prescott's own idea. Still, if she hadn't run out in front of that wagon . . .

If a cat could smile, Angel Emeline would have done so now. After all, her promotion was almost assured. All that was left was for Prescott to propose marriage to Felicity and for Felicity to accept. And since these two were destined for each other, there was no point in dragging things out unnecessarily. The sooner he proposed, the better.

After all, what could go wrong now?

In the days following that memorable Sunday, Prescott came to see Felicity each morning, ostensibly to check on Angel's recovery.

The first morning was awkward. Uncertain about the turbulent emotions roiling inside her when he was near, Felicity didn't know what to say to him, how to act around him. She was afraid he might try to kiss her again, and she didn't know whether she wanted him to or not. But he didn't try. He looked at Angel's dressings, said how well she was doing, smiled that devastating smile of his, then left a short while later.

The second morning, it didn't seem quite so strange to have him there. This time, after he looked in on Angel, Felicity offered him a cup of coffee before he started to work. Seated opposite each other at the kitchen table, Prescott shared more details about his childhood. About the good years when his parents and siblings were still alive. About the difficult years, growing up in the orphanage. About Walt and about Scrapper. About the years after he left Chicago, working and saving so he could one day have a place of his own.

The third morning, Prescott almost forgot to look in on Angel at all. Felicity invited him into the kitchen when he first arrived. This time, it was she who talked about her growing-up years. She talked about her mother's unhappiness, about her father's anger and resentment. She found herself revealing things to Prescott she'd never told another living soul. After he left, she expected to feel regret for speaking so openly, but she didn't.

By the fourth morning, Felicity was waiting for him, opening the door before he could knock. She wore her hair down, catching it back with an emerald-green ribbon she'd meant to use on a gown for Mrs. Babcock's shop. She wore her newest dress, the green one she'd tried on only once before. This time Prescott saw her in it.

"You look lovely." He placed a feather-light kiss on her cheek.

Felicity discovered she *felt* lovely when he looked at her that way.

On Friday morning, Felicity met him outside, Angel in her arms. Before she could say a word, he kissed her on the mouth. He didn't seem to care that some of the workmen had seen what he'd done. He just smiled at her, and she felt herself blossoming.

This was what her mother had told her to wait for, and now Felicity understood why. It was too deliciously wonderful to settle for anything less.

"Tell me something," she said as he placed a hand at the small of her back and guided her along the side of her house. "What made you decide to come here after you lived so many other places?"

"I thought it was to be with Walt. He's the closest thing to family I have." He gazed into her eyes. "But I think it was to find you, Felicity."

She felt a shiver of joy spread through her. Her mother had told her never to sell or leave her house except for love. Maybe it was time to sell it. "Prescott, I've been thinking—"

"Let me show you how work on the cannery has progressed this week," he said, interrupting.

He didn't need to show her, of course. She'd spent altogether too much time this week looking out the window and watching Prescott as he carried lumber and hammered nails and worked with his crew. She'd memorized the way his black hair gleamed a midnight blue after he cooled himself by dumping water over his head. She knew the color of his workshirts and the precise way his Levi Strauss trousers fit his hips and legs. She could recite by heart the commands he'd called to the men as they worked, could hear the exact timbre of his voice.

Now, as they walked the circumference of the factory,

she scarcely looked at the skeleton of the building rising up around her house. Instead, her gaze returned time and again to Prescott's face. She could see the pride in his eyes, hear the excitement in his words.

"This won't mean success for just me, Felicity. It will be a real boon for all the farmers for miles around. Think of it. They'll be able to sell their goods to folks back on the East Coast. The fruit won't spoil in a rail car if an engine breaks down along the way. It can't freeze in the cold or rot in the heat. And the cannery will be big enough to handle whatever is sent to us. Everyone in Appleton will prosper because of it. There'll be more money to buy goods at the mercantile, more money to buy dresses from Mrs. Babcock." He grinned at her. "Maybe even something as pretty as that one you're wearing."

She stopped walking, forcing him to stop, too. "My house is in the way."

"We'll make it work."

"But it would be better if you had my property, as well."

He cupped her chin with his fingers. "Not if you don't want to leave it."

He hadn't told her he loved her. He hadn't offered marriage, but deep in Felicity's heart, she believed it would happen. She believed she'd been given her most secret wish—someone to love and someone to love her. Her mother had said not to sell her house for any other reason. She loved Prescott, and he needed this land to succeed. Love had made her decision for her.

"Does your offer still stand, Prescott? Will you buy my house and land?"

He studied her face for a long time before answering, "Yes. If you're sure you want to sell, the J and J Canning Company will buy your place."

Cradling Angel with one arm, Felicity held out her other hand. "I believe a handshake will seal our agreement, Mr. Jones."

Prescott thought a kiss might be a more appropriate way to seal their agreement, but he settled for taking her hand in his. He considered proposing marriage to her that very moment. It was, after all, what he wanted and what he thought she must want, too.

But it was too soon. His plan had always been to start his business, then to take a wife. Just because he'd fallen in love unexpectedly with Felicity Blessing didn't mean he should change those plans. Until the factory was in operation, most of his time and all of his money would be tied up in the business. When he married, he wanted to be able to give plenty of both to his bride. Especially when that bride would be Felicity Blessing.

Waiting wasn't going to be easy. With each passing day, his love for Felicity grew, deepened, ripened. Every time he saw her, she became more lovely in his eyes, more desirable. He'd spent more than one night this past week thinking about making love to her. He longed to have the right to run his fingers through her unbound hair, to run his hands over her slim figure, to cup her firm breasts in his palms, to . . .

He shook off the images in his head. The sooner he got the factory up and running, the sooner he could make those images a reality.

Releasing her hand, he said, "I'll have Walt draw up the papers this afternoon."

She smiled one of those incredible smiles that transformed her face, and he thought again about kissing her. He planned to do a lot of kissing once they were married.

TEN

Walt sat forward on his chair, his face alight with surprise. "You're joking. She's agreed to sell? How did you manage that?"

"I'm hoping it's because she's fallen in love with me." Prescott grinned.

"Because she's . . . Pres, what have you been up to?"

"As surprising as you might find it, I believe you'd say I've been courting Miss Blessing."

Walt frowned.

"Don't worry, my friend. I'm not behaving the scoundrel. I'm quite serious."

"But what about Charlotte? I thought—"

"I'm afraid your sister-in-law and I just aren't right for each other. We don't have anything to talk about when we're alone together. We don't want the same things." He shook his head. "The truth is, I find Charlotte not very interesting to be with. She's pretty, but it takes more than looks to make a good wife. Marriage just wouldn't work for the two of us. She knows it as well as I do."

"All right. I can accept that. She's not as much like Rebecca as I'd expected. But Miss *Blessing?*"

His grin returned. "What can I say? I'm in love with her. I intend to marry her just as soon as the cannery is in operation, if she'll have me."

"Well, I'll be." Walt chuckled. "She's the last person I'd have picked for you."

Prescott leaned forward on his chair. "I told Felicity you'd draw up the papers for the sale of her house to the J and J Canning Company. She'd like to buy the old Simpson place. I understand their orchards used to belong to her grandfather. I guess she'd like to own them again for sentimental reasons." He didn't mention he'd first kissed Felicity in those same orchards and felt a bit sentimental about them himself. "I looked at the house before coming over here. It's just the right place to raise a large family."

"I take it you plan to live there, too." He chuckled again. "Wait till I tell Rebecca. She'll never believe this. Not in a million years."

Charlotte's face burned as she backed away from the open window. Her mother had often told her that eavesdroppers rarely heard anything nice about themselves, but this was unbelievable. How *dare* he say she wasn't interesting? Why, he made her sound positively dull. As if he were so terribly entertaining. Well, she wouldn't stand for it! Not for a minute!

Her skirts flared out around her ankles as she turned and stalked away. Of all the unmitigated gall! And he was actually going to *propose* to that woman. He'd chosen

Felicity Blessing over her. And after Miss Blessing refused to sell him her property. After all the problems she'd caused, making him redesign the factory to go around her house.

Charlotte stopped, and a smile slowly crept to the corners of her mouth. She'd get even all right, and she knew just the way to do it.

Felicity stood in the middle of her bedroom, gazing at her belongings. It was difficult to comprehend her own decision to sell her home. All of her memories were centered around this little place. Soon, probably in a matter of days, it would be leveled. It would disappear and be forgotten.

Was she making a mistake?

Prescott loves you.

How could she be certain of that? He'd kissed her. He'd told her she was lovely. He'd made her feel special. But did he really love her? He'd never mentioned marriage or what was to happen in days to come. Was there a future for them?

Angel meowed as she sat up on her bed, drawing Felicity's attention. The bandage had been removed from the cat's torso. Long white hair covered any signs of Prescott's careful stitching. Angel even managed to get around by herself now, although she obviously hated the splint that still bound her broken leg.

"What is it, pet?" Felicity asked as she reached down for the cat. She picked her up. "Am I crazy?"

Of course not. He loves you.

She held the cat at arm's length and stared hard into her green eyes. "Sometimes I'd swear you could talk," she muttered.

"Reow."

With a shake of her head, she carried Angel into the kitchen and put some scraps from last night's supper into the cat's food dish.

"Reow."

She heard the knock on her door and went to answer it, hoping it was Prescott. She knew seeing him would calm her doubts, if only for the time he was with her.

But it wasn't Prescott on the other side of her door.

"Hello, Miss Blessing." The younger woman smiled. "Do you remember me? I'm Charlotte Millard, Rebecca Johnson's sister."

Rather than being calmed, her doubts returned three-fold. Looking at Charlotte made her feel dowdy. "Yes. Of course I remember you, Miss Millard."

"I do apologize for calling on you in the middle of the day, but I wanted to speak with you if I may."

Feeling sick, Felicity backed away from the door. "Please. Come in."

"What a quaint little house you have," Charlotte said as she breezed inside. "I could not imagine how anyone could manage in a place so tiny. I suppose it isn't so bad for a woman all alone, but I'm sure you won't miss it once it's gone."

Charlotte poked her head into the bedroom, then turned around and met Felicity's gaze once more.

"You must know how pleased Prescott is that you've decided to sell. He would have done just about anything to get his hands on it. After all, it could mean the success or failure of his cannery." She laughed. "Why, I think he'd have even pretended to have some affections for you if that was the only way he could get you to agree."

Felicity felt a chill roll up her spine.

Charlotte lifted her hands in a gesture of amusement.

"You know what a determined man he is. Why, he has completely turned my head with his charm. What's a woman to do?" She walked toward the door. "Anyway, I just wanted to thank you for selling your home. Prescott and I shall be forever grateful. Now, I really must run."

With a ruffle of skirts she was gone, leaving only a hint of rose-scented cologne in the air as a reminder of her visit.

She was lying.

Felicity wanted to believe Charlotte had lied, but how could she know? It sounded as if Charlotte and Prescott had come to an agreement.

Prescott wouldn't use you that way.

But how could she be certain? What did she really know about him?

You know him, Felicity. Trust your heart. Take a chance on love.

She sat on her straight-backed chair and stared out the window. She barely noticed when Angel jumped into her lap.

Trust your heart, she heard again. *Take a chance.*

She thought back over each moment she'd spent with Prescott. She remembered the way he'd touched her, the way he'd kissed her. She remembered his smile, warm and genuine. She remembered the confidences they'd shared, the times he'd told her she was beautiful. She'd believed him because she loved him.

Maybe she was wrong about him. Maybe she would still be alone when all was said and done. But it was time she took a risk in this life.

She was going to believe her heart. She was going to believe in Prescott Jones.

ELEVEN

The days had too few hours in them, as far as Prescott was concerned, especially those days immediately following his purchase of Felicity's home. It certainly seemed fate was conspiring to keep him from having even two minutes alone with her.

On Saturday the canning equipment arrived by wagon, weeks ahead of schedule, and he had to find a place to store it all until the construction on the factory was done. On Monday one of his crew fell from a ladder and broke his arm. After the doctor had seen to the injured man, Prescott drove him back to his farm, a half day's ride away, and didn't return until after nightfall. On Tuesday a telegram arrived from the railroad, demanding a meeting with the proprietors of J and J Canning Company, necessitating an unexpected four-day trip to Boise City for Prescott and Walt.

And when he returned, Charlotte met the train and

refused to let him out of her sight from that moment on. She was like a prison guard, only sweeter and more cloying, flirting and flattering and driving him up the wall. Finally, unable to escape her, he retired for the night, determined to rise early and go to see Felicity.

But when he got up at dawn, he found Charlotte waiting for him.

"You're up early, Prescott," she greeted him as he entered the dining room. "I'm glad. I was hoping we could spend the morning together. I've missed you while you were away."

"I'm afraid I've got work to do, Charlotte."

"But surely you can spend some time with me." She placed her hands on his shoulders, then stood on tiptoe and pulled him toward her until she could kiss him. When she stepped back, there was the blush of roses on her cheeks.

"Charlotte, I think we need to—"

"You must know how I feel about you."

"No, I'm not sure I do."

She fluttered her eyelids. "But you must know you've stolen my affections, Prescott."

She was a superb actress, he thought, but not superb enough to keep him from guessing how little she actually cared for him. This was just a game to her, a contest she wanted to win.

"Charlotte, you're a lovely young woman, but—"

A scowl furrowed her brow. "I won't be toyed with, Prescott."

"I wasn't—"

"You can't seriously intend to throw me over for that old scarecrow."

He felt his temper rise. "Be careful what you say, Charlotte."

"She won't have you," she warned with a toss of her head.

"I told Miss Blessing that you and I have an understanding. I told her you'd do anything to get her land. And you did, didn't you? You even kissed her just to get it. Well, she won't have you now. I made certain of that."

He wanted to shake her until her teeth rattled, and if he didn't leave now, he just might do it. He was about to turn away when she sneezed.

"Achew!"

Then she sneezed again . . . and again and again and again.

Instinctively Prescott glanced toward the open window, and sure enough, there on the windowsill sat Angel. He couldn't imagine how she'd managed to get up there with her leg in a splint, but he wasn't about to figure it out now. Feeling grateful for the interruption, he hurried over and scooped up the cat in his arms.

"Guess I'd better take you home," he said as he stroked the cat's head. Then he whispered, "Thanks, pal."

Looking up, he found Charlotte glaring in his direction, the look filled with loathing. He considered mentioning the ugly red splotches that were appearing rapidly on her face and arms, then decided she would notice them herself soon enough.

Subduing a grin, he hurried out of the house.

The old Simpson house was enormous. Felicity's few items of furniture nearly disappeared in all the extra space. She kept moving it around, trying to decide what looked best. She moved it until she realized she was doing it only to fill the empty hours of her day, to keep herself from wondering about Prescott, to keep herself from believing the worst, to drive Charlotte Millard's suggestions from her mind.

It had been a week since she'd last seen him, and then

only for a moment. She'd heard he'd gone to Boise City, but she hadn't asked why. She wasn't sure she wanted to know.

As dawn lightened the countryside, Felicity stepped onto the spacious porch of her new home. The morning air was cool and fresh, the summer sun not yet a threat to comfort. Except for the sounds of the river and an occasional trill of a meadowlark, all was silent. She thought it the most perfect time of day.

That was the very moment Prescott came riding down the road on his buckskin, a dusty Stetson shading his face, Angel cradled in the crook of one arm.

Felicity's heart quickened the instant she saw him. Her fingers closed around the railing to support her shaky knees.

He rode right up close to her porch. One hand rested on the pommel. His posture was relaxed. Although his eyes were still hidden in shadows, she knew he was studying her with one of his intense gazes, the kind where he seemed to look right inside her soul and mind.

Finally he said, "You wouldn't believe where I found Angel. You should keep a better eye on her, Miss Blessing. She's only got eight more lives."

She couldn't think of a single thing to say.

"You look mighty pretty in the morning light, Felicity."

She ached to be closer to him. She ached to touch him.

He tipped his Stetson back on his head and peered up at the sky. "Did I ever tell you what I planned to do when I came to Appleton?" He looked at her again. "I mean besides starting the cannery."

She shook her head, not certain whether he had or not, not caring whether he had or not.

"Well, I figured I'd give myself some time to make sure it was going to succeed. Then, if I thought it would, I planned on taking me a wife. I liked the idea of a big house like this one. A big house full of youngsters." He swung down from the saddle and removed his hat, then set Angel on the first step. With his gaze locked with Felicity's, he moved up onto the porch.

Felicity almost stopped breathing.

His voice lowered as he looked down into her eyes. "Seems I bought your other place and now I want this one, too . . . as long as you come part and parcel with it. I want to see you standing on this porch every morning with the sunlight in your hair. I want to see you up in that second-story bedroom there, wearing nothing but moonlight."

A tiny gasp escaped her.

"What I'm saying is, I might have been able to wait a while to marry someone else, Felicity, but I can't wait to marry you. That's if you'll have me, of course."

He didn't give her a chance to answer before he gathered her into his arms and drew her close, his mouth covering hers. All her uncertainties melted beneath the tender assault. She wrapped her arms around his neck and clung to him while his kisses roamed from her mouth to a sensitive place on her neck.

Minutes later—or was it a lifetime?—he broke the kiss to look into her eyes once more.

"Will you marry me?" he asked softly.

"Yes," she answered in a mere whisper, still scarcely believing it was all true.

"Soon?"

"Yes."

"I love you, Miss Blessing."

Miracles did happen, she thought as she was drawn once more into Prescott's embrace. Prayers got answered and wishes came true. If anyone doubted, they needed only to see what had happened to Felicity, and they would believe.

"I love you, too, Mr. Jones. I always will."

EPILOGUE

Angel Emeline waited nervously while the archangel in charge of prayer assistance reviewed the file before him. Occasionally Archie murmured a thoughtful, "Hmm," which never failed to send a shiver of apprehension down Angel Emeline's spine.

And she'd wanted this promotion so badly. She'd been counting on being an angel, second grade.

"Well, Emeline."

She swallowed hard as her superior closed the file and lifted his gaze to meet hers.

"I see Felicity and Prescott have found one another."

"Yes, sir."

"Their wedding appears to have been quite a celebration for the citizens of Appleton, coming on the same day as the announcement that the railroad was coming up their way."

"Yes, sir. It certainly was. A great day."

"Are you aware their first child will be born in the spring?"

"Really? That's wonderful."

"Yes, it is. Wonderful indeed. I foresee a great future for the Jones family. I am pleased with the way things turned out."

Her nerves began to calm. Archie was actually pleased with what she'd done.

He flipped open the file and glanced at the papers inside again. "However, Emeline, some of your methods were a bit . . . unorthodox, should I say?"

So much for calming nerves. "Yes, sir," she answered softly.

"That poor cat could have been killed."

"I tried to be careful, sir, but I'm afraid I still wasn't used to having four legs. My timing was off and I—"

"Yes. Yes. I know." He smiled patiently.

Emeline couldn't believe it. Archie smiled? In the ages she'd known him, she couldn't recall once seeing Archie smile.

"The important thing is you helped Felicity find the answer to her prayer. And Prescott found the right woman in the process. That's very gratifying to me. I hoped he would find happiness. He deserves it. He was always a brave lad."

Emeline leaned forward, a suspicion sparking to life. Was it possible? No. It couldn't be. Archie?

He read her thoughts. "Yes, I was Scrapper. That was my last earthly assignment. I became rather fond of the boy during those years. I knew he would grow into a fine man."

"But I didn't think you *ever* left these chambers."

"Even an archangel in charge must be concerned with helping those on earth. Besides, it gives me perspective when I'm assessing the performance of others." He folded his hands in front of him. "I shall be processing your promotion papers immediately."

She grinned. She was getting her promotion. Angel Emeline, second grade. She'd done it. She'd made two people happy, and she'd earned her promotion. There couldn't be a nicer ending than that.

"May I tell the others, sir?"

He nodded. "Yes, you may tell them."

She rose from her chair.

"But before you go, about Miss Millard's rash . . ."

Robin Lee Hatcher is the award-winning author of twenty historical romances, including the best-selling Americana Series. She is the immediate past president of Romance Writers of America, Inc., the largest genre writing organization in the world with nearly eight thousand members. A native Idahoan, she makes her home in Boise with her husband, Jerry.

BELLING THE CAT

~ *by* ~

Susan Wiggs

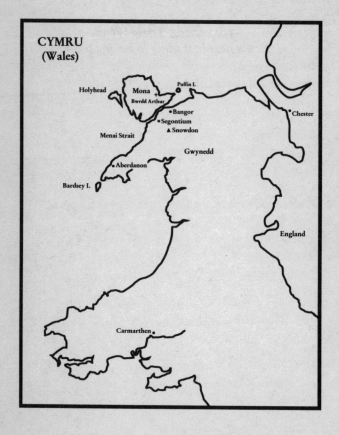

CYMRU
(Wales)

Holyhead
Mona
Bwrdd Arthur
Puffin I.
Bangor
Segontium
Snowdon
Menai Strait
Gwynedd
Aberdanon
Bardsey I.
Chester
England
Carmarthen

GLOSSARY

Bryn Melyn—yellow hill (author's invention)
Bwrdd Arthur—ancient fortification on Anglesey; local people say that it was here that King Arthur convened his Round Table
caer—fort
Carmarthen (Caerfyrddin)—"Merlin's City"
cariad—dear one
Cymru—Wales
Gwynedd—one of the four Dark Ages kingdoms of Wales
Mona (Môn)—"Mother of Wales" (Anglesey)
tylwyth—fairies

Cats became so valuable that the Welsh prince Howell the Good passed laws setting the worth of cats. Not surprisingly, a cat was worth more if it was a good mouser. Prince Howell decreed that a kitten was worth one pence. A grown cat that had not yet caught a mouse was worth only two pence; but after it had learned to catch mice, its value rose to four pence. If someone bought a cat that turned out to be a poor mouser, the buyer was entitled to one-third of the money back.

—Dr. Ann Squire, ASPCA

Who shall bell the cat?

—Aesop, fl. c. 550 B.C.

ONE

"I hate cats," Rhys muttered, glowering at the malevolent green eyes that glared at him from the shadows of the dense forest. "Truly, I do hate them. Satan's creatures, all."

"Grrr." Hodain, a lanky dog made more of sinew than flesh, halted stiff-legged in the path, his ruff standing on end and his long, yellow teeth bared.

Rhys drew up his exhausted warhorse and stopped. He sensed more than saw the movement in the low-branched grove of wych elm. "Have at it, Hodain," he said, suddenly eager to be rid of the ominous presence.

The dog lurched off the path and into the grove. Terrible growls and yowls came from the thick woods, but Rhys was not concerned. His loyal dog—part wolf, part demon—fought as fiercely as any human warrior. Hodain had brought down bears and badgers and pine martens. This shadowy, feral cat would prove no match for Hodain's strength.

Just for a moment, Rhys pondered what roasted wild-cat would taste like. Then he grimaced, disgusted with himself for having sunk so low. Uttering a curse, he ignored the gnawing hunger in his belly. He put his fingers to his lips and whistled for Hodain.

He expected the huge, brindled dog to come bounding triumphantly out of the woods. Instead Hodain emerged from the underbrush, yipping like a pup, his tail tucked between his legs. Four livid, parallel tracks of blood scored the dog's muzzle.

As the great beast whimpered and huddled near Rhys's stirrup, Rhys bent and patted Hodain's head. "We've had little but ill luck since I escaped, my friend. If something doesn't change soon—"

A bone-piercing yowl echoed down the corries of broken rock that rose like the sides of a bowl around the wooded path. The sound was neither animal nor human, but some unearthly voice of an ancient soul. Like an arrow of crystal, it speared Rhys's head. He clapped his hands over his ears.

When at last the mournful noise ceased, Rhys urged his horse forward. "Make haste, Atarax," he said. "This is a place of demons. And a day for omens."

The exhausted horse valiantly quickened his pace to a canter. Rhys heard only the rhythmic creak of saddle leather and the faint jangle of harness, the soft thump of hooves on the path, and the rustle of his war sark, a shirt of overlapping slices of horn.

The evil wildcat, which had stalked his progress since he had come awake in the coastal woodlands of Gwynedd that morning, seemed to have disappeared after that last torturous yowl.

Rhys stifled a shudder. Never had he seen Hodain run from a fight. The cat must be sinister indeed. Probably a mountain lion, possibly a long-fanged manx cat.

Rhys's father, the Bard of Carmarthen, would have said the cat was a witch's familiar.

The thought of his father lowered Rhys's mood a notch farther. As a bard, Myrddin had been respected and revered. Some even believed he could make magic. Bards were men of learning, keepers of the old stories, makers of legend. Their art kept the blood pulsing proud and hot in the veins of the four ancient kingdoms of Cymru.

Uthyr Pendragon, the high king, had once listened to Myrddin's recitations in a windy hall at Chester. Old and unwed, exhausted by numberless battles, the king claimed to have no heir. Myrddin had insisted that an heir would come. This heir, this once and future king, would be bastard born, but one day he would be a greater king than Uthyr.

For that helpful tidbit, the Pendragon had banished the bard. Myrddin was sent to the savage vales in the shadow of the jagged tor of Snowdon.

With naught to do but cleave to his wife, cleave he did. By the time Rhys's mother gave birth to him, her thirteenth son, her spent and broken body succumbed to the rigors of the flesh, and she died.

As if he didn't have his hands full enough with thirteen boys, Myrddin became foster father to a squalling, colicky infant who was fast growing up to be a cocky, handsome youth.

Rhys had never liked Arthur.

So Rhys, thirteenth son of an exiled bard who didn't know when to keep his mouth shut, had been himself exiled. He had never been able to learn precisely what he had done to bring about his disgrace. He had dim memories of his father lecturing him about honor and destiny.

Then Rhys had been banished. Myrddin had sold him to the holy brothers of Bardsey Island, there to live in chastity and servitude for the rest of his days.

On Bardsey, in the relentless wind and amid the gorse and withy-beds, Rhys had grown to manhood, learning to pray to the Christ god and to hate his captivity. Finally, just before his spirit had been bowed to the point of breaking, he had escaped. The mainland had not exactly proved to be Avalon.

Rhys found himself wandering, a masterless knight on a stolen horse, in search of some way to keep from starving to death.

And to make matters worse, he was being stalked by a wildcat.

At that point, I had not yet decided whether he was worth saving. My vision, so keen that some say I am enchanted—which I am, but I know better than to flaunt it—revealed a disheartening sight.

He sat his huge horse as if the weight of the world pressed upon his shoulders. His hair had not been shorn in weeks. Its distinctive color pleased me—it was the hot, bright red-gold of flames on a summer night.

He was a big man, taller than most, broad of shoulder, lean of hip, long of leg. Yet his hand was gentle as he reached down to pat the mangy bag of bone and gristle he called a dog.

I wrinkled my nose and sniffed. Lord, but I hate dogs. The sight of that creature was almost enough to induce me to let the wayfaring knight pass through, all unknowing, never to cross my path again.

Just as I was about to rejoin my shadow world of verdant darkness and perfumed magic, the traveler threw back his head and began to sing.

The sun struck him, and I saw that he had a remarkable face, stamped with humor and suffering and compassion and raw, aching fatigue. His voice was as rich as the song of the wind, and I sensed a latent, undiscovered magic there, and suddenly I knew.

I had a plan. I hoped it wouldn't kill him.

TWO

Singing always made Rhys feel better. His father, a true master, would probably scoff at the simplicity of the tune and the directness of the language, but Rhys sang only to please himself, not to entertain a royal court or to impress a group of scholars.

The woods thinned ahead, and the terrain fissured down toward the coast. Brown marshes and clumps of sycamore, bitten by wind and salt, were hunched along a pebbled shore. On a sloping field, white cattle grazed. The road here was broad and well trodden, so Rhys knew he was nearing a stronghold or town.

"Well, God be thanked," he said under his breath. "I misliked those damp woods."

He hoped he would find a friendly welcome in the new place.

An arrow whizzed past his head and *thunk*ed into a tree trunk behind him.

Rhys blew out a disgusted breath and ducked low, his cheek touching Atarax's neck.

He uttered a command to Hodain. The dog slunk low and crept forward, ears flattened and tail aquiver, to sniff out the attackers. Rhys bent over the neck of his mount and held his shield in front of his chest.

His shoulder still ached from the last battle he had fought.

And nearly lost.

He tossed aside the depressing thought and concentrated on the present challenge. There was a long, straight stretch of clear roadway between Rhys and the dark forest beyond the coastal clearing. He would have to risk a run for cover.

Feeling apologetic, he pounded his heels into the tired stallion's sides and urged him to a gallop. More arrows and darts sprang from the fringe of boulders and the low growth of heather at the edge of the clearing.

The attackers were Saxon dalesmen, no doubt, trained from the cradle to hate Britons. An arrow glanced off Rhys's shield, scraping the already battered bullhide.

He gritted his teeth and prayed Hodain would chase off the brigands. Another arrow nearly parted his hair in a new spot. "By the Christ," he grumbled, urging Atarax even faster, heading for the dense woods before the arrows found living flesh either in him or his horse.

Hodain's furious baying rose above the angry buzz of arrows. A grim smile tightened Rhys's mouth. Hodain might have failed to scare off the wildcat, but there was not a man alive the dog couldn't intimidate.

Shouts and curses sounded from the tumbled rocks. Rhys halted his warhorse in time to see a handful of men in wolfskins and leather breeches disappear into the woods, Hodain nipping at their heels.

Letting Atarax subside to a walk, Rhys hung his head in weariness as Hodain loped to his side. Absently he reached into his saddle pouch, extracted the last of his barley bread, and tossed the morsel to the dog.

A sea mist had curled in from the coast, bringing with it a damp chill. The fog was thick; smoky tendrils slithered along the ground and then swept up to obscure the land from view. There was a lucent, unearthly quality to the mist. It turned the trees and rocks to ghosts and mellowed the hush of the waves on the shore.

He cursed under his breath. In the fortnight since he had, in the teeth of a storm, escaped Bardsey Isle in a leaky coracle, the weather had been more enemy than friend.

He wondered how long the horse would hold out. The beast was extraordinary by any standards, as the trader in Aberdaron had been quick to point out. Bred from the big-boned horses in the south of Gaul, Atarax was made to carry a fully clad warrior into battle. For a stallion he was remarkably gentle, though quick to get his blood up when he scented danger.

Rhys would have made arrangements to pay the trader, but the trader had turned out to be a cutthroat, holding a blade to Rhys's neck and demanding all his valuables.

Since he had nothing of value save Hodain, Rhys had been obliged to knock the trader unconscious and steal the horse. Then Rhys had worked his way up through Gwynedd, accepting challenges and winning, by turns, his war sark, shield, and weapons. No one would ever guess the holy brothers of Bardsey had kept him as pure and stupid as a newborn babe.

As he tried to peer through the mist, Rhys heard hoofbeats.

"Now what?" he said, groaning. Yet even as he did, he

readied himself for battle. Checked his spear and throwing ax. Gripped the pommel of his sword. Strapped his bullhide shield to his forearm.

His mind turned as cold and empty as a frozen lake.

Aye, he had the mind of a killer—blade-sharp, remorseless. *That* was Rhys of Snowdon.

But as the attackers—six of them—burst into view from the misty shore, Rhys swore under his breath. These were no marauding Saxons, but well-armed soldiers on fresh horses.

"A killer," he said, feeling a familiar distaste. "I cannot fool even myself."

Even as he charged along the pebbled shore, he saw that two of the warriors were young and beardless. A truly ruthless knight would scythe them down like marsh reeds. Rhys merely wedged his spear between the horse's forelegs, causing the animal to stumble and topple its rider.

Rhys turned his horse to begin the second charge. He peeled his lips back in a feral grin. These knights were better armed and better fed than he. Their shields were marked with some symbol. He did not recognize the device, but it was a dragon of sorts, indicating that the men served some wealthy stronghold.

Jamming his war spear against his shoulder, he rode toward the leader. With his cheek against Atarax's sweating neck, Rhys whispered like a father to a child. "Come on, come on, come on ..."

Atarax galloped straight at the lead warrior's horse. The lesser beast veered off at the last instant.

Rhys gave chase. He herded men like sheep, cutting off their retreat at the end of the meadow, unhorsing the other young knight. Rhys cracked the dull side of his ax against the youth's knee, disabling him. As the warrior clutched his knee and cursed, Rhys winced. "That does hurt, doesn't it?" he asked, not without sympathy.

Their weapons and trappings were fine. They would net Rhys a tidy ransom.

When a steel-spiked mace caught him on the shoulder, he almost welcomed the pain. The knights were giving him a good, honest fight this day. He did not doubt that he would prevail. He did not mind paying in blood for the privilege.

He laughed as the sporting blood heated and bubbled through him. He threw himself into the challenge of ducking blows, veering out of the path of axes and javelins.

Battle was always noisy, and despite the insular mist, this day was no exception. He heard the screech of horses and the heartbeat of galloping hooves. The rusty clang of steel against steel. Shouts and curses, cries for mercy or revenge. After the interminable silence of Bardsey monastery, the blare of battle was a melody to his soul.

Within minutes he had unseated four of the warriors. Two of those lay dazed on the ground; another two were chasing their mounts, trying to corner them and grab the reins.

The head warrior, thick-bodied and determined, had yet to fall. If Rhys brought him down, he knew he could get them all to surrender.

He and the man positioned themselves for the final clash—lances seated, horses poised and quivering. His opponent had a ruddy face and a thick neck. He had the look of a capable fighter—cool-headed and determined.

The stallion's blood was up; Rhys could feel the animal's pulsing excitement.

This was the moment, then. The final charge. Then six warriors would be his prisoners.

His heart exulted. No more poverty, at least for a while. No more wondering if he would collapse of starvation. Perhaps he could even relax long enough to find a woman.

The world narrowed to an armed man on a horse, charging toward him.

A streak of midnight lightning cleaved the field between the galloping horses. At the same moment, evil green eyes flashed like sunstruck emeralds. A high-pitched yowl caused the very leaves on the trees to quiver.

"Shit!" Rhys sawed on the reins, but he was too late. The terrified stallion squealed and reared. Trained by instinct, he then dropped his forelegs to the ground. His sharp hooves pawed the earth, seeking to crush and shred the hell-bent creature.

The raven-coated cat hissed and bristled, arching its back and then coiling itself. Its fangs were long, gleaming like ivory. It leaped at Atarax, sinking its claws into the horse's neck.

The stallion went wild. He snapped his back, turning his body into a catapult.

Rhys knew, just for an instant, the unexpected glory of flying.

They carried the broken and bloodied warrior across the Menai Strait to the stronghold on the Isle of Mona. It was low tide, and the crossing was easy, even for me. The mist lifted and I watched, unable to decide.

On the one hand, he was obviously without property. He, his huge stallion, and the brindled fleabag all had the smell of want about them.

On the other hand, he had nearly defeated six well-armed warriors.

The stranger was large and brutish. He might be crude and unmannered as well.

On the other hand, he had the most endearing cleft in his chin.

All dilemmas, I decided, should be so delicious.

"My lord, there was a score of them, at least," said a deep, ale-soaked voice.

"Aye, my lord. A giant, bloodthirsty horde of barbarians!" said another.

Rhys blinked himself awake. He lay upon a straw pallet in a large, high-ceilinged hall. Timbers blackened by generations of hearthfires patterned the roof.

Mentally, Rhys took stock. He sensed the comforting presence of Hodain stretched out at his side. He felt a few fiery aches—shoulder, upper arm, back of head, the usual places—and decided he was no worse injured than any man beset by six warriors and an evil spirit in the shape of a cat.

Unnoticed in the shadows, he watched and listened while he pondered his options.

"See that?" a young man asked, baring his forearm to a portly, handsome man with a snow-white mustache. The man wore an arm ring and brooch of red gold; Rhys guessed he must be the lord.

The youth's forearm bore a shallow, livid streak. "They tried to take me prisoner," the lad said, "but I fought my way free."

"Either that," said a startling, female voice, "or your shield strap chafed."

Rhys squinted at the group around the fire, but he could not see her. She did have a remarkable voice. It was low and musical, rippling with a knowing mirth. The very sound of it reached for him, touched him like a brand.

He'd never had a woman, never known the texture of her skin, the scent of her hair, the taste of her lips, the music of her laughter sweet in his ear.

And God, he wanted one. This one, he decided, would do nicely. Sight unseen. The sound of her voice alone was enough to make him burn.

"I think they were trained in the ways of the old Roman Legions," a warrior said, dousing the laughter with a loud, angry shout. "Hideously dangerous, my lord."

"A pity," said the white-haired lord, "you were only able to capture the one."

"We were lucky to escape with our lives," a young man insisted, rubbing his swollen knee.

"You should probably just kill that one, my lord." The other youth pointed the tip of his sword in the direction of Rhys.

Hodain lifted one black, serrated lip. He showed them one yellow, tusklike fang. And he gave a single, threatening growl.

"Perhaps not," the youth said hastily, sheathing his sword.

"He might be worth ransoming," the lord said, holding out his horn mug to a serving boy.

"Then again," said that amazing female voice, "he could be worth nothing at all."

THREE

"Let him sleep off his defeat," said Roderick, the chieftain of Bryn Melyn. "We've other matters to discuss this night."

Sirona tightened her grip on her drinking goblet, feeling the age-worn smoothness of the hollowed horn. She stared straight ahead, not daring to look at her father. Roderick was lord of the mightiest stronghold on the Isle of Mona. His rippling fields of barley and rye provided grain for the Pendragon's army. Now the high king wanted more than grain from Roderick, but Sirona knew it was she who would pay the price.

Thick as the warriors' boasts, a veil of peat smoke hovered in the hall. Wisps trickled lazily to the louvers in the roof, along with the smells of meat and mead and men's bodies.

On a pallet in a dark corner, the fascinating stranger

slept on, unmoving, guarded by his ill-tempered dog. Briefly she studied the prisoner's hulking shape—broad chest rising and falling with even breaths, long legs lolling past the end of the pallet, great shaggy head cushioned on his arm. She burned to know the manner of man he was, but their meeting would have to wait for a private time.

While the men carried on with their banquet, their boasts growing more improbable with every new sip of mead, Roderick let the silence settle and draw out to the point of discomfort. Sirona knew it was her father's way of getting her attention and whetting her curiosity for his announcement.

She could not abide being made to wait. So at length, with a determinedly bored smile, she turned to him, pretending she had no idea what he was about to say. "What other matters, Father?"

For a moment, they looked at each other with unmasked affection. She saw Roderick, known to all Gwynedd as a great war chief, but beloved by her simply as Father. He had a powerful, compact build, ruddy cheeks, and a huge cloud of white hair to match his bountiful mustache.

When he looked at her, he smiled as if he could not stop himself. She loved that about him—the way he loved her, unquestioningly, yet always with a very male, paternal sense of bafflement and exasperation. She, in turn, loved him with so much of her heart that she had none to give to any man, for none measured up to the greatness of her father.

Roderick touched Sirona beneath the chin and studied her. "You look more like your mother every day."

"So I'm told by the householders."

She knew he was trying to distract her, and for a few

moments she played along. Her mother had died when
Sirona was but a toddling babe. According to retainers
who had served the chieftain for many years, the lady of
Bryn Melyn had been excessively beautiful and clever.

Like me, Sirona thought. She knew this without vanity, in fact with some little desperation. Being comely
made her suspicious of the reasons men paid court to her;
being clever let her see through empty flattery or veiled
ambition.

Roderick settled back on his tasseled cushion. He
angled his head toward another stranger who broke bread
with them that night, seated amid the warriors at the cir-
cular oaken table that had graced the hall of Bryn Melyn
since time immemorial.

The dark-robed traveler had a high-bridged nose like a
Roman and wore his hair cut short and blunt. He did not
lift his cup as often as the household knights; nor did he
talk as much. He did, however, listen intently to all that
the men were saying.

"He's an emissary from the high king, isn't he?" Sirona
asked. "Uthyr Pendragon sent him."

Roderick nodded. He had long since ceased to question how Sirona seemed to know so much of his affairs.

"His name is Owain. He tells me the Saxons are raiding the coast again, and the Mercians in the east are hammering away at the borders," Roderick said.

Sirona took a sip of her mead, savoring the honeyed
wine and peering over the rim of the cup at the visitor.
Owain had the typical courtier's paunch around his middle and a watchfulness that sat ill with her. His gaze
darted from one person to the next, assessing, cataloging,
taking the worth of a man with a single sweep of the eyes.

His gaze reached hers, and she noted shiny black eyes,
thin mouth, twitching nose. Not unlike a rat.

Sirona could not help herself. Very slowly, she set down her cup. She sent the king's man her greenest, hottest glare. Like an invisible lightning bolt, her inhospitable stare struck him. He squirmed like a bug on a pin, inching back until the bench he sat on upended, and he sprawled onto the earthen floor.

His comrades guffawed and teased him about not being able to hold his liquor. But never again would he raise his eyes to Sirona.

Men were so easy.

"Does the high king send his jester as emissary these days?" she asked.

"You are sharper than an arrowhead," Roderick muttered. "If your mother were alive—" He stopped himself and shaded his face with his large, work-hardened hand.

"Finish, sire," she said gently. "Please, you so rarely speak of her."

Reluctant humor tugged at his mouth, and he lowered his hand. "She would applaud you. In sooth, daughter, I did love the lady excessively, but I never could master her will."

She touched his hand. "You mastered her heart, Father."

His bushy white brows shot up. "*Cariad*, that is exactly what I wanted to speak to you about. The matter of *your* heart."

"Oh, no." She darted a glance at Owain. A familiar feeling of dread sank like a fieldstone in her belly. "Father, we have been through this—"

"The high king needs me, Sirona." He squeezed her fingers.

She snatched her hand away. "Fine. Then go to him. Take an army of warriors to fight the Pendragon's border wars. But leave me be, Father."

His face, noble and long-jowled, became implacable, as if a spell had turned him to stone. She saw the square jaw tighten, the chin thrust up. "I could be gone for a year or more. The king has sent Owain to—"

"Do not say it!" She held up her hand. "Just leave me here with a few household knights. We shall be fine. Safe."

He thrust his trencher away. "You slay my appetite, daughter." He drained his cup of mead, then spat into the rushes on the floor as if the drink had turned bitter.

She closed her eyes and caught her breath. Then she forced herself to look at him, at the naked love and fear in his face. "I understand why you think I need a protector in your absence. Why not just that, Father? Why not assign a warrior to defend the stronghold while you're away? You have wealth enough to pay an army of fighting men."

"That's not enough. Silver and gold make whores of men. I want a man to make a deeper pledge—to you, not to my wealth. I want him to give you all that he has. His heart. His soul. His life if need be." Roderick hugged her. "Because that is what *I* gave your mother."

If Sirona's tears had not all dried up many years before, she would have shed a few just then. "Ah, Father. Such a man does not exist. You were the last of that breed." She gestured imperiously at the warriors who lounged at the round oaken table, belching and boasting and slopping their mugs of mead and heather beer into the rushes.

Roderick narrowed his eyes speculatively. "If I found a good one for you, would you marry him?"

She laughed, covering a prickly thrill of prescience. She herself had taken a tentative step in that direction, but her father must never know. "Even if you did find such a man, and I did happen to marry him, what about—"

"Never mind about that, young lady," Roderick snapped.

Sirona planted her elbows on her knees and scowled into the firepit. "I have no interest in any man," she lied.

Roderick pressed his thumbs to his temples. "I am finished arguing. Come morning, you will meet with Owain."

"No," she said. "He concerns me not at all." Turning to a more interesting topic, she added, "Look, Father. The barbarian captive seems to be astir."

"You must tend to his wounds. In the morning, I'll see about selling him back to his kinsmen."

"He has no kinsmen," Sirona said with complete certainty. "At least, none who would buy his freedom."

"And how would you know that?" Roderick asked.

Sirona lifted her brows in a look of innocence.

"I'll deal with his comrades-in-arms, then," said Roderick.

"He has none of those, either."

"Then what about the hordes of barbarians that attacked my men?"

Suppressing intemperate laughter, Sirona shook her head. "This stranger came alone, save for that smelly mongrel at his side and his superior warhorse."

"But my soldiers said—"

"The stranger fought them alone," she said matter-of-factly. "He would have defeated all six of your best warriors except for—" She broke off and rose from her cushion. "Excuse me. I just remembered I left some herbs boiling. I should make him a poultice."

With a steely stare, Roderick pinned her where she stood. "Young lady, answer me true. Except for what?"

"A most unfortunate occurrence." She folded her hands in front of her tunic, cast down her eyes, and tried to look demure. "His horse reared and threw him."

"Ah." Roderick inhaled laboriously, and she knew he was trying to keep his famous temper in check. "And can you tell me, daughter, what might have caused that horse to rear?"

"Father," she lied through her teeth, "I haven't a clue."

FOUR

"I am the chieftain's daughter." The nudge of a slippered foot stirred Rhys out of his half-sleeping state.

"What?" He scowled into the night-black emptiness, pierced only by dying embers in the central firepit.

"I am the chieftain's daughter." Exasperation tinged the voice, but he recognized the silky, almost insolent tone. She was the woman he had heard speaking earlier, who had seduced him with her voice alone. "My name is Sirona," she added.

Sirona. It slid through the darkness like a supple, velvet song. Without even seeing her face, he was half in love with her already.

"How do you do?" His voice sounded rough with sleep. "I am Rhys of Snowdon. My lady, can you tell me the name of your father, and what place this is?"

Gentle fingers brushed his brow. Her touch startled

and pleased him. "You *did* suffer a blow on the head. My father is Roderick, lord of Bryn Melyn on the Isle of Mona."

Worse yet, thought Rhys. He was trapped at an island stronghold. He could not see her, but he had a sense that somehow she could see him.

"Well then, come on," she said at length. "I need to dress your wounds and clean you up before they present you to my father in the morning."

"It's the middle of the night, my lady Sirona," he protested. He felt Hodain's warmth against his thigh. Why hadn't the dog warned him with a growl that someone approached him while he slept? Hodain had never failed to do that in the past.

"Not quite the middle," she whispered, and humor tinged her wondrous voice. "It is just past moonrise. Everyone else is asleep. Can you walk?"

"I—" Rhys paused and stretched his legs. He realized, with a start, that someone had removed his horn sark and tunic. He was clad only in his leggings and soft leather boots bound by strips of rawhide. "Yes."

"Then come along." Unerringly, her hand found his, and she tugged him upright.

Her touch was as soft and light as the brush of the wind. He could feel the smoothness of her skin, and his pulse quickened. As he came to his feet, Rhys expected Hodain to protest, but the dog slept on.

"Where are we going?" he whispered.

"Shh. And mind the men. They sleep every which way, like corpses on a battlefield."

While he pondered that unsettling image, she led him through the hall and to a doorway. Rhys promptly smacked his head on the lintel. Pain blossomed like a bursting star.

"Graceful, aren't we?" she purred, and again the laughter touched her voice.

"Seeing in the dark is not a skill I've mastered," he muttered. "Among other things."

"What other things?"

"Perhaps I'll tell you when I come to know you better."

They emerged into the garth, a yard of trampled earth with outbuildings leaning against the picket walls. The moon was a low, perfect circle of light, bathing the rugged profile of the hilltop fortress in a white glow. The stars emitted a cold blue light. Beyond the northern walls, the roaring sea leaped up at the cliffs.

Sirona turned to face him and dropped his hand. "I love the night."

His words evaporated on a gasp of wonder. Never, not if he had lived a thousand lifetimes, had he seen such a woman.

Her beauty dimmed the light of the moon, and for a moment he could only stare like an idiot. Her hair was bound by a thin silver fillet on her brow. The locks, of purest black, fell dead straight from crown to hip. By contrast, her skin was the palest, richest cream, touched with roses at the lips and cheeks. And in the middle of all that exquisiteness, the eyes.

They were a green so luminescent that he could discern it even in moonlight. They were the green of a new leaf with the sun behind it. Long, wide eyes, uptilted at the corners, lashed by thick black fringes, set off by the dark, perfect arch of her brows.

Those brows clashed as she huffed out a breath. "I was hoping you'd be different."

"What do you mean, lady?"

She held a thick bundle of clothes under one arm. He studied her dress, a long shift with an overtunic, cinched at the waist with a jeweled girdle that had a bulky pouch of soft leather hanging from it. She looked as slim and supple as a young willow draped in mist.

"The way you stare." She glanced at the sky. "We had best be going."

"Where? It's the middle of the night."

"So you've said." She took his hand again. "Nighttime is not only for sleeping."

Her soft murmur was a siren song, and her words startled him. This was no demure girl giggling behind her hand, but a woman of frank manner and forthright desires. In that moment, he would have followed her to Caledonia and back. As he lumbered painfully along behind her, he inhaled the clear summer air, letting it caress his bare chest.

She led him out of the garth through a withy gate and along a winding path. She moved with fluid grace and made no sound when she walked. Rhys found his attention caught by the straight, glossy fall of her hair and the gentle sway of her hips. She was an altogether unusual and fascinating woman.

Perhaps he could come to terms with the chieftain, her father.

Even as the thought entered his mind, he chided himself for his own foolishness. Who was he to lust after the chieftain's daughter?

"Do you always go about at night with half-clad strangers?" he asked.

A ripple of laughter rode the breeze. "Sir Rhys, is that a warning?"

"No, but do you not worry for your safety? Your virtue?"

She ducked under a low-hanging branch. "No man will take me unless I choose to allow it." Rhys caught the

branch before it struck him in the face. "As for my reputation, I think of it not at all. If people cannot accept me
as I am, then I have no need of them."

Rhys's exile on Bardsey had taught him little of
women. Yet he sensed she was unusual—and he treasured
her uniqueness. With each step he took he fell deeper
and deeper under her spell.

"What makes you think I won't bolt and run?" he
asked.

"If you are a true knight, you're bound by your word of
honor."

"And if I'm not a true knight?"

"Then my father's men will hunt you down and kill
you. Besides, you wouldn't leave without your dog."

"True. Hodain comes with me everywhere."

"Not tonight."

A sting of suspicion smote him. "By the Christ. You
drugged the poor beast, didn't you?"

Sirona gave no answer, but she looked once over her
shoulder. He found that single, low-lidded glance so
provocative that his blood heated. Her beauty was edged
sharply by danger. He knew it was probably foolhardy, but
he found that danger, that air of the forbidden, impossibly
alluring.

She stopped at a tumble of rocks around a small pool
half hidden in shadow, half sparkling in moonlight. The
burble of a spring filled the air, and steam rose from the
water. She smiled at his rapt expression. "The Romans of
old never did uncover this one. Else they would have
built a temple around it, no?"

The shadows hung thick around the rocks, and when she
stood in their gloomy depths, he could no longer see her. He
scooped up a handful of warm water and brought it to his
lips. It had an unmistakable chalybeate tang. "No doubt."

"The waters have great healing powers." He sensed movement but heard nothing until she spoke again. "Do you need help?"

He started. Now her voice came from the pool. He had not known that she, too, was going to bathe. His father had once told him that the Roman men and women used to bathe together. Apparently the custom endured on this remote isle.

"I don't need help." In contrast with hers, his movements created a rustle of leaves, a snapping of twigs, that made him sound as large and clumsy as a wounded deer. Keeping to the shadows where she could not see him, he shed his leggings. Beneath, he wore only a clout to protect him from the chafing of his leather trousers. He hesitated before removing this final garment.

It was full dark here in the shadows, he told himself. She could not possibly see him.

Yet he could not escape the memory of her eyes, her green, penetrating eyes, flecked with deepest gold. Those glorious, uptilted eyes seemed to see with sharper discernment than any others he had beheld.

"Come into the healing waters, Rhys," she urged him softly.

Shaking off the disquieting notion, he shed his braies and stepped into the steaming pool, sinking to his waist.

A sigh of pleasure escaped him before he could stop it. He chuckled low in his throat. "I admit, you were right. The waters feel delightful."

"They have healed many a wound, Rhys of Snowdon. Is that a scar upon your chest?"

His sense of startlement returned. She *could* see through the dark. He was not ashamed of his body, but it was not his wont to expose his private self to strange maidens. Besides, he had never had the opportunity.

He nodded awkwardly. "A very old scar."

"Ah." She moved out of the shadows to an area where the moonlight struck the water, and again her beauty seized him. With the wisps of steam curling around her and her tunic clinging to every curve, she looked like a creature from another world, a place of enchantment. Her hair lay in swirling fronds upon the surface, and when she tilted her face to gaze up at him, the light filled her eyes with a sparkle so bright that it almost hurt to look at her.

"It happens to you a lot, doesn't it?" he asked. "The staring. I apologize, my lady."

Her shoulders lifted in a careless shrug. "People always stare at freaks."

Before he could ask her what she meant by that, she waded to the water's edge and took a damp cloth from the pile of her belongings on a rock. "Well then, Rhys of Snowdon. You did not bolt and run. You are a true knight."

"Aye, lately."

She touched the warm, herb-soaked cloth to the gash in his upper arm. He winced, seared by the healing heat.

"Why did you come to Gwynedd?" After cleansing the wound, she measured a thin thread of silk and passed it through the eye of a needle as easily as if it were full light of day.

He tensed his muscles in anticipation of the pain. "I came because I had nowhere else to go. I was hoping to offer my sword to a great chieftain in need of warriors."

She glanced over her shoulder at the distant *caer*. At the top of the hill, Bryn Melyn loomed like a great, brooding dragon at rest. "My father's household is full. He has no desire for another mouth to feed. Look away."

Stubbornly, he kept his gaze fixed on the deep gash. "I don't mind watching."

She glared at him. The intensity in her exquisite face startled him. Between them, an invisible cord of tension tightened. He had the most uncanny feeling that she was pushing at his will, trying to penetrate it and make him do her bidding.

"Stop it," he said through gritted teeth.

She blinked, a silky, unhurried sweep of her lashes. "Stop what?"

"Whatever you're doing," he said irritably, feeling foolish now that the moment had passed. "Just get on with the stitching." He clenched his jaw and looked on implacably.

"Since you insist." She set to work, pulling together his torn flesh. She worked deftly and steadily, and within moments, the gash was neatly closed.

Rhys felt light-headed. His stomach seemed to float upward, and he almost disgraced himself by retching. She was right. He should not have looked.

She put aside her needle and cleansed his back and shoulders and neck. Slowly the sick feeling ebbed, and he began to enjoy the long, careful strokes of her cloth, redolent of pungent herbs. Rhys could not remember the last time he had experienced a human touch.

"Where else do you hurt?" she asked.

"Everywhere," he said, just so she would continue massaging his shoulders and back. "Your father's knights were ruthless."

"You were never in any real danger. Cei likes to show off with his mace, and he sometimes gets carried away."

The back of his neck prickled. "You saw?"

She caught her lower lip with her teeth. "No. I just know Cei. Also, the bruises here"—she drew her hand along his rib cage—"are those of a mace." She smoothed her fingers over his shoulder and chest. "So tell me about the scar."

Rhys leaned his head back and shut his eyes. Her touch was magic; he wanted her never to stop. "When I was very small, a band of raiders descended on our farmstead in Gwynedd, in the green shadows of Snowdon." Even now he could picture the immense mountain, swathed in mist, with lesser tors grouped like sentinels around it. His father had been an indifferent farmer, but that had not stopped the raiders from looting the stores. "They set fire to one of the huts. I heard a cat yowling within, so I rushed in to rescue it."

He felt her hands tense upon his back. "Ah, then you were injured by falling timbers while saving the life of a cat?"

He sank into the water up to his neck, wincing at the heat. "Nay. I was scarred by the cat. It bit and clawed me, ripping into me as if I were its prey. It would have torn my eyes out if I'd let it. Damned cat," he muttered, then sank beneath the surface of the water. After a moment, he came up for air. "I've hated cats ever since."

She took in her breath on a hiss. "Do not judge them all by the actions of one, and do not hold a creature responsible for what she does out of fright."

He was puzzled by her spirited words. "It was a long time ago." He dove under a second time, gulping mouthfuls of the warm, faintly iron-tasting waters. When he came to the surface again, he stared up at the glorious night sky. The full moon cast its glow over the rocks, turning them to solid black shadow. The light played in the delicate wisps of steam rising from the pool.

An overwhelming sense of well-being swept through Rhys. He felt more alive than ever before. Every individual bone and sinew in his body pulsed with vital awareness. The blood sang in his ears. His heart surged in his chest.

Because of *her*.

When he raised his gaze to Sirona, he went completely still, transfixed.

Her face had, from the first glimpse, fascinated him, but some unseen force allowed him to look deeper now, to see the dark complexities of her. She was a sensual creature; she had a silkiness about her that tempted him to hold her and pet her, to spoil and coddle her. Even so, he also sensed her fierceness, lurking just below the surface.

"I'm staring again," he whispered, his gaze never wavering.

"Yes," she whispered back, "but there is something different about the way you're staring at me now. Perhaps you see more than a woman's face and form."

"Not perhaps. For certain. I see shadows in you, Sirona, and needful things and dreams, but they are all hidden inside you."

She nodded slowly. The yearning in her eyes reached for him, pulled at him, yet she did not speak. Whatever secrets she held inside would stay there until he found a way to set them free.

He was not certain which of them moved first. But at some point he realized that their hands were touching, fingers twining together. With the gentlest of tugs, he drew her close. The water made each movement as smooth and light as silk blowing on a breeze.

He said, "Sirona," and slipped his arms around her waist, pressing her against him. He knew she would feel his need for her, and he was glad, for something in him wanted her to know the power of his feelings.

Filled with a sense of wonderment, holding his breath in trepidation, he bent to kiss her. It was a simple thing, a kiss, when one thought about it in abstract terms, yet the actual act was rife with intricacies he had never even begun to imagine.

As his lips touched hers, he caught the sweet musk of womanhood that clung to the dark, hidden places of her. Their mouths brushed; their sighs mingled; and both Rhys and Sirona seemed to be catching their breath, waiting, holding back, even as they reached for completion.

He slid one hand up over the curve of her breast. The soft, damp swell of it filled him with lust, but he kept his hand moving, up to her smooth white throat and then to the delicate angle of her jaw. He stroked her there, tenderly, relentlessly, until her mouth opened to his.

No one had taught him this. Indeed, the compulsion to do so came from some part of Rhys he barely knew. He wanted to reach inside her, to gather her into him. She stiffened and then relaxed, letting him find by taste and touch the things he could not see with his eyes.

At first, he did not press his advantage. He merely savored the taste of her and the texture of her ever-softening lips, parting slowly, inviting him in. At last he let his tongue explore, and it was an exquisite sensation, more achingly sweet than clover honey.

She surged against him. The idea that her hunger matched his was staggering. Only when her fists pressed at his bare chest did he, with the greatest reluctance, move back.

"I think the healing waters have done their work," she said.

"Aye, that and more," he admitted, still dazed by their encounter and by the heat that coursed through him. It was as if the pool were a crucible and he the metal all melted down, ready to be poured into a new shape.

"Rhys," she whispered, and for the first time he could

hear a quiver of panic in her voice. "What have you done?"

He felt the need to reassure her, this strange, self-possessed, night-loving creature who suddenly seemed so vulnerable. He touched her beneath the chin and brought her gaze to his.

"Sirona, it was a kiss, no more."

"I've never been kissed before."

He could not help himself. He laughed outright, his mirth echoing in the hollow enclosed by the rocks.

She jerked back. "Do you mock me?"

"Certainly not," he said, struggling to contain his amusement.

"Then why do you laugh?"

"Because, *cariad,* until you, I never even touched a woman."

His purity could not be a lie. Men did lie, and no doubt this one was capable of deception, but surely not on such a matter as this.

In fact, the lies usually slanted the other way. Untried youths began from the age of twelve to insist that they bedded women often. These willing, eager, undyingly appreciative women always lived on some remote, elusive farmstead where they could neither confirm nor deny the lads' boasting.

Now here was this stranger, who had ridden out of the mist and into my life, freely and cheerfully admitting that he was a virgin.

I found it as intriguing as it was unusual. The stranger was a beguiling man indeed. He was beautiful in a rugged, powerful way, with his reddish hair and battle-scarred body and blue eyes so full of humor and tenderness and pain.

The feeling of certainty that had gripped me when I first

saw his face returned. Everything changes, I told myself, pretending it was easy, trying to accept these new things that set fire to my dreams and awakened my longing.

Therefore, I decided he should be put to the test. That is, if he was not killed outright, first thing in the morning.

FIVE

"I am known to be a fair man," Roderick stated. The chieftain subjected his prisoner to a long, assessing stare. "If I were not, you'd be dead. Instead, I'll have to settle for reducing you to beggary."

"You're too late," said Rhys. "I'm already poor."

Sitting at her father's side, Sirona tried to stifle a yawn. As lady of Bryn Melyn, she had duties. Appearing at the crack of noon was not a task she cherished, but she had taken the time to dress well. Beneath a tunic of emerald silk, she wore her favorite gown of black, shimmering with threads of silver and gold.

The meeting took place in the atrium. The open-roofed court in the center of the stronghold, roughly paved with worn and crumbling limestone, was a legacy of the Roman host that had once occupied the isle.

The high sun of midsummer showered down on

Roderick, who sat in formal array upon a thick-legged stool. Rhys stood before him, looking more hale than he should after being attacked by six warriors. He was bareheaded, his hair richly red and gold in the blazing sunlight. He wore a clean tunic, one she had given him. It was too tight and gaped open at the throat, the leather lacings trailing down his chest. He had no beard, keeping his face shaven and smoothed by pumice in the old Roman style.

She forgave him the vanity. His face was far too beautiful to hide behind a beard.

She took a deep breath, thinking of the night before, the cool darkness and the hot spring and the way he had stood so still and been so grateful as she had cleansed his wounds.

Ordinarily, the taking and ransoming of a prisoner bored her senseless.

But not when the prisoner was Rhys of Snowdon.

The guards had bound his wrists with leather straps. At a nod from Roderick, they forced Rhys to his knees. Yet even so, with the full sun pouring down over his head and shoulders, he looked as proud and strong as the crag of Snowdon.

"My lord," he asked, "what is your will?"

Sirona watched his lips move, and she remembered his kiss. She made a little involuntary sound in the back of her throat.

Roderick looked at her sharply. Sirona prayed he had not seen her in the grip of that sudden, raw yearning. She cleared her throat and pasted on her customary bored, disdainful look.

Roderick stood and flung his gilt-edged cloak over one shoulder, displaying a fabulous amber brooch with the Bryn Melyn dragon holding the huge stone in its talons. Hands on hips, he walked in a slow circle around the prisoner.

Roderick was an imposing man, the lines of his face severe, hiding a wonderfully soft, sentimental nature he allowed only a few to glimpse.

"You fought six of my best warriors," he said. "You wounded four of them."

"They are valiant men," Rhys said. "Particularly in the stories they tell."

Sirona sniffed and put a hand up to her mouth to hide a smile. The men-at-arms, standing in a line against the wall, shuffled their feet and grumbled among themselves. Owain, the king's man, paced back and forth, shooting resentful glowers at the prisoner.

Roderick clasped his hands behind his back. "I have been thinking of a price to set for your ransom."

"My lord," said Rhys, "that is a waste of your time."

Roderick stopped and turned to him. "Oh?"

"I have nothing. Naught but my war sark, my sword and shield—which are in bad condition—my dog, and my horse which are not for trading."

Sirona felt a stab of suspicion and blurted out, "I think you lie. You speak the tongue of a man of learning. You fight like a trained war—"

"And how would you know my style of fighting, lady?" he asked.

She swallowed hard. What *was* it about this man that made her forget all her cunning? "I, too, doubt the boasting of my father's men-at-arms. And *you*, sir, are trying to change the subject. Surely you have a noble family somewhere. A wealthy clan that would pay for your freedom."

His face went hard as if the muscles beneath the tanned flesh had turned to stone. "A wealthy clan, lady?" A burst of acid mirth escaped him. "By our very size, my family makes a clan, though hardly a wealthy one. And it is a bitter thing, making a man buy his freedom."

"That is the way of the world," she said haughtily. Something small and dark sank inside her. Did he not remember their kiss? Did he feel nothing but rancor when he looked at her by light of day? "It is the way of a world built by *men*, not by me. *I* am not responsible for the practice of ransoming."

She was, however, responsible for his capture. When she thought of that, a scarlet flush stained her cheeks.

"I will let you buy your freedom." Roderick looked from Rhys to Sirona and back to Rhys again. "With your horse."

Rhys rose from his knees so quickly that the men-at-arms drew daggers and surged forward.

Roderick held up a hand to stop them. He planted himself in front of Rhys, and his eyebrows shot up. So did Sirona's. Rhys was a full head taller than Roderick.

"My lord, if that is your requirement, then you must kill me where I stand. For I shall give that horse to no man." He glanced at Sirona. "Or woman."

"Then you had best compose a message for your people, asking for payment in gold."

A mirthless laugh burst from Rhys. "My 'people' have no gold, unless you count their dreams. I am the thirteenth son of Myrddin, the Bard of Carmarthen."

A silence blanketed the gathering. Sirona did not even draw a breath. Neither did anyone else. The seconds crawled past. She could hear the low mumble of bees in the pear trees beyond the atrium wall. She could hear a lark beating its wings as it rose toward the sun. She could hear the pounding of distant waves and the thud of her heart in her ears.

After several moments, Owain recovered and rushed forward. "He is the spawn of Myrddin the Enchanter!"

Rhys whirled around to face Owain. As he moved, he lifted his bound hands. The muscles in his arms corded and strained.

The thick leather bonds snapped as if they had been made of grass.

Sirona froze, watching him, wondering if in his anger he would slay Owain where he stood, slay him with his bare hands, using no weapon save rage.

Rhys kept his hands clamped to his sides. "Myrddin the *Bard*. He is no enchanter."

"Uthyr Pendragon was put under a spell by him!"

"The only spell binding the Pendragon is the spell of lust," Rhys snapped. "My father had nothing to do with his dalliances with other men's wives."

Owain planted his feet wide and set his hands on his hips in blatant challenge. His wide arm rings flashed in the sunlight. "Your father had *everything* to do with Uthyr's fruitless marriage. The high king will pass from this life with no worthy successor."

"There is an heir," Rhys said quietly.

Sirona, with her uncanny sense of hearing, caught the whisper, though no one else did. She shivered.

"My lord," Owain barked, "kill him now. He is the son of a dangerous, exiled man. Kill Rhys of Snowdon and take his horse."

Murmurs of assent rippled through the assembled men. Cei shook his fist. "We should kill the horse, too, or at least offer it in sacrifice. It's probably under an enchantment as well."

"Cei speaks the truth," someone else shouted. "No ordinary horse is so large and swift."

"Silence!" Roderick roared, holding his hand aloft. "Listen to you, crazed by a lust for an honorable man's blood." The chieftain glared his men into submission. "I have this past fortnight sought a husband for my daughter."

A horrible dread seized Sirona. "Father—"

"Is it any wonder I could not find one among you?

Ambitious, weak-willed creatures all. Perhaps providence has brought the prisoner to me for a reason."

Not providence, thought Sirona, but my own foolishness. Flames of humiliation seared her throat and breasts and cheeks. "I'd rather marry a toad."

"Maybe I *am* a toad," Rhys said mockingly. "After all, since I have an evil enchanter for my sire, one never knows." He tossed his head. The red-gold hair rippled like fire on the breeze. "*I* would rather marry an otter hound bitch."

His insult raised her hackles. "You churl, you—"

"Hush, child, and listen." Roderick took her cold hand in his and drew her away from the assembled men. He led her through a low arch in the wall and stopped at a vine pergola in one corner of the adjoining patio. At the base of the gnarled plant was an urn, crumbling with age.

Roderick turned to face her, lowering his voice. "I spoil you. Indulge you too much. In this, I will not be swayed. The high king summons me. I must go. Meanwhile, Saxon and Mercian and Hibernian Celt alike would dearly like to plant their banners in my stronghold. And I don't have to tell you, daughter, how men populate a new place with their own kind."

She shuddered and snatched her hand from his. "Do not seek to frighten me, Father. It won't work. I'll be fine on my own."

His ruddy face lost its color. "That is what your mother said," he whispered. "The day before she died."

She touched his arm. The old, bewildered sorrow ached inside her. "Father, it's not your fault Mother took sick and died during your absence."

"She was not sick."

Sirona frowned, cocking her head. "But you've always said—"

"*I lied.*" Leaning back against the cracked wall, he dropped his head into his hands. "I was to be gone a sennight, no more. But I forgot something important. It takes a Saxon only seconds to kill." He squeezed his eyes shut. "Of course, with your mother, they took more than seconds."

"Father, what are you saying?" Sirona swallowed the bile rising in her throat. "That my mother was killed by Saxons? You never told me."

He opened his eyes and shook his great, white-haired head, like a large dog shaking off sleep. "I had hoped I'd never have to, but you push me to it. Now do you see, Sirona? Now do you understand why you *must* take a strong, worthy husband?"

She wanted to run and hide in horror, but she stayed where she was, a prisoner of her father's affection and of her own astonishment that she had never, in all the years of her life, known the truth about the way her mother had died.

"Why didn't they kill me, too?" she asked.

"One of your mother's women took you away to the countryside and hid you until I returned." Roderick's voice still shook. "I did love her so. But never could I sway her stubborn will to mine."

"And who decreed that a chieftain should govern his wife's very will? Other chieftains, surely. Not their wives."

He cupped her cheek in his hand. "You have grown up to be even more cunning and beautiful than she. Sirona, I need to know you will be safe, under the protection of a husband."

"Father, please. I beg you. I am not ready. I have no wish to marry."

"That is not an excuse I can offer the high king. I am determined to find a man who can defend this stronghold, match your own wit so you'll never grow bored, and above all, love you as I do."

At her father's words she felt a stab of hope, yet at the same time she knew happiness with a man was an impossible wish. "What makes you so certain Rhys of Snowdon is this man?"

His eyes gleamed with knowing. "Because you yourself brought him here."

Sirona prowled restively back and forth, back and forth. *That* had been a mistake, the result of one moment of weakness. She had given in to her need when she should have been strong. Rhys had appeared in all his splendid masculinity, and she had *wanted* him, so badly that she'd forgotten to count the cost of having him.

The ceaseless low roar of the sea crashed beyond the walls. Salt air mingled with the scents of flowers and ripening fruit, and Sirona was suddenly desperate to safeguard her freedom. "He does not want to marry me."

"That is his pride speaking," Roderick said.

"A match between us is absurd." Yet in her heart she had known it would come to this.

"Nay," said her father. "Rhys desires you with as much of his heart as I once desired your mother."

"He has a *dog*, Father."

"Aye, that he does."

"I *hate* dogs."

"You'll learn to tolerate the beast."

"But what about the legacy from my mother?" She smoothed her hands down the sides of her shimmering black gown.

"Whether you keep it or not is a matter for fate to decide. Sirona, heed me. This is not a thing I do lightly. Rhys of Snowdon will have to prove himself worthy. I shall put him to the test, and if he fails"—Roderick pushed away from the wall—"he shall forfeit his life. And you shall marry Owain."

Sirona's eyebrows shot up. "Don't you think that's a bit extreme?"

Roderick set his jaw grimly. "I want to make certain he is well motivated."

"And what will you do to me, Father?" she asked. "How will you make certain *I* am motivated?"

Roderick did something he had never done before. He went down on one knee before her and took her hand. Pressing it to his heart, he said, "Sirona, I lost your mother to the Saxon hordes. All these many years I have lived with the guilt of having left her. I wonder. . . what her last moments were like. What her last thoughts were. Did she scream out my name as she died?"

"Father!" Sirona fell to her knees and pressed her cheek to his chest. His gentle hand came up to stroke her hair. Her heart wept, even though her eyes could not. Reluctantly, and with great tenderness, she said, "You leave me no choice."

SIX

Roderick strode back out to the atrium. Looking pale and subdued, Sirona followed him.

So, thought Rhys, the father had gotten his way after all. Had Roderick of Bryn Melyn beaten his daughter into submission? No, her skin looked as pure as ever. She displayed no hint of tears. Nor did her father, who regarded her with something akin to worship, seem the sort to raise a hand to his daughter.

Rhys planted his feet wide apart and waited for the chieftain to open the second round of the game. Since Rhys had, in a temper, broken his bonds, no one seemed inclined to tie his wrists again. For the past several minutes, he had paced freely through the atrium, pondering his predicament.

At first, shock had prevented him from absorbing the full implications of Roderick's suggestion. Then, while father and daughter had conferred, it had dawned on

Rhys. The prize Roderick offered was rich beyond measure: this stronghold. Sirona. All of it, his. He could
scarce believe his good fortune. He hoped she would forgive his initial reluctance.

Roderick settled himself on his stool. "So, Rhys of
Snowdon. I choose *you.*"

"My lord, I am honored."

Owain loosed a snort of disgust.

Rhys glanced at Sirona. Even in defeat she looked
magnificent, her shiny hair catching the sunlight, her
emerald-green overtunic shifting in the breeze, and her
strange black gown clinging, shimmering with her movements as she seated herself.

"But first," said Roderick, "I set you to three tasks. If
you accomplish them, you take possession of this
stronghold and of my daughter in marriage."

Keen interest kindled in Rhys. "Three tasks, you say?"

"If you fail at any one, you forfeit your life."

"You give me great incentive to succeed, my lord." His
smile felt only slightly forced.

"Also, if you fail," Roderick said, "Owain will have her."

Sirona sat as if frozen by horror, her face pale, her eyes
wide and disbelieving.

With great tenderness, Roderick reached out and
smoothed his hand over her hair. Then he stood and faced
Rhys, not reaching his height but making up for the lack
with pride and bluster. "I do love my daughter well. The
tasks I assign you are designed to prove that you are worthy."

"What be these three tasks, my lord?"

Roderick flung one corner of his cloak over his shoulder, a casual gesture, so Rhys was caught off guard when
the chieftain's arm shot out and twisted into the fabric of
his tunic. Roderick put his ruddy face very close to Rhys's.
"Do I have your attention?"

"My lord, you will have my fist in your face if you don't unhand me."

Black mirth danced in Roderick's eyes. "An excellent time for me to let go." He stepped back. "I would have you perform three tests. One to prove the strength of your body, one to prove the strength of your mind, and one to prove the strength of your heart."

"I never before noticed any weaknesses therein. But I would know the exact nature of these tests, since my life is forfeit if I fail."

"Of course," Roderick said. "First, I want you to take Sirona to the mainland for the trading fair in Bangor. You will bring back seedlings to plant an orchard of apples."

Apple trees? Rhys wondered. To prove his worth? "A strange request, my lord." He decided that the chieftain must truly want him to be his son. "That is all?" he asked.

"That is the entire extent of the first task."

Rhys was certain there must be a hidden peril in the task, but since Roderick would be sending Sirona with him, the danger could not be mortal. Seedlings for an orchard. How very odd. Or perhaps not so odd. Tending an orchard would demand that he stay and nurture the saplings. Months and then years would pass before he could reap the fruits of his labor.

"I accept," said Rhys.

"The second task is this. You must sing a song that makes my daughter weep."

Sirona sniffed disdainfully. "I have not wept since I reached womanhood. I never weep. *Ever.*"

Rhys was not put off by her skepticism. Myrddin the Bard had had little to do during the early years of his exile. Out of sheer boredom, he had instructed his sons in the bardic arts. He had taught all thirteen of them to tell stories that brought grown men to their knees with sadness, and to sing with the emotional resonance of an ancient harp.

"I accept," Rhys said again.

"Excellent. Last, you must bell the cat."

Rhys frowned. "I beg your pardon?"

Roderick drew a length of chain from his belt. Attached to the thin red-gold filament was a tiny golden bell that clicked softly as he placed it around Rhys's neck. "After you have accomplished the first two tasks, you must bell the cat."

Sirona softly hissed in a breath and rose to her feet. Anger flared and leaped like sparks in her eyes. She opened her mouth to speak.

Roderick held up a hand. "The bell belonged to my late wife, of beloved memory. You may have noticed a rather large black cat hereabouts."

Rhys grimaced at the unpleasant memory of the shadow creature that had caused him to lose his way in the mist. "My lord, I did notice."

"Aye, well, she needs taming. Place that bell around her neck, and your tasks will be complete."

This was by far the strangest of the three commands. Sirona looked as if she might burst into flame at any moment. She appeared magnificent and dangerous— drawn up to her full height, shoulders thrown back, her eyes narrow, and her chin set with defiance.

Rhys suspected that he was the only one who could see her hands, the way they were clenched white-knuckled into fists at her sides. This, he knew, was not anger, but fear, sharp as the scent of blood. He alone glimpsed the vulnerability in her, and his heart softened. She was about to be given to a virtual stranger; he could not blame her for her reluctance.

Roderick folded his arms and waited.

Rhys said, "I accept."

Without making a sound, Sirona padded out of the atrium, her long black hair swishing as she walked.

"Do not take these tasks lightly," Roderick cautioned him. "I know I seem a kindly man, but the moment you fail, I will kill you."

The words dropped into the quiet atrium like stones into a well. Rhys shivered as if a gust of wind blew across his soul.

Rhys of Snowdon must not succeed at his tasks. True, the marriage was a promised thing, but only if he managed to perform all three tests.

I should not have allowed matters to go so far, but the unquiet grief of a chieftain for his murdered wife had touched me in a soft, raw place that throbbed and bled inside me. And so, in a moment of weakness, the pledge had been made. Rhys of Snowdon would be given the chance to win himself a wife.

Unless. . . The soft place inside me turned hard with fear. If he failed, the fault would be his. No marriage would be made. Now, I am not completely heartless; I intended to see to it that Rhys got the chance to flee rather than face execution for failure.

I felt a twinge at the thought of never seeing him again. He was by far the comeliest man I had ever encountered.

He was the only man I had ever kissed.

But he was not for me. Fate had favored me with a gift I could surrender to no man. It was a lonesome, melancholy treasure that gave me as much pain as it did delight.

My path was clear. I could not expect Rhys of Snowdon to understand, only to leave our lives as he had found them, never to return.

SEVEN

The next morning, in the garth, Hodain announced the arrival of Sirona with a low-throated growl of warning. The dog generally liked people, but he had taken a pointed dislike to Sirona. Rhys considered, then instantly dismissed, the notion that somehow she meant him harm.

He watched her approach. In Sirona, the quality of beauty took on new meaning. She was grace and mystery and wisdom, possessing an allure so powerful that some might call her a witch.

Once again, she wore the shimmery black gown beneath an overtunic and mantle that blew back on the breeze. The dress glistened and rippled with her movements, outlining her lush curves and sinewy, long limbs. Her hair was bound back by a silver fillet over a sheer veil.

She led her little hill-bred mare to the block and mounted with her customary fluid elegance. Giving her mantle a negligent shake, she turned to Rhys.

Hodain loosed another growl. Rhys snapped his fingers to silence the dog.

"Shall we go?" she asked.

Rhys glanced at the great hall of the *caer*. Roderick stood in the open door, his hand raised in salute. Rhys had given his word of honor to his host. He would not try to flee. Why would he, when such rich rewards awaited his return?

He nodded curtly and angled Atarax toward the gate. Hodain trotted ahead with a proprietary air. A straight Roman road cleaved the broad, yellow hill leading down to the shoreline of the strait.

Only moments after they left the fort behind, the holy silence of the island closed around them. Some fine, rare quality of the air made the day seem uncommonly soft. A mist as light as a babe's breath hung over the wooded rises. Each separate droplet held a fragment of the sun's brightness. The trees and rocks themselves seemed animated with a life of their own.

He glanced back at Sirona and blinked at what he saw. Somehow, the misty softness had surrounded her with a radiance—not the ordinary glow of the morning sun, but with an incandescence that made her more startlingly lovely than the moon at midnight.

"Is something amiss?" she asked.

"No."

"Are you greatly displeased by this task?"

He slowed his horse so that they rode abreast. With his tail held aloft like a war banner, Hodain forged ahead.

"I am not displeased," Rhys said.

"Yet you are oddly silent for a man."

He grinned. "I can remedy that."

"Do not bother," she said quickly. She looked with interest at his flashing smile. He sensed that she was not accustomed to good-humored men.

"This is a curious task," he said.

"How so?"

"Well. If I had such a daughter as you, Sirona—"

"*No one* but Roderick of Bryn Melyn has a daughter like me," she said with assurance.

"I said if. And if I did, my tests for her suitor would be far more difficult than simply buying trees for an orchard."

She lifted one dark-winged eyebrow. "Ah. And what would your tests be? Slaying dragons? Pulling swords from stones? Finding grails? That sort of thing?"

"On the other hand," said Rhys, "perhaps Roderick made the tasks easy on purpose, for who would have such a sharp-tongued wife as you?"

"No one, if I get my way in this."

"Me, if I get *my* way in this. I might regret it forever after, Sirona, but I *will* win you."

For a moment their gazes locked. The sunlit depths of her eyes entranced him. He fancied he could see the memories there, that she recalled two nights before as vividly as he. She moistened her lips and parted them, and her face was filled with such yearning that he nearly reached across and snatched her into his arms.

"We are meant to be together," he said. "I cannot explain why I know this is so, but my heart tells me it is."

"I wonder if you would believe that if I were the daughter of a slave rather than a chieftain." She sniffed daintily and trotted ahead of him. Still the sunlit mist surrounded her, clung to her, melted around her. Entranced, Rhys followed, holding his silence, for she seemed to value that. She did not stop until she reached the shore of the Menai Strait.

"We shall cross here." She had halted at the muddy, pebbled bank. Scuttling creatures the tide had left behind darted for safety under rocks. Far off in the east, the giant, stony peak of Snowdon reared above the clouds, brooding down with a forbidding glare.

Some distance away, Hodain stood chest-deep in the shallows, facing the mainland and barking.

"We'd make a better crossing there," said Rhys, pointing in the direction of the dog. Hodain had found a spot where the current was slow, meandering beneath the slender shadows of trees along the shore.

"We'll cross here, and that's final. I know the way of the tides." Sirona did not even pause to see if he agreed or not. She poked her regal face into the wind and urged her mare forward.

As he followed her into the turbulent, shallow water, Rhys grumbled, "I begin to see why your father regards this as a test. It is a test of my patience."

The sound of her laughter echoing off the water rang like bright, chiming bells. Rhys gritted his teeth. She was a bossy, mocking woman. He should be wishing for a rogue tide to sweep in and carry her off. Instead, *he* wanted to sweep her up and carry her off. He could die a happy man with the music of that laughter in his ears.

They forded the strait, wading their horses ashore not far from the old Roman auxiliary fort of Segontium. The legions of Magnus Maximus had once manned the outpost against pirates who plundered copper from the mines of Mona. Now the conquerors were but forgotten ghosts.

A summer wind whispered through the empty, crumbling halls of Segontium. Ivy crept over the defensive earthworks and red sandstone that had once made up the great walls of the place. An aqueduct had tumbled into disrepair. The barracks, granaries, shops, stables, bathhouses, and strongrooms echoed with emptiness. Atop one cracked pillar was a spread-winged eagle carved in the stone. Its beak and taloned feet were open, hungry, ready to seize and consume.

In their relentless way, the Romans had been as savage and ruthless as the hordes of Saxon and Jute that now poured westward, battering at the doors of Gwynedd, seeking to plunge the kingdom into darkness and tumult.

Sirona halted her mare beneath a great wind-harried oak tree. "This is where they said good-bye," she told Rhys.

"Who?"

"Maxen and Elen, his princess. Maxen Wledig, as the Welsh called him, lived as fast and furiously as a storm, marrying a beautiful British princess and then being put to death in the prime of his ambitions."

Sirona reached up and plucked a green twig from the oak. "She used to march with his legions, but on his final campaign, he made her stay behind." She turned her pale face away, and though she looked into the distance, she seemed to see nothing but the shadowy past. "Elen was with child, but still she begged to go with him, to no avail. He marched to his death before their child had reached her fifth summer."

She shivered, although the wind off the sea was soft, almost balmy.

"You know the old stories well," said Rhys.

"The Romans called her Queen Helen of the Hosts." Sirona smoothed her hand down over her gleaming gown. "I am descended from her on my mother's side."

Just for a moment, Rhys pictured Sirona as her warlike kinswoman might have been, strong and dark, fearless, incomparably beautiful.

Hodain, who had been sniffing along the wooded track leading away from Segontium, stopped and let out a growl of warning. The dog's legs and tail went stiff, and his ruff stood on end.

Rhys drew his sword from its ramskin sheath and

motioned to Sirona. Bangor was less than an hour's ride away, but between here and there, the path was rife with brigands. "Stay here. I'll go see what's ahead."

He spurred Atarax and galloped inland, where the land sloped upward to the gloomy green woods surrounding the great mountain ranges. Ahead, Hodain raced into a ravine folded between two rearing hills. Behind came the clop of hooves.

"I told you to stay back," he shouted at Sirona, hauling on the reins and blocking her way. "Wait at the old fort."

"I'm coming with you." Her voice sounded tighter, more shrill, than it usually did.

"No, Sirona. There could be danger."

She bit her lip. Her face was as white as the mist that shrouded the distant peak of Snowdon. "I think perhaps you should—"

A crash sounded in the woods. Hodain barked and lunged. Cursing, Rhys pounded his heels into the sides of the stallion and galloped into the verdant shadows. The thick, leafy arms of oak trees seemed to reach for him.

"Rhys!" Sirona called out, and he thought she would beg him to protect her from the marauders. Instead she said, "Rhys, I am sorry!"

Just as his mind seized upon her treachery, he felt a stone crack into his temple. He toppled sideways off his horse, unconscious before he hit the ground.

I have never known the taste of guilt before this day. But now I know its flavor, and it has a bitter tang, like the taste of rust or blood.

The men who had been lying in wait wanted to cut his throat and take his horse, but I forbade it. I had hired them for a purpose, but that purpose was not murder. It had never been my aim to cause him harm.

I merely wanted him gone.

But when I saw him lying there on the leaf-strewn track, his handsome face like something out of a dream, I felt a jolt of unspeakable emotion.

I made them drag him to dry shelter within the old, empty halls of Segontium, perhaps to the room where Maxen and Elen had loved and where she wept for him until she had no more tears. The magnificent horse, though a tempting prize, was left nearby with reins trailing. I even insisted that they leave that execrable dog behind. Loyal half-wit that it was, it would protect Rhys with its life if strangers should happen by and threaten him.

The men wanted to go straight back to Bryn Melyn. But as I walked away from Rhys of Snowdon, warrior knight cruelly wronged by fate—by me—I thought of his kisses and the words he had whispered in the dark. Perhaps it was because the spirit of my kinswoman was strong here; perhaps it was because of the sick guilt, but I felt the ancient magic pulling at me, the wildness screaming from the shadowy depths of time.

The change was unusually painful—a breaking and pulling and wrenching sensation; but as always, it happened in secret and without a sound, and the men, all unknowing, wandered back across the strait without me.

And I did what I always do when the world presses upon me. I joined my spirit with that of my ancient mothers, and I set myself free.

EIGHT

"A fine fix you've gotten yourself into," muttered a clipped, cultured voice.

Rhys scowled and shifted on the uneven ground. The rich green scent of moss and leaves surrounded him. Instantly he thought of Sirona and knew she had betrayed him. He opened his eyes, took one look at the face hovering above him, and closed them again.

"Tell me this is a nightmare." He flung his arm over his brow.

"Here now! After so many years, is that any way to greet your father?"

Rhys kept his arm in place as a shield. "Just how many years *has* it been?" he wondered aloud. "Two? Three, since you visited me at Bardsey?"

"I only come when you need me," Myrddin said softly.

A pause. A long, uncomfortable pause.

Rhys groaned and pushed himself up on his elbows.

His head throbbed from the blow he had taken. He looked into the face of Myrddin, his father, and the image seemed to pulsate and brighten painfully at the edges.

Myrddin was strikingly handsome; his line was that of Briton and Roman and Celt, and the best qualities of those races resided in him. He was tall, powerfully built, and intelligent, but some latent strain, probably Celtic in origin, had given him a big heart, a glib tongue, and a decided lack of common sense.

"How did you find me?" Rhys braced up on the heels of his hands and leaned his head back against the red stone wall. The knot on his temple throbbed like a second heart. For a moment, stars pricked his vision.

Myrddin handed him a skin flask. "Here. This will make your head feel better."

Rhys scowled and sniffed the contents of the flask.

"You always were the suspicious one." Myrddin furrowed a hand through his abundant chestnut hair and let loose with a long-suffering sigh.

"Tell me, why should I trust the man who sold my freedom to the holy brothers of Bardsey?"

"Son, I had my reasons." Myrddin's deep gray eyes held shadows of pain. "It was your destiny to go there, just as it was your destiny to escape."

Despite all the years of loneliness and uncomprehending hurt, Rhys, too, possessed the blood of the Celt. Some long-buried, mystical part of him loved his father. He took a quenching drink from the flask. Like all his father's finest potions, the fiery liquid tasted delicious and imparted a warm, luxurious, and false feeling of well-being.

"You," Rhys said, handing back the flask, "are a dangerous man. And you haven't answered my question. How did you find me?"

"Easy!" said a cheery young voice.

Rhys groaned. "Not you, too. Begone, brat."

Laughing as if Rhys had made a joke, Arthur dropped down from his exploration of the crumbling wall walk. "Lucky for you," he said with great earnestness, "Father decided to make a journey to Bangor."

"Aye, lucky me." He tried to look disagreeable and severe, but there was something wonderfully golden and fey about his little foster brother. The boy had grown tall and sturdy as any farmstead lad, but he had not lost the twinkle in his eyes. Rhys couldn't help the grin that tugged at the corners of his mouth.

"Luckier still, Hodain sniffed us out and led us straight to you."

"Ah. I *am* blessed."

Arthur squatted beside Rhys and gave him a hug. Caught off-guard, Rhys hugged him back. Tenderness heated his throat and eyes. After a moment, he pushed the lad away. "Off with you, rodent, else I'll show you what fists are for."

"*A verbis ad verbera*," Arthur said with a merry laugh. "From words to blows." He scrambled up a broken wall. "Look, Father! The barbarian host approaches! I'll smite them ere they see another dawn!" Unsheathing his dagger, he loosed a war cry and lost himself in fantasy.

Rhys stood and leaned against the wall. He glared at his father. "Teaching him Latin? Haven't you done enough damage?"

"There are certain things the boy needs to learn."

"Aye, like farming and cattle breeding. Face the truth, Father. He's a charming little tadpole, but hardly a king."

"Not yet, at least," Myrddin said. "Listen, Rhys, I don't expect you to understand why I—"

"Father!" Arthur shouted from the broken rampart. "You're not listening, Father!"

Rhys lurched over to his horse. Odd that the brigands had not taken Atarax or his harness. Perhaps the horse had not allowed itself to be caught. "He's not your father, boy."

Arthur hunched his shoulders up to his ears.

Rhys muttered a guilty oath, led Atarax over to the wall, and let the lad sit on the great beast. "Here now, I didn't mean to grieve you, Arthur."

"When are you going to stop being mad at Father? All he did was—"

"All he did was sell me to the Roman Christian Church, like a victim to the lions," Rhys spat.

"I wish you would at least try to understand," said Myrddin. "It wasn't the gold. It was a journey you had to make."

"Never mind, Father." Rhys passed a weary hand over his pounding brow. He had no faith in his father's visions. He lifted Arthur from the horse, pausing to ruffle the lad's yellow hair. None of this was Arthur's fault.

"I must be going," he said. "Fare you well, and for God's sake, don't let any king's men see you."

Myrddin took Arthur by the hand. "We're coming to Bangor with you, Rhys."

"Who said I was going to Bangor?" He got that familiar, unpleasant, twitchy sensation he always felt when his father guessed things with uncanny accuracy.

"You must go to Bangor to find the woman."

"What woman?"

Myrddin sighed heavily. "The one who has managed to get you so twisted up with desire that you can't even think straight."

Rhys felt a blaze of temper, but he forced himself not to show it. She had tricked him. By now, he knew that. But what else would she do?

"She would go to the fair, for certain." Myrddin gave

Arthur a boost onto his horse. The lad kept a good seat on the long-haired gelding. One day he'd be a fine horseman.

Rhys gave a snort at his father's words. "Why would she do something so foolish? For once, Father, you are wrong."

As usual, his father was right. As if Rhys had been no more than a stone in her shoe, Sirona had removed him and continued her journey to the trading fair.

Rhys, Myrddin, and Arthur stopped on a grassy slope above the town and surveyed the market. Silks and embroidered fabrics brought by sea traders lay folded on benches. Herds of sheep and pigs and white cattle were crowded into holding pens. Wickerwork cages of chickens and pigeons teetered in tall stacks. Rhys saw plenty of sacks of grain and seed; he would have no trouble buying apple seedlings. Women cried out, offering food and drink, and other women, with softer cries made more with the eyes and hands, offered darker pleasures from the doorways of their wattled huts.

Rhys spotted Sirona instantly. Her lovely gown caught the sun's rays as she moved between the rows of benches and carts. She stopped at a cart heaped with freshly caught fish. Rhys thought her interest in buying herring was a task ill suited to a chieftain's daughter, but he had ceased to be surprised by anything she did.

"*That* is the woman?" Myrddin asked.

"She is beautiful," Arthur said. "Is she a goddess?"

"Not quite," Myrddin said cryptically. "By the staff of Mithras, son, where did you find her?"

"It happened quite by accident, I assure you."

"I've never seen one. Oh, there is a record of one who graced the court of Agricola back in the days when the Legions marched across Britain. I always thought it a hoax, and yet, I think I am not mistaken."

"You speak nonsense, Father. Now is not the time for obscure historical lessons." Rhys scanned the woods beyond the slope. The forest was strangely silent when it should have been alive with the chitter of wood warblers and flycatchers. "You and the boy had best come with me."

"No, we'll wait here. Go and fetch the woman, Rhys. You must hurry. Her men are probably off at the carnal house. If you move swiftly, she'll be yours."

Rhys felt an unexpected rush of elation at his father's words. Dismissing his faint sense of unease, he nudged his horse down the slope and into the midst of the marketplace. At a hitching block, Atarax garnered the usual admiring stares. Rhys secured the tall horse, then plunged into the crowd.

The sharp reek of fish drew him to the cart laden with herring. A few women stood with cloths held to their noses, but Sirona did not seem to mind the smell as she murmured something to the fish seller.

Rhys seized his chance. He clamped one fist around her upper arm and passed the other behind her waist. "My lady, it is a pleasure to see you again."

She caught her breath and regarded him through narrowed eyes. "I should have put you in a coracle and set you adrift."

"I would have drifted right back to you." He liked the feel of her in his arms, her delicate, fine-boned strength and the firmness of her muscles beneath silky flesh.

"You're a fool, Rhys of Snowdon. Why didn't you just disappear when you had the chance?"

He stopped and held her close, oblivious of the shoppers and tradesmen jostling past them. All humor fled from him as he studied her small, angular face and her remarkable uptilted eyes. "I want you, Sirona." He had never spoken truer words in his life. "I will do anything to have you."

She made a choking sound, almost a sob, but she had sworn she never wept and she did not do so now. "Please," she whispered, "let me go."

"*Rhys!*" The shout was not loud, but it reverberated with such harsh alarm that he let go of Sirona.

Although this gave her a chance to run from him, she stood where she was, searching the crowd. "Who calls you?" she asked.

"Rhys!" Myrddin shouted again. He was four rows over, moving past a forge barn hung with a display of iron tools.

"My father," Rhys said.

She studied Myrddin in his homespun tunic and leggings bound with rawhide. "*That* is Myrddin the Enchanter?"

"That is Myrddin, my father." Rhys felt a stab of wry amusement. "Did you expect him to be wearing silk raiments and a turban decked with stars and moons?"

"Of course not. He *is* remarkable, though not in the way I expected. I do see where you get your looks."

Rhys felt unexpected delight at her words. Perhaps she was not as indifferent to him as she tried to appear. He took her hand in his and pulled her along toward Myrddin. "Come, he must have found some trouble. Light of God, but he works fast." They reached him in a moment. The bard's face was pale, his eyes wide. Above one eye, a livid goose egg stood out. "Father, did you suffer some accident?"

"It was no accident. They took the boy, Rhys," he said. "They took Arthur."

"Arthur!" Sirona said in a harsh whisper. "Not—"

"Yes." Myrddin spared her only a tiny nod of greeting. "The very one."

"*Who* took him?"

"Saxons."

The word lanced Rhys through with a shaft of ice. He knew the bite of Saxon rage; he bore the brand of it on his very chest.

Myrddin absently fingered the swelling bruise on his head. "There were six of them. Too small to be a raiding party."

"But enough to kidnap the lad."

"I realized that too late. One of them laid me low with the blunt side of his ax." Myrddin pointed toward the distant peak of Snowdon. "They left at a gallop."

Before Rhys could respond, Sirona stepped forward and put her hand on Myrddin's shoulder. "Then so shall we."

At that moment, I did not wish to reveal my uncanny sense of dread. In sooth, I could scarce explain it to myself. I only knew that when Myrddin revealed the fate of the boy, I experienced such a cold thrill of foreboding that it felt as if my heart had frozen in my breast.

I knew virtually nothing of the boy called Arthur save what I had heard sung long ago by a wandering harper. If the legend be true, Arthur was the once and future king. Even if it were not true, he was a little boy in mortal danger.

He would be less than nothing if Rhys did not reach them in time.

I knew without asking that Rhys would die for the boy. And that if things came to such a pass, I would feel responsible.

NINE

Rhys had never enjoyed fighting. The brothers of Bardsey were not particularly peaceable men; in fact, they fought as hard as they prayed. Rhys had joined in as boisterously as any of the postulants and novices, but it was always with a sense of resigned duty that he had bested all others in wrestling and wargames.

After he had left the holy place, he'd fought to defend his own life, not for pride or pleasure. He found these fights for survival a grim and nasty business.

This, today, was a higher cause. Today he would fight for the life of a boy, an innocent victim.

Rhys had seen the devastation that could be wrought by lawless men. He had seen burned-out villages strewn with silent, broken, bloodied corpses. He had seen what a Saxon's ruthless rage could do to a woman or child.

For the first time, as he bent over the pumping neck of Atarax, Rhys knew the power of protective fury. He felt stronger and fleeter than he ever had before. His blood surged with determination.

The outlaws were fleeing into the deep, uncharted heart of the hills, where the forest grew so thick the sunlight never penetrated. The land rose on the rocky breasts of the mountains. It was treacherous terrain, not unknown to Rhys, who had grown up in the shadow of Snowdon. He understood its perils, the caves and crumbling rocks, the death pits dug by the Saxons and the ancient, haunted burial tombs.

Hodain, with his nose low and tail high, led the way. The summer-green forest of crack willow and lichened oak and hazel sped past in a blur. Atarax flung up rich-scented moss and earth with his hooves.

Somewhere, far behind Rhys, Sirona and Myrddin rode in flagrant disregard of his orders.

The thought made Rhys's temper flare hotter. What could they, a woman and a wounded man, bring to bear upon Saxon warriors?

Still, he wasted no time arguing, for every second squandered was a second lost. At every curve of the winding path, at every outcrop of rock, every steep cliff leading toward Snowdon, he feared to see the murdered body of Arthur.

No, he told himself. If murder was their intent, they could have slain him on the hill above the town.

He rode past secret lakes, surrounded by stones, flashing with darting fish. He studied the gouges made by the hooves of small, unshod Saxon horses, and he pressed hard to overtake them, even passing Hodain, who ran as swiftly as a wolf on the hunt.

Rhys thought about the fight to come. He had worn his horn sark out of habit today, but no helmet. He had his buckler and sword, but no other weapon.

The Saxons had chosen the place where they would

make a stand, as Rhys had known they would once they realized their horses could not outpace his. He could see a narrow clearing ahead where the ground became somewhat level. A shadow flickered in the trees.

They were waiting for him.

He reined his horse and tried to decide how best to approach them. Hodain bounded up, his tongue lolling, his ears perked. A few moments later, Sirona arrived.

"Curse you, woman," Rhys said between his teeth. But in his heart, he was not cursing. "You should have stayed back."

"We must save the boy. Don't spend your rage on me."

"Where is Myrddin?"

"He had to stop, for his horse stepped in a hole and went lame."

Rhys passed a hand over his sweating brow. "Perhaps he'll stay out of trouble."

She studied the rise of the woods ahead. Her eyes were greener and more full of shadows than the forest itself.

"Stay on horseback," she said.

He was stunned that she had so quickly guessed the Saxons were waiting in ambush.

"And go in at a gallop, for there are two waiting above. One in the trees and another on that outcrop of slate."

He squinted at the distance. He saw boulders and trees and a cataract crashing down a rocky gorge, but no sign of Saxons lying in wait. "Likely I'll gallop right onto a Saxon war spear," he said.

"No! They are expecting you to approach slowly. Cautiously. You must do the unexpected."

"How do you know about the two above?"

"I have keener vision than you." She became fierce and avid, leaning forward in the saddle and clutching his arm, her sharp nails digging into his flesh. "Rhys, you must trust me on this."

He was not certain what convinced him—her touch, her fierceness, or his own impatience. He found himself nodding, wheeling his horse, and pounding in his heels.

Atarax reared out of sheer excitement, then sprang forth on his powerful back legs. Baying loudly, Hodain raced up the hill. As he hurtled headlong into the Saxon trap, Rhys braced himself. Perhaps Sirona possessed that special, intuitive magic some women were gifted with. But now was not the time to doubt, to question.

Atarax exploded through the bowing hazel and willow trees. Because he wore no helmet, Rhys saw a movement above. At the last second he veered, and the waiting Saxon crashed to the ground. Rhys heard the dull snap of a breaking bone, the rush of air from emptying lungs.

A sense of wonderment glowed inside Rhys. Sirona had been right. If he had been riding any slower, the barbarian would have landed on him, probably slitting his throat before he hit the ground.

He charged up the bracken-infested hill. Arrows whizzed past. She was right about the warrior on the outcrop, too. This one used better judgment than the first. He peered over the edge of the great rock, took one look at Rhys on his racing horse, and stepped back, raising a cry of alarm.

Thus ended Rhys's advantage.

Four of them, armed and mounted and clad in wolf-skins, awaited him on a narrow, flat section of the glade.

For a moment, they did not even look human. They were stone men, cold and soulless. Then one of them raised his battle-ax and surged forth. A silver arm ring flashed in the sunlight. Saxons never used money rings—unless they were in collusion with a man of another tribe.

Incensed by the idea, Rhys dropped his head and charged. He had no thought for his own fate but found himself gripped by the fervent hope that Atarax and Hodain would not be wounded. The dog went for one of the horses, nipping at its hocks and nimbly eluding a wickedly curved disemboweling weapon wielded by its rider.

The first Saxon came on, drawing so nigh that Rhys could see broken veins in the man's ruddy cheeks and hatred in his eyes. But, strangely, he could see more than that—the twisted heart of a dispossessed man.

And the cunning of a trained killer.

That same unerring, instinctive wisdom guided Rhys. He knew the precise instant the Saxon would swing his ax. Rhys lifted his sword arm. The heavy blade slashed out, cutting the air cleanly, stopping the lethal arc of the ax.

The two weapons met with such force that the clash startled birds from the trees. The impact reverberated up Rhys's arm, chilling his blood, jarring his bones, numbing his fingers.

With a roar, the Saxon swung his other weapon, a mace bristling with iron spikes.

Rhys ducked his head. The mace whirred by. As he straightened, Rhys brought up his sword, catching the tip under his attacker's chin. The Saxon fell screaming from his horse. He lay on the ground, clutching his face while the blood seeped from between his fingers.

The whole encounter had lasted a matter of seconds. Yet Rhys felt as exhausted as if he had fought a battalion.

And the next two Saxons came on together.

The fallen warrior's sturdy hill pony trotted in a panic back and forth, barring the path for a moment. Rhys squeezed his knees around his horse and urged the big stallion forward. Hodain nipped at the pony, herding it out of the way.

The two Saxons separated, one going to each side of Rhys. Even as his sword deflected one blow from an ax, the man on the other side of him went for his undefended flank.

Before he felt the pain, he felt the breathlessness. The ax struck him square in the middle of the back, hard enough to knock him from his horse. The horn sark prevented him from being cleaved in two. In a daze, Rhys staggered to his feet.

Atarax sidled, then reared and scraped the air with his hooves. Harried by a relentless Hodain, two of the hill ponies squealed and threw their riders.

Rhys ducked in time to elude a swinging mace. Even as he straightened up, the Saxons rushed him, one from the front, one from behind. The one in front held a spear aloft, the flinty head aimed at Rhys's unprotected neck.

Though he was tempted to duck right away, he waited until the spear was in flight, for then the warrior could not change his mind. Then Rhys hit the ground rolling.

A terrible cry sounded. The spear had found living flesh—in the Saxon who had been rushing Rhys from behind. He fell, cursing his comrade-in-arms and watering the musty forest floor with fresh blood.

Rhys turned to face the other two Saxons. The hot, sharp smell of their comrade's blood incensed them. One ran forward, roaring like a charging boar and brandishing a cudgel.

The spear thrower came on with another weapon, this one fashioned from straps of hide, the ends spiked with iron nails. Rhys felt the ugly lash of it ripping into his thigh. He heard a thud and then a yelp from Hodain, and the dog lay still, stunned by a blow from the cudgel.

The two warriors backed Rhys against the sheer rock face of the hill until he had nowhere to retreat except over the crashing cataract.

Such a quick death was beginning to look attractive to him. Frantically he warded off blows, but they kept coming, battering, clanging, until he saw nothing but defeat swimming like a red tide before his eyes.

Thus he would die, failing Arthur, failing Myrddin, failing Sirona and her father. The whisper of death was close now, urging him to slacken his muscles, to still his movements, to let down his defenses.

He let out a snarl between his gritted teeth. But his defiance meant nothing. Two blows caught him at once, the nailed whip lashing his side and the club striking a glancing blow to his head.

He opened his mouth to scream, but no sound came out. He heard instead a familiar, feline yowl.

Blessed bones of Christ. The evil cat. The malevolent spirit had come to see him die.

Sweat and blood ran down Rhys's brow. He put up his sword to take the brunt of a blow. He blinked to clear his vision.

In a streak of black, the cat descended from the rocks above.

Rhys hunched his shoulders in anticipation of the impact. Instead the cat sailed past him, landing squarely upon the face of the Saxon with the cudgel.

The man yelled and dropped his weapon. Long, thin forelegs wrapped around his head. Razor-sharp claws raked the warrior's eyes, his face.

Rhys confronted the other Saxon. He had no clearance to thrust with his sword, so he simply doubled his fist and drove it into the Saxon's jaw, shattering the bone.

The other warrior staggered back while the cat clung. He managed to wrench a knife from his leg binding and stabbed blindly. The cat shrieked and was flung several yards from the warrior. It lay unmoving on the forest floor.

Rhys hurled himself at the remaining Saxon. His

sword battered the knife out of his hand. The Saxon stumbled and fell back.

Panting, Rhys pushed the tip of his sword into the hollow of the Saxon's neck.

"I'm sending you to hell from whence you came," Rhys said, panting, drawing air between his clenched teeth. A shudder racked him. He had never killed a man before this day.

"*Wait!*"

Rhys planted his foot on his victim's neck and looked up at the speaker.

It was the last warrior, the one who had waited at the top of the cliff.

In front of him, snug against his chest, he held Arthur. And he had a knife pressed to Arthur's pale, unprotected throat.

I am not wont to perform selfless acts or to put myself in peril. That is for foolish mortals who treasure such nonsense as love and loyalty and honor.

Anger, then. That is what I would call it. Though I bled and ached from blows, though it would have been simpler to lie there and bleed my strength into the earth, I let the anger rouse the savage within me.

While the two men faced each other—desperate, bleeding, filled with hate—and the boy between them shook with fright, I staggered up and seized the red-hot blade of my rage.

TEN

The cat was alive.

Rhys took note of this offhandedly, marking it as an insignificant thing, particularly at that moment. He had never imagined that his thoughts, while he lost his last battle, would be of a feral black cat. He saw it from the corner of his eye, dragging itself up and darting up a tree behind the warrior who held Arthur captive.

Arthur looked tiny and fragile against the big-boned Saxon. He trembled like a leaf in the breeze. Yet even from a distance, Rhys saw something extraordinary in the boy's face and posture. The flash of defiance. The steeliness of courage.

Much good would it do him now.

Though he kept his stare riveted on the blade at Arthur's throat, Rhys saw the cat creeping out on a limb of the huge oak tree.

Under his foot, he felt the nervous rasp of his captive's breath.

How to prevail? The other Saxon stood too far away to rush him. A simple pressing of the hand, and his knife would sink into Arthur's neck.

I can't do this alone, thought Rhys.

The leaves of the oak tree stirred and sighed restlessly. Rhys loosened his grip on his sword, preparing to relinquish the weapon. He would offer his life for Arthur's. Perhaps that would satisfy the enemy.

Just as he prepared to speak, the cat dropped from the oak bough. Its claws raked down the Saxon's face and over the hand that held the knife.

Arthur plucked the knife from his captor's hand, turned, and stabbed him in the thigh.

And then, with a choked sob, the boy ran from the clearing.

Rhys was still half-dazed as he raced after the lad, crashing down through the oak forest, calling Arthur's name.

There goes gratitude. I risk life and limb, and for what?

For a clearing littered with bleeding Saxons and a few milling horses. The last man sat up, felt his neck and muttered a few thankful words, then ran in the direction of the stray horses.

Much to my amazement, the dog survived, lurching up and shaking its great, brindled body. It sat in a nest of dry leaves and began to lick its bleeding leg. It was all I could do to creep away and hope my wounds would heal.

Oh, for a sunny spot on a window ledge!

Rhys caught up with Arthur some ways down the hill. The terrified lad ran pell-mell, stopping only when Rhys called his name. Arthur turned abruptly and flung himself into Rhys's arms.

For a moment he simply held the boy, feeling awkward as he reached up and stroked the spun-gold hair. "Are you all right, lad? Did they hurt you?"

"No, but I was scared. I should have fought him, Rhys, as you did. I should have—"

"Hush." Rhys held Arthur away from him. "You were wise to wait for me. It takes no special courage to fight."

A thumping sounded, and Myrddin came trotting up on Arthur's pony with the lame horse on a lead rein. He dismounted before the horse halted and lurched forward a few steps. "Thank God!" He pulled Arthur into the shelter of his arms. "Christos, Arthur, I thought we'd lost you."

"Rhys defeated all of them, and then the cat appeared and scratched their eyes out."

Myrddin let out a shuddering breath. "A cat, you say?"

"Aye, a huge, mean black one."

"Ah. So I thought. By the light, Rhys, that horse of yours runs like the wind."

"I'd best see about finding him, and Hodain and Sirona as well."

Myrddin boosted Arthur into the saddle. "Are you all right, son?"

It took Rhys a moment to realize Myrddin was speaking to him. "Some bruises and cuts." He glanced down at his thigh and grimaced at the seeping blood. "Nothing serious."

"I'll leave you to find your wife-to-be, then." Myrddin winked. He mounted with Arthur and turned down the hill.

Rhys shook his head, watching them go while a little ache formed in his throat. Myrddin drifted in and out of his life like a mist off the sea.

Feeling weary and ill used in his heart, he trudged back up the hill.

Hodain lay in a pile of leaves, licking his paw. Atarax had found a clump of clover to graze in. Neither Sirona nor her horse was in sight.

"Where have you got to, woman?" Rhys muttered. He glanced up. The western sky blazed with the colors of evening. The horses of the Saxons had all fled into the hills. Even the injured warriors had managed to pick themselves up and escape.

A cold dread seized Rhys. If they had taken Sirona—

He did not allow himself to finish the thought. As he strapped on his weapons and mounted up, he nearly shook with urgency. He would find her if it took a lifetime.

Two hours later, he had found nothing. No trail of footprints or hoofprints. No broken twigs or trampled underbrush. Twilight yielded to a thick, dense darkness, and his urgency was fast rising to panic. Hodain kept his nose low, busily scouting the area, but to no avail. Rhys lost his sense of direction, but he did not stop.

If he had any judgment at all, he would get a night's rest and then make his escape. But he kept thinking of Sirona, her strange beauty and her soft voice, her healing hands and the quiet melancholy that lived in her soul. He remembered how it had been when they'd kissed. Magical, yet achingly real.

He did not know what it was like to bind his heart in love, but he was beginning to find out. Loving meant worry and frustration and desire and joy. Though he had only just met Sirona, he knew he could love her.

If only he could find her.

The night shadows turned the trees to long-fingered monsters that tore at his head and shoulders as he passed beneath the branches. He heard the trickle of a stream and decided to water his horse. He nudged Atarax toward the sound and waited while the stallion sucked noisily at the water.

And so he wandered through the crawling hours of the blackest night of his memory. When dawn glimmered on the horizon, a fine, stinging spray of rain started. Rhys's nerves were frayed. His heart was breaking. How could a woman simply disappear?

Roderick of Bryn Melyn would kill him, and at this moment Rhys would welcome death.

Hodain trotted over the sodden carpet of moss and ferns. He gave a muffled bark.

Hope stirred in Rhys as he nudged his horse forward.

She lay in the shelter of a rocky crevice, scowling at the dog. "Get away from me, you beast," she said peevishly, pushing at the inquisitive gray muzzle.

Rhys dismounted and rushed to her. Before he could think, he hauled her into his arms and held her fast, stroking her silky hair. "Sirona. What happened? Are you hurt?"

"I am fine."

"How came you here? Did you get lost?"

"Certainly not. I never get lost."

"Where is your horse?"

"I suppose she wandered home."

He pulled away and cradled her face between his hands. After a night spent in the woods, she should not look so remarkably lovely.

"By the Christ, woman. I thought I'd never find you."

For a moment, she leaned her satiny cheek into his hand. Then she pulled away. "You were not supposed to seek me out. Don't you understand, Rhys? You should have seized the chance to get away when you could."

"No. I gave my word to your father. Besides, I want you, Sirona. I love you."

Her breath caught. She looked away. "Don't."

He smiled and turned her face back to his. "It's too late, *cariad*."

"There are things you don't know about me, Rhys."

"Then tell me. I want to know everything."

"You do not." She hugged her knees to her chest. For the first time, he noticed that she moved stiffly and even winced a little as if in pain. He wondered if she had suffered some accident, yet her extraordinary gown shone in the early morning sun as if it were new-made only the day before. "Rhys, tell me this," she said softly, as if the very trees and rocks had ears. "Why do you get so angry when people say your father is an enchanter?"

"I don't."

"You lie. You almost came to blows with Owain over it."

"Because *he* lied. My father is no sorcerer, mumbling spells, putting curses on kings."

"You and I both know that magic takes on many forms. It's not all incantations and potions."

As she spoke the words, an incredible feeling of rightness washed over Rhys. She was the first person to understand the distinction. Myrddin had special gifts, but his powers were subtle, more a product of a keen mind, a vivid imagination, and good timing.

He took her hands in his. She tried to pull back, but he firmed his grip and made a hushing sound in the back of his throat, the sort of noise one would use to soothe a skittish filly.

"Please," he whispered. "I am grateful to you for realizing that. You're an extraordinary woman, Sirona."

Her lucent green eyes held a world of sadness and secrets. "More than you know, Rhys."

He leaned forward and kissed her, at first lightly brushing her lips with his and then pressing, shaping his mouth to hers and taking in her breath with his own. He had thought he knew what it was like to kiss her, but he was wrong. It all felt new and different—as if she were not a stranger, but a treasured friend, lost and then rediscovered.

The taste of her, the smells and textures uniquely hers, awakened old, deep longings. He used to have only vague desires, alone on his pallet at Bardsey. Back then the yearning was a sharp, sweet stab, a craving as intense as the need to draw air while holding his breath underwater.

Now Sirona gave a face to the dark dreams of his nights. He wanted her and her alone—not for her beauty or her wealth, but because of who she was, the things she said, and the strange, sad look in her remarkable eyes.

He fancied he could feel her heart in her fingertips as she curled her fists against his chest and clung to him. Her need was urgent, as raw as his, a pressure building like steam in a lidded cauldron.

He pressed closer yet, aligning their bodies so that the embrace became fuller, more intimate.

She resisted him, her movements sharp and quick as she scrambled to her feet in the blink of an eye. She was as nimble a woman as he had ever seen.

"I must go back," she said.

He stood, gritting his teeth at the pain in his thigh. "Why are you afraid of my touch, Sirona? You know I would never hurt you."

She hugged herself as if the summer had suddenly turned cold. "Just go, Rhys. Away from here. Away from me."

The mere thought of never seeing her again filled him with bleakness and, worse, a dread that something terrible would happen to her. "We'll both go back to Bryn Melyn," he said.

"Fool!" she said. "My father will have you killed, for you have not done as he bade you."

Rhys lifted one side of his mouth in a crooked grin. "By God, Sirona, do you think, after all I have endured in the past day and night, I'm incapable of buying seedlings at market?"

And so he prevailed just this once. The previous day and night had left me weak and weary. The ancient magic had healed my wounds, but not completely; still some stiffness remained. I found myself oddly acquiescent, and I was surprised to realize the reason why.

I trusted him.

Sadly for him, he trusted me, and the thought that I would have to shatter his dreams of a future with me brought an ache to my heart.

Since he had come into our lives, I had been seized by a broader range of emotions than I had ever thought possible. He stirred me to anger, to melancholy, to towering joy and unabashed lust. Try as I might, I could not feel indifferent to him.

This worried me. His next task was to make me weep, and I greatly feared that he had the power to break my heart.

ELEVEN

"It was nothing," Rhys said, his mouth a twist of irony. "That's what I told the chieftain. He was well pleased when I returned with the seedlings. And so I get to live to proceed to the next task."

His only two listeners, Hodain and Atarax, eyed him dolefully. They were in the horse shed, a small, close hut lit by the setting sun streaking through gaps in the walls. The big dog had licked his wounds clean and was curled in a nest of straw, and the horse stood tethered between two posts.

Rhys peeled off his shirt and slung it over the half door that divided the byre. He was weary and sweaty, yet oddly pleased with himself. He had managed to rescue Arthur and to return with Sirona. All that remained was to wash down his horse and himself, then return to the hall for a celebratory feast. It was midsummer eve, and people were arriving from all over the countryside to observe the festival of fire.

Rhys bent and scooped water from a bucket, sluicing it over his head and shoulders, shivering with the chill.

"Nothing at all," he repeated, dousing the horse next. "Fighting barbarians, rescuing fosterlings, searching the forests for a lost maiden, it is all in a day's work for Rhys of Snowdon. Or so I told the chieftain. Remind me to drink more than my share of mead tonight."

Midsummer was a favored time, the dances and rituals all suggestive of growth and light, fertility and bounty. At moonrise tonight, a great bonfire would be lit, fed by offerings from the chieftain, his priests and advisers, his warriors and servants—and his daughter.

"They used to sacrifice horses," Rhys said offhandedly. "I think it was the Christ priests who put a stop to the practice. So I suppose Christians are good for something."

Growling, Hodain lifted his head and flattened his ears.

Rhys braced his hand against the stallion's flank and turned to see the black cat slip soundlessly through an opening in the eaves. On dainty feet it crept along a stout rafter beam, settled above Rhys, and calmly set about licking its paws.

"My newest companion-in-arms," said Rhys. "But at least I can say one thing in your favor. You joined the fight at a most opportune moment." He narrowed his eyes. "You're an unusual little beast, ranging so far afield, attacking grown men rather than hunting birds or rodents. And how is it that you can cross water to reach this island?"

The cat ignored him and continued to preen. The sun struck its sleek, blue-black coat and turned its eyes to twin emeralds.

"You're enchanted, aren't you?" Rhys said, but speaking the words aloud made the whole idea ridiculous. Still . . . He fingered the golden bell he wore around his neck. He had no idea why belling the cat was so important to Roderick, but he had sworn to do the chieftain's bidding.

Taking the chain from around his neck, Rhys edged toward the cat. "Here, puss," he called softly. "Here, puss."

The cat crouched, frozen, green eyes glittering. Rhys's hands shot out. The cat sprang up with a hiss and a baring of teeth. Seemingly without effort, the creature leaped to a higher beam, well out of reach. There she settled again, watching, tail twitching, a growl rumbling low in her throat.

Rhys decided he was too weary to pursue the infernal cat. He replaced the bell and turned his attention back to his horse, smoothing his hands over the muscled hide, feeling grateful to be the master of such a magnificent animal. Atarax nickered and swung his great head around, nuzzling Rhys's ear.

Rhys chuckled. "So much for your fierce reputation." Because no one was about, Rhys did something he never wanted a living soul to see—he let the horse kiss him on the mouth.

In the shadows above, the cat made a hissing sound.

"Ah, what does a cat know of the bond between a warrior and his horse?" Rhys asked. He continued to groom the horse, examining hooves and hocks, combing his fingers through the thick, tangled mane and forelock.

"There was a time," Rhys went on, "when I myself did not understand the vagaries of my own heart." He pressed his damp palm against his bare chest. "I felt comets and shooting flames, but the longing was formless. Painful. I knew not what it meant."

He finished washing Atarax and loosed the crossties, bringing the animal to a bin of honeyed oats. "The moment I met Sirona, I knew." He pictured her lovely, pale face, her abundant black hair, the fire and passion and need in her eyes.

"It *is* love," he confessed to his mute listeners. "She grew angry when I told her so, but I think she simply needs to get used to the idea. My need to cherish and adore her is more powerful than any faith I ever felt at Bardsey. Is that blasphemous? Very well, then I blaspheme. But it is the truth. I want to greet each day with her in my arms. I want to watch ten thousand sunsets with her, to share her joys and her sorrows. It is why I came back, you know. I could have gone away, lost myself in the forests of Gwynedd, but I came back. Not for a stronghold or a cache of silver, but for her. For Sirona."

He exhaled wearily. "And so now, the second task. I am commanded to sing a song that makes her cry. They say her tears dried up when she became a woman, and she has never wept since. That is something I do not understand. For I have wept. When the sunlight touches the mountain peaks, or the curlews mourn the passing of summer, when I remember how I learned to laugh at my father's knee, sometimes my heart weeps."

His shirt tucked beneath his arm, he opened the gate of the byre and looked westward at the wide sky on fire with brilliant light. The low, parallel hills led down to cliffs clad in rocks and heather. The lonely, seaswept island contrasted starkly with the river-fed forests of his youth.

Just for a moment, he let himself admit that his father had loved him enough to teach him how to love. And to teach him how much it hurt.

•   •   •

The frightening thing was, he moved me. In all the years of my life, in all the generations that had gone before me, this deep turmoil of emotion had never happened. I thought I knew what love was. I thought it was the warm, comforting feeling of a father telling tales by the fireside or the settled, pleasant knowledge that one's world was secure and predictable.

Rhys of Snowdon taught me that sometimes love could be taken to extremes; control could go awry, and desire was not warm but hot, not comforting but unsettling.

I, to whom dreams of love had been forbidden, was learning to dream again. I, who had vowed never to love, began to long for the ecstasy of total surrender.

The fault lay in the lap of Rhys of Snowdon. And with a feeling akin to cold horror and self-disgust, I realized that I loved him. Even simply standing there in the doorway, with the evening sunlight playing over his bare shoulders and chest and damp hair, he exuded an allure that taxed my powers of restraint to their limit.

Ah, his magic was strong, though he knew it not. He lacked the flashy sorcery of his sire; Rhys's magic was subtle, the tug of a string attached to my heart. I regarded him with a sort of quiet awe, a thing I'm not wont to do.

He threatened all that I was and all I held dear. Yet at the same time, he offered whirlwinds and wizardry and a joy that lifted my heart to the stars.

Clearly, I had a choice to make. But as I watched him, shirtless, caring for his horse and speaking the secrets of his heart aloud, I realized I had no choice, or perhaps the choice had been made long ago. For Rhys of Snowdon was a man who could do the impossible.

He could make me cry. Because he made me care.

I had one last chance to stop his campaign to win my heart, one last chance to preserve, at whatever cost, my gift.

• • •

The feasting was already in progress when Rhys entered the yard in front of the hall. He had gone to the chalybeate springs to bathe and was clad in a clean tunic and leather leggings. His harp was in a pouch tied at his waist. Dancing sunwise around the fire, warriors and women cavorted to the thump of skin drums and the scree of pipes. Hodain and the other dogs foraged for scraps beneath the tables.

Roderick sat in the lord's seat at the head table, his face florid and laughing. Beside him was Owain, the king's man, eyes dark with malevolent shadows. On Roderick's other side, Sirona sat unmoving.

For a moment, Rhys merely stood and stared while the dancers swirled around him. She was splendid tonight, her shining hair forming an inky veil around her exquisite face. In just a few short days, he had seen her in many moods—laughing, taunting, fearful, fierce. Yet always a melancholy splendor clung to her and made him want to pull her into his arms, to kiss her lips into a smile. Though surrounded by merrymakers on the most joyous festival of the year, she looked alone and lost, holding a horn cup and gazing at the dancers without seeming to see them.

Seized by a feeling so powerful that his chest hurt, he made his way through the crowd and stopped before the chieftain, sinking to one knee and then rising slowly.

"Well done, Rhys of Snowdon," Roderick said. "The first of the three tasks is accomplished."

"It is an honor to serve you, my lord." He turned to Sirona. "And you as well, my lady. I do thank you for your help." He couldn't help adding, "And for the special welcome you arranged for me at Segontium."

Her green eyes flared wide, then fled from his stare. Her black gown glistened as she turned away.

"Ah, you wound me," Rhys confessed, pressing a fist to his chest. "There is nothing you can do that I won't forgive, Sirona."

"See, daughter?" Roderick said. "He is a man of tender heart."

"What do you expect from a man who kisses his horse on the mouth?" she retorted.

Rhys froze, first in embarrassment and then in shock. That had been a private moment, with none present to witness it save Hodain . . . and the *cat*.

An icy wave of suspicion rolled over him. "What are you hiding from me, Sirona?" He searched her depthless green eyes, and he saw, mingling with the reflected flames of the bonfire, a flicker of desire. Ah, she wanted him, for all that she cloaked herself in cool regret.

"Hiding?" she said. "I cannot imagine what you mean."

A blare from a horn broke through the moment. The pipes and drums dwindled into silence, and people turned toward the main gate.

"Ah, Christ," Rhys said under his breath, letting go of Sirona. He stood and waited while his father and Arthur made their way across the yard to the chieftain's table.

Arthur grinned and clasped Rhys's hand. Myrddin sent Rhys a cordial nod, then bowed before the chieftain.

"My father," Rhys said. "The Bard of Carmarthen. The boy is called Arthur."

Rhys could feel the onlookers' curiosity as if their stares held the sun's heat. In a way, he was relieved that Myrddin had come. Now everyone could see he was no evil enchanter.

Almost everyone. Owain gripped his drinking horn so tightly that his knuckles shone pale. The shadows in the eyes of the king's man deepened with hatred ... and fright.

What surprised Rhys was that Owain's horrified stare was directed not at Myrddin, but at Arthur.

"You are welcome to Bryn Melyn," Roderick said. A wave of his hand summoned food and heather beer. Arthur settled himself at the head table, while Myrddin went to stand by the fire.

Rhys took his place beside Sirona. He knew he should be hungry after the ordeals of the past two days, but instead his stomach felt taut and twisted, his tongue clumsy and thick.

"You never explained," he said, "what you meant with that remark. . . ." He felt his ears heat. "About the horse."

She sent him a beguiling smile. "I simply meant you are a man of soft sentiment."

The coil of suspicion in Rhys's gut eased as he put aside the ridiculous notion. Sirona might have been outside the hut earlier; surely that was the logical explanation for her uncanny knowledge.

"And to you," he said, "sentiment is weakness?" Before she could answer, he grabbed her wrist and forced her to look at him. "What it means, my lady, is that I am not afraid to love. Can you say the same of yourself?"

The world fell away, and it was just the two of them staring into one another's eyes. He felt drawn to her, and somehow he sensed that she wanted him, all of him, wanted to melt into him and become part of him. But most of all, what he saw when he looked into her pale and beautiful face was uncertainty.

"I cannot," she whispered at last. "I don't know what is happening to us, Rhys."

"I do. We're falling in love. Is that so terrible?"

She caught her breath as if his words were a striking

fist. Her throat, very white above the neckline of her dress, worked convulsively as she swallowed. A soft sound escaped her—a wordless whimper of denial and despair.

"No," she said, her voice low and trembling. "You're wrong about me, Rhys. This talk of love and marriage and growing old and fat with contentment is your dream, not mine." With a quick, subtle movement, she wrenched her wrist from his grip and fled the courtyard, leaving through a side gate that led to the cliff-topped north coast.

Rhys swore and started after her, surging up from the bench and finding a path around the bonfire. Myrddin stopped him just as he was passing the firepit. "Let her go for now, son," he said quietly.

Roderick and his guests had moved close to the bonfire for the ritual offerings. In times past, cattle and horses and men had leaped the fire; now the revelers made symbolic gestures, tossing in oak boughs and clusters of mistletoe, wicker effigies, bits of cloth, herbs, and other small treasures.

Rhys glanced down at the pouch containing his harp. For a moment, the temptation seized him. Burn his harp and destroy any chance of singing for Sirona.

As if he sensed his son's thoughts, Myrddin put a hand on Rhys's arm. "All women are great mysteries," he said, pushing a drinking mug into his hand. "Some more than others."

Rhys glared at his father. "Why are you suddenly so interested in my life?" he asked. "Are you afraid the brothers of Bardsey will demand recompense because I left them?"

Myrddin waved away the question. His soft brown eyes filled with unspoken regrets. "You have started a new life for yourself. I'll not deny your right to choose. Despite what you may think of me, Rhys, I want you to be happy."

"You have an odd way of showing it." Rhys tossed back the contents of the mug. The flavor surprised his palate, for he had expected to taste heather beer and instead tasted honey and herbs.

He glared at Myrddin. "I should have known."

Myrddin had the grace to look sheepish. "Sit you down, Rhys. I want to tell you something."

"Lies? Wild tales? Along with drugged mead, they are your specialty." Yet Rhys found himself sitting beside his father near the fire, moving close so the revelers, who had started to dance again, did not trip.

"That is for you to decide," said Myrddin. "I am a bard, Rhys. Telling stories is what I do."

Rhys planted his elbow on his knee and stared into the flames. Wood was scarce on the Isle of Mona, so fires were usually fueled with peat or dung; but because it was midsummer eve, great oaken logs burned with the offerings.

Yellow flames, with hearts of the purest blue, wrapped around the logs and thinned to hot nothingness. The drink Myrddin had given him spread inside Rhys like a forest fire, racing through his limbs to his fingertips, to his head. Yet instead of the fuzzy oblivion of drunkenness, he suddenly saw with remarkably sharp clarity—the flames and dancing sparks, the blue-ringed moon rising in the night sky.

He thought of the task ahead and blew out his breath. "Father, I'm in no mood for storytelling now. I have something important to do tonight."

"Oh? And what must you do?"

Win Sirona's heart. Rhys forgot that he did not trust his father's potions and held out his cup for a refill. "I must sing a song. I must make Sirona cry."

"Indeed."

"In the first place, to make her cry, I would have to hurt her. I don't wish to hurt her."

"Son, she is already in pain. Perhaps, with the tears, the healing can begin." Myrddin thrust a stick of white ashwood into the fire. Sparks flew upward, and the wind snatched at them.

"In the time before years were counted," Myrddin said in a low, rhythmic voice, "the *tylwyth* sometimes wove special properties into ordinary things."

The warm, tingly feeling surging through Rhys intensified. With an effort of will, he said, "I have no time for fireside tales about fairies. I must go and find her."

"The *tylwyth* are no longer with us," Myrddin went on, ignoring Rhys, "not as they used to be, but on occasion they speak to us—through the innocence in a child's eyes or the song of the wind off the lake. We just need to learn to listen for them."

"Father, with all respect, I must—"

"They gave their gifts to a very special few. One such gift was a beautiful gown woven of black threads and shot through with skeins of brilliant, shining color—emerald and gold, ruby and silver and sapphire. This they gave as a gift to the most clever woman in the land."

Rhys had more pressing errands than sitting there listening to Myrddin's tale, but he felt indolent and fanciful, and when he stared into the flames, an image took shape.

Wavering and flickering before his eyes, a shadow within the fire elongated. He saw, with the remote aloofness of a dreamer, a woman dancing with sinuous grace. She wore the shimmering gown, and it was Sirona, yet not Sirona. It was every beauty and grace that had ever belonged to a woman.

"When she wore this gown," Myrddin continued, "she had a singular power. The power to change her shape."

The leaping, translucent image in the fire shifted. The pupils of the knowing green eyes narrowed and elongated, and the dress covered all of her, and Rhys found himself looking at a sleek black cat.

"No!" he roared, jumping up, hurling his mug into the flames and shattering the wavering image.

The ring of standing stones, high on a cliff above the crashing sea, had long been a favorite place of mine. Now that night had fallen, I embraced the wildness in me and then set it free, leaping from stone to upended stone, feeling the awesome power of the ancients.

As my feet connected with the rough, rocky surface of the silent monuments, still warm from the sun, part of me remembered other times, other lives.

The gift of the tylwyth had been given here, at this very spot. She had been an ordinary mortal, though her restless soul had brought her here, running from parents and priestesses who would bind her against her will to a husband she did not want.

She had thrown herself weeping upon the altar stone, and she wept so long and so hard that none of her daughters or their daughters, upon reaching womanhood, forever after shed a tear.

When she lifted her head, she saw that the midsummer moon had risen. The light glinted off something very bright, lying across the altar stone.

It was the gown, of course. The same one passed to the chosen daughter of each generation since time out of mind. I know this, because the history was woven into the very fabric of the garment.

My father, though a loving man, foolishly tried to hide the gown from me, but destiny led me to it, as it should.

Since the magic was woven, each wearer kept the gown until her daughter grew to womanhood. But my mother was cruelly murdered before she could pass her gift to me, so I seized it recklessly, knowing upon first finding the dress in a coffer that the dress was of me, and I was of it.

There was no one to tell me that I must suffer for possessing the gift, or to warn me that it would one day be taken from me. I knew only that I must wear the gown and surrender to the still-living spirits of all the women of my line, giving myself into their care until it was time for me to care for another.

I remember the first time the ancient power engulfed me. It was like being swept up by a comet and carried far away from myself, from all that I knew, everything I believed.

There was pain and exultation and terror and the pure delight of utter freedom. Perhaps I lost consciousness slightly; perhaps I do each time the change sweeps over me. But so intense was this new power that for the longest time, I was able to push aside the melancholy and the yearning—the curses that came with the magic.

Even now, I told myself that my gift was enough.

And the very instant the thought crossed my mind, I knew that for the first time in my life, I was lying to myself.

Possessing this power was no longer enough. My heart was hungry in my breast, and I tried to deny what I was feeling, what it was that I wanted, needed, craved.

I had no name for this need, but it was the thing that I saw each time I looked into Rhys's eyes.

The depth of my own longing frightened me. And robbed me of my usual acute senses.

The unthinkable happened.

Rhys burst out onto the cliff, breathing hard as if he had run the whole way from the caer.

He saw me. Our eyes locked, and in the moonlit depths of his, I saw the knowledge, burning bright as a flame.

For a moment, I was paralyzed by utter shock. Then I did the only thing I knew how to do—I ran.

TWELVE

"Sirona!" Rhys's shout echoed through the shadows of the standing stones. The stones were oddly reassuring, silent sentinels of another age, forming an embracing ring of power.

He paced up and down on the thick carpet of sea grass. Such a thing could not be. The one woman he loved—the only woman he could ever love—could not possess that sort of power.

Yet the coincidences were uncanny. Sirona knew of things only the cat had seen. When the cat was near, Sirona was not, and he never spied the two of them together.

Sirona. Sirona. Sirona. He could defend her stronghold to his last breath. He could safeguard her life with all his strength, put food in her belly, and keep her warm at night. He could love her until the stars burned themselves out.

But there was one thing he could not do. He could not set her free from the curse that chained her soul.

Unless . . . He touched the pendant around his neck. Unless the bell made a difference.

After you have accomplished the first two tasks, you must bell the cat. The dark certainty flowed over Rhys, wrapped around him, and filled him with resolve.

"Sirona!" he said, barely whispering.

A shadow broke away from the shelter of a stone. She had been nearby all along.

She looked small and slender and fragile, but then she threw back her head, tossing her glossy hair, and her unshakable pride seized his heart. It was a great vanity to think such a woman could ever be his, yet his heart knew nothing of vanity, only of pure, raw wanting.

She looked at him, and the moonlight silvered her, the gown glimmering. He sensed a struggle in her, part of her seemingly entranced by him, another part looking ready to flee.

Carefully, as if he were approaching a wounded creature, he went toward her. He wanted simply to touch her, to stroke her silky hair and whisper in her ear and feel the heat of her body against his, to assure himself that she was fully a woman.

He wanted her so badly it was painful, but he could not let her see his hunger.

"Sirona, I've come to tell you something," he said.

She stopped and moistened her lips with a darting pink tongue. "Yes?"

"I love you."

"No."

"I have loved you right from the start, before I even saw you, when you were only a voice in the dark."

"How can I believe that?" she asked in a low, rough voice.

"Because it is my pledge to you. A promise I will never break."

"Men have made promises to me before, but their vows sprang from lust—for me, for Bryn Melyn, for my father's wealth." She took a step back, and the distrust in her eyes slashed at him. "How much plainer can I be, Rhys? I can't—I don't want—to marry you."

He reached for her. It was a mistake. With a sound that was half sob, half snarl, she fled again.

Biting off a curse, he strode after her. She sought the shadows of the moon-silvered standing stones, moving like a wraith or a ghost. He realized that she sought the ultimate escape, that of transforming herself into a wild creature he could not love, an animal that knew no affection, only the cold instinct of survival.

He reached into the shadows, and his hand touched something silky. The sensation chilled him.

Then he caught her wrist and shuddered with relief. Though her bones felt fragile in his grip, he pulled her toward him until he held her in his arms.

"Let me go," she said desperately.

The slow boil of anger surged up in him. "Not until you listen to me."

She tossed back her hair. "Speak, then."

"You accuse me of coveting your lands and your wealth. Well, let me tell you, my lady, if I wanted only lands and wealth, I could find a much more pleasant means of getting them than putting up with you."

Her look of incredulity almost made him laugh.

"So don't flatter yourself that I would go to these lengths simply because you have a pretty face and a rich father."

"You have spoken." Her voice sounded thinner; she was less sure of herself now. "Let me go."

"No. For you see"—he began to stroke her back, his hand smoothing over the texture of her gown and the shape of her body beneath—"there is still the matter of my loving you. And I do, Sirona. With all that I am. I care not who or what you are. I love you." He bent and brushed his lips across hers. "I love you."

"Don't," she said softly, helplessly. "Please, don't."

He ignored her and held her closer still, filling his senses with the scent of her hair, the taste of her mouth, the satin smoothness of her skin. Only when he felt the harp pressing into him did he remember his promise to Roderick.

Reluctantly, he lifted his mouth from hers. "Sirona, I gave my word to your father—"

"I shall listen. But I warn you, nothing makes me weep. Nothing. It is not something I can do."

He took her hand and led her back to the center of the stones, where the moonlight made a frosty pool on the sea grass. "All I ask is that you listen."

She sank to the ground, the light-catching dress spreading around her. She drew her knees to her chest and regarded him with such a hopeless skepticism that he thought he would fail and even feared before he began.

Then he told himself that whatever else Myrddin might be, he was a master of bards and had taught his son well.

Rhys sank to one knee before her. She seemed startled by his almost reverent posture. She tilted her head to one side, and her lips parted slightly. She looked bemused and expectant and a little sad, just vulnerable enough to make him want to hold her in his arms and never let go. Her eyes held the sadness of never weeping, of keeping it all in—the grief, the melancholy, the loneliness, year after year.

He took out the harp and touched the aged, curving

wooden frame. Never before had he caressed the strings with such delicacy, and he realized inspiration sprang from looking at Sirona and imagining what it was like to stroke her.

She shivered as if he had actually touched her.

Rhys started to sing. Always, it was as if pure magic stirred him. As if the words were fed to him by the gods, he sang with a stark, powerful clarity that surprised even himself.

He sang of whirlwinds and firestorms and tempests. He sang of endless summers, of flowers that had souls, and of what the waves whispered as they sighed upon the shore.

Sirona regarded him in mute amazement. She was a woman of high culture, but apparently she had never yet heard a student of Myrddin the Bard.

And then the words formed in his mind; he sang of a woman whose heart ran wild. A woman who begged the mystical forces to release her, to give her power over her own destiny, power to love with an unfettered heart.

He sang of that very first woman amid the standing stones, and of the tragical Elen and all the generations of women who came after, and then of the one woman who had the power to end the discontent and distrust, if only she dared.

He sang the ballad to its mournful conclusion, to the lone horseman who rode away with the name of his beloved soft upon his lips. The woman grew old and lonely, each endless day a string of regrets for what might have been . . . if only she had dared to love.

The last plaint shivered from the strings and died a slow, quivering death into the night air. Rhys set the harp on the ground.

For the first time since he had begun to sing, Rhys looked at Sirona.

Her eyes were larger and more haunted by shadows than ever. She put a trembling hand to her cheek and gasped.

"I have not felt tears since I was a child," she whispered brokenly, then pressed a hand to her mouth. "They taste bitter, like the sea."

"Ah, Sirona, *cariad*." He cupped his hands around her trembling shoulders and touched his lips to her cheek, tasting the sharp salt of her tears. "I'm sorry, so sorry," he whispered. "I never wanted to hurt you."

But his words and his touch seemed to draw yet more grief from her, more sobs that sprang from her ancient, aching soul.

"So sorry," Rhys whispered over and over again. "More than you know."

He expected her to curse him for bringing her grief, to push him away and flee once more into the shadows. Instead she clung to him, curling her fists into the soft linen of his tunic and lifting her damp, shining eyes to his.

"How did you know?" she asked. "How did you know?"

"You told me," he said, his mouth hovering just a breath away from hers. "In a thousand ways you told me, Sirona. Each time I saw the melancholy in your eyes. Each time you turned away from me and pretended you didn't care."

"I did care," she confessed. "That is what made me so afraid. So terribly afraid."

He kissed her deeply, his tongue sliding into her mouth, echoing the desires of his body. She answered him with an eagerness that matched his, opening her lips for him, catching his tongue between her teeth while a soft moan hummed in her throat.

The heat and the desire built. In desperation he wrenched his mouth from hers and stood.

"Do not stop," she said, surging to her feet. She placed

her palm flat upon his cheek. "I want you to make love to me."

"Why?"

"You say you love me. Is that not reason enough?"

"For me, it is." It was painful to move or even to speak, he wanted her so badly. "What about for you?"

"I want you, Rhys. I do." As she spoke, she dropped her hooded mantle to the grass. Then, with unsteady hands, she parted his tunic at the neckline and rolled it down his arms, baring his shoulders and chest until he wore nothing save the golden bell on its filament around his neck.

She caught her breath, staring at his naked chest with the ornament gleaming in the moonlight.

"Sirona, are you sure?" he asked. "You must be very, very sure."

Slowly, she released her breath and nodded.

"Say it, *cariad*. I must hear you say it."

"I'm sure," she said. "Please. I need . . . want . . . "

"What?" His voice was rough with urgency.

"You. Your touch. Your love."

His heart seemed to turn over in his chest. "You have it, *cariad*." He drew her close, cradling her head to his chest. "You have it."

He felt clumsy and ignorant, but he found the back laces of her gown and loosened them, peeling the garment over her shoulders and breasts and then lifting her to help her out of it. As he dropped the dress to the ground, she stared at it for a moment.

He feared she would grab for it and hold it like a shield, demand that he stop. In that instant, he felt a searing hatred for the age-old garment. It was a curse upon its wearer, a curse upon the woman he loved.

Then she looked back at him, and at last he saw what he had hoped for, prayed for—trust. She had chosen him.

"I will make you glad, Sirona," he said, removing her shift and watching with awe as the moonlight showered her. She was made of alabaster dusted by silver, her hair a glossy curtain spilling over her shoulders and down her back. "I will love you till the end of time," he vowed, "and leave you no room for regrets." He threaded his fingers into her hair. "I am so awkward and inept with you, Sirona."

"No." She turned her head to kiss the palm of his hand. "You are never that."

Her assurance liberated him. It was true, he had no practice in the arts of seduction, but he had the heart of a man deeply in love and the desire to please her.

Keeping his gaze fastened to hers, he unlaced his boots and leggings and removed them; now he wore nothing but the bell of the *tylwyth*.

Her hand shook when she touched it, and she winced as if the shining metal burned her. Then she slid her arms around his neck.

He sank to his knees, bringing her with him, so that they knelt on her mantle and faced one another, imprisoned like postulants within the circle of stones. Her gaze skimmed his body, and then her hands followed, sliding over shoulders, knotted muscles of his back, buttocks and thighs, and finally his manhood, bringing a hiss of painful delight to his lips. He threw back his head and gritted his teeth.

Too soon, he told himself. Too fast. When he regained control, he held her close and whispered into her hair. "You do delight me more than I can bear, Sirona. Would that I could make you feel half of what I feel." He slipped his hands down her sides and bent to nuzzle her neck.

"I think," she said with a shudder, "you have succeeded."

"I've barely started." The waves hurled themselves at the cliffside, thundering like the blood in his ears. His heart sent its message to his hands and mouth, and he laid her back and loved her as if he had done so a thousand times.

He covered her breasts with his hands, marveling at the soft weight of them. He tasted her throat and then moved his mouth lower, lower. She gasped and arched upward, and his mouth took her fully and then slipped down to find the mystery and the darkness of her. He gently pushed her knees apart and in the moonlight saw how she was made, the nest of curls and the delicate petals and tiny bud. He tasted her. She cried out, sobbing, protesting, even as she clutched at him. She tasted of sea foam and mystery and dark sweetness, and when she pulsed against him and lifted her hips, a profound wonder shook him that he could know her so intimately.

He kissed his way upward—flat, taut middle, dark-crested breasts, arching throat—and when his mouth touched hers, she gasped. Her legs went around him and drew him close. He thought for a moment that their joining would be impossible, and she was still pulsing and softly moist, and she sheathed him within her depths.

He stopped kissing her long enough to gaze into her face, and hers was aglow.

"Ah, Rhys, Rhys," Sirona said, looking up at him. The intimate bond was a deep amazement to her, but she knew she lacked the words to tell him what she felt. She knew only that she wanted him with her, in her, until she was part of him and he was part of her.

So this is love, she thought, and her heart opened like a blossom to the sun. It was fearsome, but not in the way she had expected.

He loomed above her, more solid and substantial than the ancient stones themselves, and the moonlight limned his beloved form—shaggy hair, broad shoulders, strong arms braced on each side of her.

And between them, hanging there and swaying with each thrust, the bell of the *tylwyth*.

She closed her eyes, knowing she had a choice to make, knowing any choice would hurt. And then she knew nothing. Her mind emptied and opened, and she became light as mist, floating upward, sent aloft by him. Her passion coiled tighter and tighter until she cried out, grasping his shoulders, lifting herself toward him, wanting, wanting. . . . Red fire flashed behind her tightly closed eyes. She was mad, feverish; she had the delicate chain in her hands, and she lifted her head to kiss him deeply, endlessly, and then the very fiercest part of her convulsed and burst into flame, and somehow the hands grasping the chain pulled it up and over his head, down and over hers, the transfer as smooth and compelling as the sinuous tandem movements of their loving. She felt Rhys shudder, felt a ripple of muscle, and their bodies seemed to meld together in mutual surrender.

For long, long moments, neither moved or spoke. She loved his weight upon her. It was precious and solid, and she could not bear the thought of being without him.

She listened to their breathing, and to the sea, and she saw the shadows of the great standing stones long upon the grass.

And for the second time in her life, she wept.

Dawn came, a miracle dawn, the sun racing up to meet the sea, setting fire to all it touched. Rhys came awake when the light warmed his face.

For a moment he was disoriented; then he felt a warm presence curled next to him.

Sirona.

His soul sang her name. Last night all his dreams had come true. Loving her was a pagan delight, and they had slept the past few hours with only his shirt over them, her mantle under them.

Her silky head stirred beside him, and she blinked.

"Good morning, *cariad*," he said. "It is a beautiful morning." He groped for his flask and took a drink of sweet spring water before handing the flask to her.

She drank and set it aside. "Rhys?"

"Yes?"

"I wonder if it is always like this between a man and a woman."

"I don't know. I only know that with us, it is magical, like finding where the morning mist is born or where the waves begin."

"I never knew—never suspected—love could be this way."

It was the first time she had mentioned love. He knew it had been there all along, but to hear her say it filled him with pride and delight.

"Kiss me, *cariad*," he said.

She pressed her hands to his bare chest and propped herself up. Her breasts swung softly, enticingly.

"Ah, *cariad*," he said. "You are so—"

He broke off, hearing the tiny rattle of the golden bell. She heard it too and frowned. "What . . . ?"

The bell was around her neck.

"Oh," she whispered, grasping the golden bauble. "Oh, no. No, no!"

"Sirona—"

"Stay away from me!" She jumped up and tugged on her shift and gown and mantle. Bumbling, he pulled on his clothes.

"Sirona," he said again, "don't run away. Talk to me."

"I have nothing to say to you. How does it feel, having tricked me?" She sidled toward one of the standing stones as if seeking shelter in its ancient, mystical shadows. "I never knew love was such a lethal weapon, Rhys. You should have explained that to me."

He shoved his feet into his boots. "I did not place that bell around your neck." He backed her against the rough surface of the stone and pressed his palms against the granite. "Think about it, Sirona. Think about the way I touched you, kissed you, last night. You wanted that." He pointed to the bell. "It was you who did this."

She closed her eyes and remembered the wonder and terror and joy he had given her, remembered taking the chain with her own hands, taking it from him just as she had taken his love.

"How does it feel, Rhys? Like a great victory? You'll be able to go to my father and tell him you accomplished both remaining tasks in one night. You made me weep, and you belled the cat. How proud you must be." She beat her small fists against his chest and sobbed. "How proud you must be. How very, very proud."

He took her chin in his hand. The tears poured from her eyes. "Tell the truth, Sirona. The only thing I made you do is love me."

"And I do," she whispered brokenly. "God help me, I do."

THIRTEEN

Sirona raced down the hill, away from the circle of stones. With Rhys's calls still echoing in her ears, she ran toward the coast to a favorite place of hers. Looking north to Puffin Isle, she stopped upon a flat-topped hill surrounded by a lynchet. The thick earthen walls had probably been built before the Romans had come. In the middle stood a great, thick disk of stone known as the *bwrdd*, or table. The hill crested at a cliff, the sheerest and loftiest on the Isle of Mona.

She went through a gap in the old, mounded wall and headed down a slope toward the sea. Rockrose thorns tore at her dress, and she froze, staring down at a black thread that unraveled from the weave. She closed her eyes and willed forth the change, awaiting the painful, ecstatic moment of her transformation. But the wildness that poured through her was different; it was the searing desire for Rhys that possessed her. The gown was an ordinary garment now, at least for her. Still it held the magic of the ancients, but not for her. Never again for her.

She grasped the hated bell at her throat, intending to rip off the offensive ornament, to fling it far into the sea, even though she knew such an act would only be symbolic, useless. Rhys had conquered her. Every part of her. It had been a most tender conquest and she the most willing of victims.

She should feel shame, self-disgust, disappointment, but instead she felt only the piercing wound of elation, the knowledge that she was beloved of Rhys, that he wanted *her*—not for her beauty or her father's wealth, but because he looked at her and saw something he cherished.

A thin shout, like the cry of a gannet, drew her attention. She looked up at the cliff edge.

At its highest point, two figures struggled.

Sirona gasped softly. It was Arthur and Owain, locked in a bitter fight as chunks of earth and rock rained down the treacherous side of the cliff. The drop was sheer, sculpted by wind and sea.

Sirona threw back her head and called Rhys's name. Then she climbed back up the slope, cursing the slow awkwardness of her mortal form even as she ran.

She and Rhys reached the old hill fort at the same time. He looked at her with a heart-catching expectancy in his eyes, but she would not allow herself to think of that now.

"It's Arthur," she said, panting.

Sirona would never forget the look on Rhys's face. This was a man who loved with the fierce protectiveness of a mountain lion. Like a sunbeam strengthened and magnified through a bead of water, he focused his gaze on Arthur. His fist tightened; then he raced to the land's end.

"Owain!" His bellow filled the endless sky.

Sirona rushed after Rhys. Her skin was cold with fear. Owain was treacherous; she had sensed that from the start. His attack on the boy merely confirmed it.

When he gained the edge of the cliff, Rhys plucked Arthur out of Owain's grasp and pushed the lad to the ground. Sirona knelt beside the terrified boy. Yet even though he trembled, he had blood beneath his fingernails and a very unchildlike flintiness in his eyes.

"He was in league with the Saxons," Arthur said. "He gave them silver rings to abduct me." He shuddered, and then his fear for himself dissolved into concern for Rhys. "Stop them," Arthur cried. "They'll both fall!"

Rhys and Owain were evenly matched for strength. Locked in a deadly embrace, they had fallen to the ground, fists flying as the turf beneath them crumbled from the towering heights down into the sea.

Sirona paled. In that moment she realized that she could not lose Rhys, that no cost was too dear to spare his life. She saw Owain take the upper hand, pinning Rhys beneath him, locking his hands around his throat. A terrible, struggling gasp came from Rhys.

Sirona reached desperately for the wild power of the cat, but she no longer possessed the gift. She had surrendered it, and now she was as helpless as any woman.

Or as strong as any woman.

She strode forward with her chin held high and her eyes as hard as gemstones. "Owain!" she called.

He froze, his hands still clamped around Rhys's throat. Beneath them both, the turf cracked and fell away. Rhys's lower body hung precariously over the edge.

"At the Pendragon's orders, you came across the forests of Gwynedd to take me as wife. Let Rhys go, and I will do as you bid."

Owain blinked. Slowly, finger by finger, his hands relaxed. He straightened and walked toward Sirona. Rhys lay unmoving, and Sirona's heart lurched. She prayed he had only lost consciousness.

Owain grabbed her wrist and gave a nasty laugh. "You sell yourself cheaply, woman, for the life of Rhys of Snowdon."

"He is," she stated, "more dear to me than my own life. And you will know that, Owain, every time you look at me, touch me, take me to your bed."

He dropped her hand as if it were a live coal. "Curse you, woman! You would dishonor me with every breath you take."

"But it would be the truth."

Owain turned away from her. Before she could stop him, he seized Arthur by the arm. "You've surrendered your honor for Rhys of Snowdon," Owain snapped. "Now you have nothing to trade for the boy."

Sirona closed her eyes, but she could not escape the hopeless sight: Rhys unconscious, in danger of falling to his death. Arthur in the clutches of the ruthless man to whom she would be forced to surrender.

A wildness rose in her. This feeling was unfamiliar, different from the transformation from woman to cat, but infinitely more powerful. As she stood there, a wholly new spirit slammed through her with the force of a tempest. And though she had never felt it before, she knew a shock of recognition. This strength, this power, was her feminine will, as wild as any creature of this world or beyond. She felt bountiful, endless, and from the very depths of her being, she reached across time and space, using every aching fiber of magic within herself to cry out a wordless summons.

The moment passed in a blink of time, and then there

was only the hollow wail of the wind and the ceaseless snarl of the sea below the cliffs.

Seconds later a drumming sound, more regular than the pounding of the waves, filled the air.

Arthur struggled against his captor. "Look!"

Up over the rise came her father and Myrddin, leading all the warriors of Bryn Melyn. Hodain raced to Rhys's side and nudged him.

Owain's hand twitched and then closed more tightly on Arthur.

Fury welled up in Sirona. "Think hard on what you are about to do, Owain," she said. "If you harm the child, you'll have an army of warriors to face."

No one spoke, but the howl of the wind was deafening. Finally, after what seemed an eternity, Owain moved away from Arthur and stalked, with shoulders hunched, down the hill.

After a few steps, Owain turned and clenched a fist. His knuckles were beaten raw. "A curse upon you all." He faced Sirona. "I spit upon your offering. I would not have you to wife if you begged me."

"For that, I am thankful," she said.

Myrddin tossed back the hem of his shabby mantle and shouted, "Begone, Owain. Tell the Pendragon he can no more change destiny than he can bend the path of a river."

With a groan, Rhys rolled away from the cliff edge and stood. He looked briefly, expressionlessly, at Sirona. The blandness in his face tore at her heart, for she knew he had heard her offer to Owain.

"Are you all right, Arthur?" Rhys asked.

The lad nodded.

Rhys started down the hill. He walked past the stone table. Myrddin hurried forward, stopped Rhys with a hand on his arm.

"My son, you wanted to know why I sent you to Bardsey." He nodded at Arthur, who had boosted himself upon the stone table and was pacing its circumference, surveying Roderick's warriors as if he were a battle commander.

"That is why," said Myrddin. "Because you would give your life for a boy who would be king."

Rhys stared at his father, then with a muffled cry drew Myrddin into a fierce embrace. Sirona held her breath. With all her heart she prayed he would turn to her, prayed he would see what was in her soul.

He looked. Even as he moved away from his father, even as he pulled her into his arms, she felt his love and her own meld like two metals in a crucible, burning hot and forging a bond so strong it had the feel of eternity.

EPILOGUE

"Believe me," Rhys assured his wife, "it is the right thing to do. Even my father thinks it is safest to burn the gown."

Sirona regarded him with wide, wounded eyes. When she looked at him that way, he wanted to fling himself at her feet and promise her the moon.

He forced himself to stay firm. "The treacherous garment has meant nothing but heartbreak. You know that, don't you, *cariad?*"

"Yes," she said forlornly. She held it draped over her arms. There was a gentle swell in her middle that had not been there a few months before when they had married.

They had pledged themselves the very day Owain had slunk off in defeat. Roderick had declared a holiday. Myrddin had dubbed the spot Bwrdd Arthur, and Rhys had pledged his heart, his sword arm, and his soul to Sirona.

She had pledged the same, and now she was expecting

their first child. It would be born come spring, just when the apple trees they had planted began to blossom.

The babe would be a daughter, if Myrddin's divinations could be trusted.

Roderick had taken his legions to serve the king. Bryn Melyn was Rhys's now. Myrddin and Arthur had joined the household.

Sirona stared wistfully at the gown. The autumn sunshine streamed down over the grassy lawn in front of the hall, and smoke plumed from the fire burning in the pit. "I suppose it must be done," she said.

"My love, if you'd rather not—"

"No, you are right. When I chose you, I chose with my heart. The part of me that was ruled by the old ways is free now. That is how it has always been with the women of my line. I had no mother to teach me this, but I did learn it from you. From our trials together."

He touched her chin, brought his lips down to hers. "I do love you, *cariad.*"

"I know. That is why I can burn the gown. Because you love me, and I love you." With exquisite sadness and joy in her face, she held the gown over the flames in the firepit. "And," she added, "that is more magical and enduring than anything in this world or the next."

Just for good measure, I let a single, sparkling tear slip down my cheek. Rhys had given me the gift of feeling sorrow and joy, pain and pleasure, and the fine agony of loving with my whole heart.

Because of him, my life is now infinitely richer, its textures deeper and somehow more real.

And so I let the gown drift into the firepit, where the hungry flames licked at it, then devoured it.

The babe made one of her sweet, quickening movements, and I knew then that my small deception would be understood and forgiven . . . one day.

The black gown that fed the fire this day was a forgery, a duplicate. The real gown, that ancient masterwork of the tylwyth, was hidden away in a coffer.

I'm saving it for my daughter.

Susan Wiggs has won many awards for her work, including the RITA Award from Romance Writers of America for Favorite Book of the Year.

In addition to being a militant romance writer, feminist, and butter sculptress, Susan Wiggs has recently become a Christmas tree farmer. Though rarely impulsive, she suddenly moved from Texas to an island in Puget Sound, where she lives with her husband, Jay, her daughter, Elizabeth, the world's most ill-mannered dog, and two hundred noble firs.

Although she has convinced her family that toiling away at a writing career makes her a candidate for martyrdom, she secretly believes it's the second-most fun to be had.

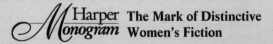